PLAGUE JOURNAL

A Novel

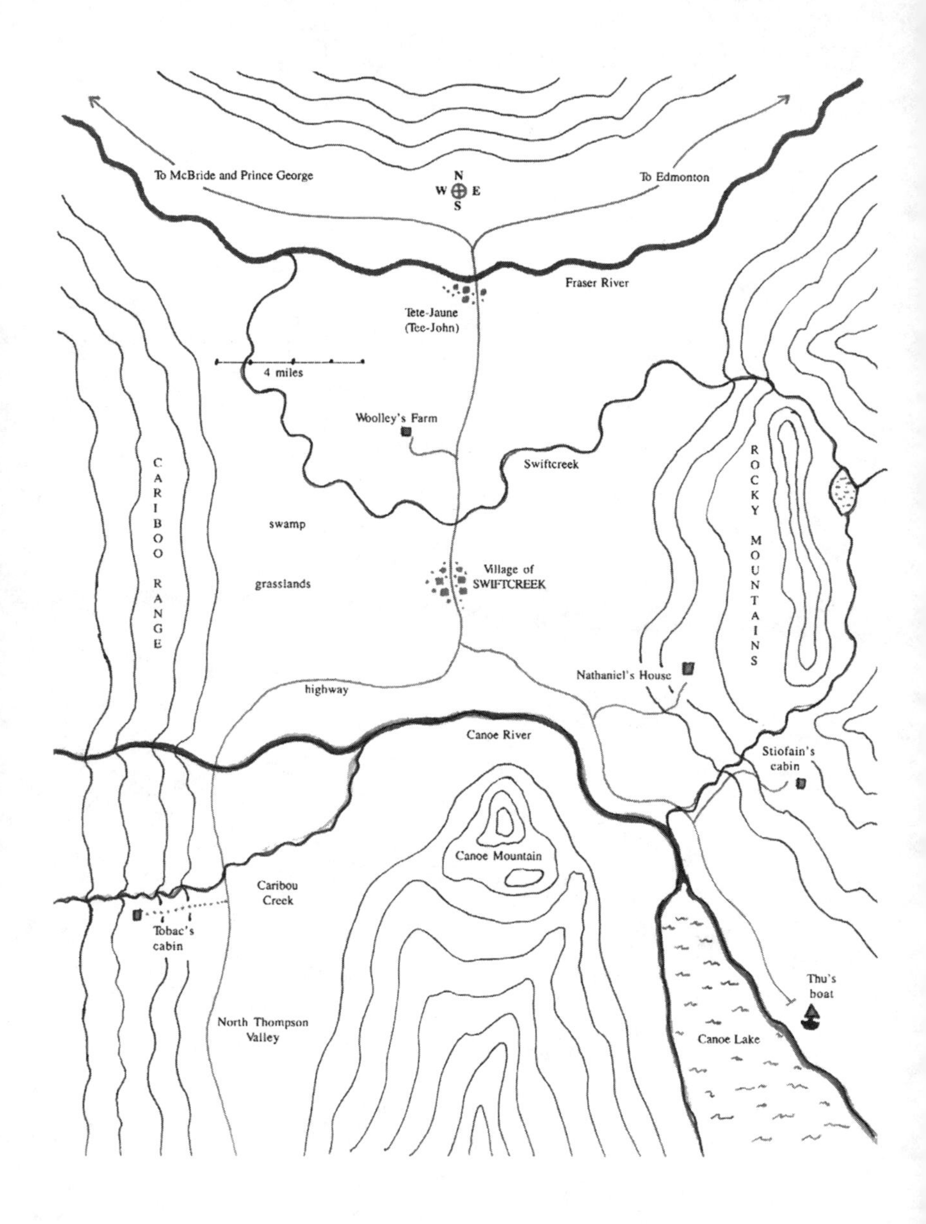
To McBride and Prince George
N
W
E
S
To Edmonton
Fraser River
Tete-Jaune
(Tee-John)
4 miles
Woolley's Farm
Swiftcreek
CARIBOO RANGE
ROCKY MOUNTAINS
swamp
grasslands
Village of
SWIFTCREEK
Nathaniel's House
highway
Canoe River
Stiofain's
cabin
Canoe Mountain
Caribou
Creek
Tobac's
cabin
North Thompson
Valley
Thu's
boat
Canoe Lake

MICHAEL D. O'BRIEN

PLAGUE JOURNAL

A Novel

IGNATIUS PRESS SAN FRANCISCO

Cover art by Michael D. O'Brien
The Last Homely House

Cover design by Roxanne Mei Lum

ISBN 978-0-89870-981-0 (PB)
ISBN 978-1-68149-378-7 (eBook)

Library of Congress catalogue number 96-75778
Printed in the United States of America ∞

For Sheila

We were frightened the moment we saw him, but we did not run away, we stood and watched him. He came on us as if he would run over us. But before he reached us he began to spread and spread, and grew bigger and bigger, till at last he was so big that he went out of our sight, and we saw him no more, and then he was upon us.

George MacDonald, *Lilith*

Lost is our old simplicity of times;
the world abounds with laws,
and teems with crimes.

Anonymous, *Pennsylvania Gazette*, 1775

Vancouver, British Columbia, Sept 30

Dear family,
You're probably going to be surprised at finding *this* stack of papers in my trunk at the cottage. By the time you read it someday, I'll be dead and gone, and there won't be much chance to explain it.

It came into my possession by accident. Well, not quite by accident, but it would take too long to explain that now, and anyway you get to read about my part near the end of the story.

The guy who wrote these pages was the editor of *The Swift-creek Echo*, which closed down some time back. It was written on foolscap in tiny handwriting. He filled every inch of space on every sheet of paper, both sides—I guess because he wrote it on the run and didn't have much paper at his disposal. I just spent a month deciphering the whole mess and typing it into my computer.

Anyway, read it for yourselves. You'll see he was a smart guy, even though he tended to run on about his ideas. He could be pretty boring. *The Echo* was like that, too. He was the quiet type. Nice kids, smoked a pipe, and always looked like he belonged somewhere else. Half the town hated his guts, and the other half thought he was a hero, though they didn't always get what he was saying. I don't know what to think. Judge for yourselves. You can read it or not, whatever you like. I don't think it makes much difference.

Cpl. Frank McConnell, R.C.M.P., retired

The beast and the white hart circle each other. The beast is a serpent coiling and leaping across the sky, seeking to entrap the hart. The beast has power. Darkness and confusion issue from its mouth. It alters its shape and becomes a bear. When it moves again, it is a leopard. It uncoils and is all three. Its tail drags a third of the stars from the sky. It rears on its hind legs and lunges forward, its claws raking the air and its mouth roaring obscenities. The hart tilts his rack of antlers and steps forward. He charges and pierces the beast's chest, but the beast's claws tear gashes in his throat. Blood pours slowly through space.

One

New Year's Day. Our place, Swiftcreek, B.C.
Zizzy gave me this scribbler for Christmas, and I promised her I'd write in it, so here goes. She must have worked for days to decorate it, because the cover is a mosaic of hundreds of tiny images clipped from magazines and mail order catalogues, glued together into quite an original work of art. Mauve, violet, and lavender colors predominate. Exotic nineteenth-century heroines, herbs, flowers, miniature landscapes, and her favorite Renaissance paintings are arranged into a garden of earthly delights —the kind of delights that appeal to a ten-year-old girl.

On the first page of looseleaf, she has pasted the old logo from my adolescent periodical, *The Quill* (total subscriptions during its heyday numbered forty-seven). Beneath the drawing of the quill she has penned an inscription in flamboyant calligraphy. It reads as follows:

To my Father, the best writer in the world.

A slight exaggeration. When I unwrapped it on Christmas morning and read the dedication, I had to suppress a laugh, then suddenly I choked up. Tears in my eyes. Big hug.

What a sweet kid. If only I could have been a better dad for her and Bam. If only, if only—the refrain of my life.

"It's for you to write in, Poppa", she said.

"What'll I write?" I asked.

"Thoughts and secrets, and things you want to remember—the good things." She smiled at me. "Not like the stuff you write for the paper."

"This is so beautiful, Zizzy, I don't want to touch it. It's a treasure. I couldn't bear to mess it up."

"You're supposed to mess it up!" she laughed. "That's what it's for."

Interesting insight for a giggling ten-year-old. A work of art that you're supposed to mess up? Like my life, I suppose. Well, life *is* messy, pardon the cliché.

* * *

March 6.
The mind is a mosaic, or, more accurately, a swirling multimedia art form. I think about the mind-brain relationship constantly. How does it work? Why does it work? Chimps and crayfish figure things out within the parameters of their limited world views, but only man thinks about thinking.

Which I am doing at the moment.

Zizzy wants me to write "good things". Thoughts and secrets and memories, she says. Yet two months have now passed, during which I have not found a free minute to collect my thoughts, to pick my way through the filing cabinet of recent events in search of a single archival treasure.

Most treasures are fleeting. I dip into the reservoir and pull out a few:

Memory: A child's smile, intimate but enigmatic: Waving goodbye, Bam hikes up Delaney mountain alone on snowshoes, as I did when I was his age. Waving hello, Zizzy builds a tree fort halfway up a giant cottonwood. Ascent is natural to children; it is their instinctive hunger for transcendence.

Memory: Ziz pretending she's a ballerina after seeing a video of *The Nutcracker*. Arms extended for balance, tremulous at her first rise upon the point of her running shoe. Confident in her beauty, but untested. A fledgling, she has wings but cannot yet fly. This is the delicate moment, the first of many incidents in the long passage from childhood to adulthood. It needs the parent's smile of encouragement and boundless (sometimes faked) confidence. Blunders are common at this point. Let the wise parent beware.

"You are my Dad," the smile asserts, "and I love you, but I must have my own quest, and my own private interior, where I explore the terrain of my undiscovered self."

Memory: The pure contentment of waking from a sleep that is so deep and so restorative that you regain consciousness as if it were the first day of creation. Forgotten is your habitual fatigue and sadness and consciousness of failure. Gone is the knowledge that you are a bitter, middle-aged, single parent. You are rubbing sandman's dust from your eyes, gearing down to be a responsible adult for yet another day, when what to your wondering eyes do appear but half a dozen teddy bears, seven dolls, a stuffed monkey, and a statue of the Blessed Virgin, ringing you on the rumpled quilt of your bed, each gazing upon you with great affection. And a note:

Breakfast will be Served shortly!
In Bed!
Happy Father's Day Poppa!

The smell of toast, frying bacon, and eggs.

Memory: I am six years old, lying on the silvery, mica-flecked sandbanks of the creek. I am wearing only swimming trunks, and the sun is burning on my back. I am watching the slow, exhausted lashing of battered salmon as they arrive at the last cascade of Swiftcreek, their ancestral spawning beds. They have completed the five-hundred-mile journey from the sea. They will give birth and die. For the first time in my life, I feel the immense dignity of life's determination to prevail over death. I fall passionately in love and slide down into the cold waters of the creek to join them. I am a fish.

Memory: The first snow, two, maybe three years ago. It falls at dusk, late afternoon. The world is hushed, and the children run out through the back door and hurl themselves into it, making snow angels. After hesitating, I run out, too, coatless, and fling myself in between them, making a man-sized angel between the cherubim.

Memory: Deep winter. Bam, Ziz, and I are curled up together on the couch in front of a blaze of pine knots in the fireplace. Our hands dig into the greasy popcorn bowl while a blizzard howls outside the picture window. I light a candle and begin to read to them from Tolkien's *The Hobbit*.

* * *

"Stop right there, Dad!" Zizzy commanded, sitting upright. "Read that again."

"Read what again, Honey?" I asked.

"The part about the stone."

"The stone?"

"Please, Poppa, before it's gone from my mind."

Bam explained: "I think she means the part where they're running away from the dragon's lair. You just read it a minute ago."

"I did?" I said, genuinely puzzled. Whatever they were referring to was definitely gone from my mind. I must have been reading on automatic pilot. I quickly scanned back a few paragraphs and found the section where the dwarves and the hobbit flee through the underground passages, hoping against hope that they will escape Smaug the Dreadful.

"You mean where they're running up the stone stairs?" I asked.

"Yes, that's it", Ziz nodded dreamily, entranced by an obscure illumination. "Read it again."

" 'Though all the old adornments were long mouldered or destroyed, and though all was befouled and blasted with the comings and goings of the monster, Thorin knew every passage and turn. They climbed long stairs, and turned and went down wide echoing ways, and turned again and climbed yet more stairs, and yet more stairs again. These were smooth, cut out of the living rock broad and fair; and up, up, the dwarves went, and they met no sign of any living thing, only furtive shadows that fled from the approach of their torches fluttering in the draughts.' "

"*Cut out of the living rock*", Zizzy breathed, staring into space. "Oh, that is so *beautiful*!"

Bam and I laughed. We think she's a hopeless romantic.

Bam, in his thirteenth year of life, hates emotional excess. In recent months he has been exploring the male mystique of stoicism and big muscles.

"The dwarves wouldn't have called it *beautiful*", he corrected his little sister in the driest tones of condescension. "They were interested in making things. *Useful* things, not pretty things. Tunnels, underground cities, swords, tools—"

"Poppa?" Ziz ignored him. "Isn't Tolkien a genius at finding just the right word?"

I nodded. He sure was.

I was busy pondering the fact that I had read the passage—aloud no less—without directly engaging my conscious mind. With a jolt I realized that the brain can function simultaneously on more levels than one. How utterly bizarre!

What did it mean? Was my brain fragmented, and, if so, did it mean I was crazy? Or was I a prototype of some new kind of man: *homo sapiens multiplex*, a superior being who can rub his tummy and pat his head at the same time?

Zizzy's request had alerted me to the hidden dangers of complexification: a lack of focus, compartmentalization of thought, the loss of attention, an indifference to the illuminating moment.

I stared into the fire, my eyes blurring. Strangely I heard a fragment from a poem by Robert Frost, the words rising unbidden from memory: "Something there is that doesn't love a wall."

Now where on earth did that come from? And why did I hear it now, at *this* moment? Is there a central routing office at the core of the brain? A tiny secretary who directs all inquiries to the appropriate department? Or is there an omni-index that cross-references every scrap of meaning absorbed by the mind during its life? Then cross-references the cross references?

The word *stone*, for example. Through my mind there flashed a series of images:

The Tolkien passage I just read.

The Frost poem about tumbling stone fences in a field—"Mending Wall", I think.

The time when I was eight years old and had finally mastered the art of stone-skipping, sending a flat, black disk of slate across the waters of Canoe River, touching the surface twelve times before it sank.

The red stone Bobby MacPhale pelted me with when I was

fourteen years old, knocking me to the ground and giving me stitches in the forehead.

David's five smooth stones, one of which killed Goliath.

My grandfather Stiofain's stone cross, which is now hanging on a nail at his cabin down the road.

The stone that rolled over the entrance to the cave where I hid during the forest fire so many years ago.

The stone that rolled away from Christ's tomb.

My grandfather Stiofain saying to me, "Tanny, our hearts are like stone, and only suffering carves them into bowls big enough to catch the joy." Incomprehensible to me at the time, but unforgotten.

And so forth.

I tore my eyes away from the fire, shut down the mill-race of memory, and resumed reading to the kids.

* * *

May 20, Swiftcreek
Pick a word, any word, and see what the index comes up with. Try Love. Or Hate. War? Truth, maybe? Wife? Maya?

No, not wife. Not Maya. Definitely not Maya.

How about the word *pain*?

Doc Woolley says the brain is basically a machine, with a driver attached, but a driver who is conditioned by the instrument he thinks he controls. There is something not quite right in this concept, but I'm not sure what it is. So far, I've been able to locate and distinguish several levels of function that I loosely group under the title *Myself*. Me. Nathaniel Delaney:

1. intellect—data, ideas, rational concepts.

2. imagination—the inner theater. All kinds of images and dramas pop up on the screen, with or without an invitation.

3. emotions—raw surges of feeling, some pleasant, some not so pleasant.

4. the body—the senses (self-explanatory).

5. Grandpa Delaney insists on the category of the spirit. "A man's soul", he calls it. I'm undecided about this department,

having received no absolutely convincing evidence about the question from the other departments. Although there are tremors on the edge of consciousness that indicate undiscovered dimensions of our being, for the moment one can conclude only this: the human person is complex, unpredictable, a mystery. Above all we are not machines.

* * *

June 8. Our house
My daughter, Zöe, and my son Tyler have embarked upon an adventure. A real adventure.

They have gone away on a four-day school trip to Vancouver. I dropped them off at the bus, then came home to a hollow house. I'm all alone for the first time in ages. I find myself floundering in an unexpected hiatus of silence. I "hear" Bam and Zizzy laughing and talking in the backyard, which is impossible, so it must be some kind of residual memory, maybe a minor bug in the index, or just the automatic pilot humming along oblivious to real-time. Who knows? Sometimes I turn around to see where the voices have come from only to catch myself, the fool of a not unpleasant hallucination. I laugh, scratch my head, then as an afterthought I rub my tummy.

* * *

That was all I could write. The mind-mosaic swarmed with multicolored stories, images, fragments, but none of it would gather itself into a coherent form, and I couldn't seem to force it to do so. Was it writer's block or general burnout? In any event, the index was locked.

I went out on the back porch with a cup of coffee and my pipe. The sittin' stump in the yard had been rain washed and sun dried, and it seemed to beckon me to meditation. I sighed. I was too tired for meditation. Thinking takes effort. But I sat down on it anyway.

A squirrel descended the tree upside down and scolded me for disturbing his projects. Or maybe he was just making his policy statement. A male, no doubt, establishing the borders of his little geopolitical world. Size means nothing when the territorial instinct is at work. Possibly he was just scolding me for my shallowness, my heaviness, whatever—my many failures.

"Easy for you, Chip! Easy for you to judge!" I said. "You are neither complex nor a mystery to yourself."

This infuriated him, and he launched into a diatribe against the follies of mankind.

"Chip," I said in a conciliatory tone, "it's not my fault."

His arch look implied that it certainly was my fault.

Spreading my arms wide, I protested: "Do *I* look like I invented the neutron bomb? Do *I* look like I invented the concentration camp?"

"Blame shifter!" he accused in a nasty little voice. "You're all blame shifters."

I sighed again.

When she climbed onto the bus this morning, Zizzy turned, ran back down the steps, and gave me an extra good-bye kiss.

"While we're away, Poppa, don't be lonely. Promise?"

"Sorry, kid. Can't help it", I said. "You're not even gone yet, and already I'm lonely. I love you."

She grinned and gave me her best schoolmarm look. "Maybe you'll feel better if you write in your Christmas journal."

"A capital idea, my dear young lady! I shall hurry home and do that very thing."

"You can write the following, Poppa: 'My daughter, Zöe, and my son Tyler have embarked upon an adventure. A real adventure.' "

"Excellent!" I replied. "Why, Miss Delaney, you and J. R. R. Tolkien have an uncanny genius for finding just the perfect word."

And so forth. We were interrupted by the impatient bus driver, the impatient teachers, and the impatient fellow students. Honk-honk, roar, gusts of diesel exhaust.

Well, I obediently wrote it down in the journal. But for now I am busy trying to rub my tummy and pat my head, lapsing into the private mental journal I keep whenever I am not talking to squirrels.

* * *

Royal York Hotel, Toronto. August 14
I'm here for the national press convention. It's hot as blazes out there on the streets, but my room has air conditioning, thank goodness. Ziz must have smuggled the journal into my luggage. I've been remiss. Months have gone by, and I haven't had a chance to write in it. I've been too busy, as usual.

The kids will be having fun with Grandpa Delaney at his cabin. I miss them. I would like to call them, but Grandpa doesn't have a phone.

I was a bit miffed when the convention staff informed me upon arrival that my speech had been dropped from the schedule. No explanations, just weasel talk. They sent the press association's PR man to handle me, and ooh, is he good at what he does. He said that somebody in clerical staff had made a big mistake, overbooked the speakers and underbooked the conference rooms. Profound apologies. His eyes shifted left for a split second. Next year, he said, they want me to be keynote speaker.

Yeah, right.

Obviously it has something to do with my latest editorials. I've been drifting from the comfortable center. More accurately, from their concept of the center. Of course they wouldn't for a minute admit that's the real reason.

I ran into Pete Stanford in the lobby this morning. I haven't seen him in years, not since he was a reporter at the *Vancouver Star*. We're about the same age, mid-forties, but he looked ten years older than I. He seemed to be in rough shape, trembling hands and a haunted look in the eyes.

He put on a hail-fellow-well-met mask for about thirty seconds, then sagged. A troubled guy. He said he had been looking forward to hearing my talk and was surprised to see it wasn't on the schedule. He wanted to know what happened, so I told him.

* * *

"They dropped me", I said.

"That's nuts", he growled. "They didn't drop any of the jerks." He named a few hacks. "So how come they dropped you?"

"I don't know for sure. Probably PC issues."

"What! You? Politically incorrect?" He shook his head in disbelief.

"Yeah, I guess I am."

He laughed humorlessly. "C'mon, Delaney, that can't be the reason."

"Sure could."

"You? A fascist?"

"No, Pete", I said, as pleasantly as possible. "I'm not a fascist. I'm not even conservative. Not what they mean by conservative."

He looked at me curiously. "Then what the hell *are* you?"

"I don't rightly know. Haven't figured it out yet."

He pursed his lips, removed his glasses, and stared at the floor.

"The medical ethics stuff?"

"That's my guess. It's considered downright distasteful, and very bad journalism, to publish an honest opinion these days. Have you noticed?"

"Yeah, I've noticed. Some of us are more equal than others, right?"

"Precisely. We're living in Orwell country now, Pete. When did it happen? How did it sneak up on us?"

"It's not that bad yet."

"Yet? If the Supreme Court says it's perfectly all right to give your grandma a lethal injection, or cut a child to pieces in the womb, it can't be all that bad yet, eh?"

He didn't answer.

"So, anyone who still calls it murder is a slandering, hate-mongering rabid dog and should be sued for libel, right?"

"At the very least, he's an embarrassment", Pete mumbled.

"So, pal, I'll understand perfectly if you want to disassociate yourself from me. I don't think anyone's noticed us talking yet."

I said it rather sardonically. He stared into my eyes hard.

"Thanks for the insult, Nathaniel. Just when I was about to offer you a drink."

Then he punched me semi-hard on the bicep and grinned crookedly. "I'm buying", he said.

He took me up to the revolving restaurant on top of the CN tower. At 1800 feet, it's reputed to be one of the world's tallest structures. That's a foothill where I come from, but when everything else is far below your line of sight, and even a huge city like this looks like a scattering of tiny dice, your perspectives alter somewhat. I expect they have inscribed on the roof, "Neither God nor man can sink this ship." Only God would read it, of course.

The view was Zarathustrian. There we were, a century after Nietzsche, two little overmen—*übermenschen*—revolving in the eternal circle. The waiter brought our drinks, and we stared out the glass windows, watching the world rotate around us. Magnificent view of Lake Ontario. You could see the curve of the earth.

Pete's macho joshing didn't last long. Saying nothing, he stared glumly into the depths of his imported Dutch ale, while I swirled a swizzle stick in my vodka and orange juice. To break the uncomfortable silence, I asked about his family. I was pretty sure I had heard he was married.

"My family? Which family?" he said miserably.

"Your wife, kids?"

"Had two. Two wives, four kids between them. Two families, not necessarily at the same time, mind you."

"Had?"

"Both over."

"I'm sorry", I said. "Care to talk about it?"

"Not much. It was my fault."

"My marriage is over, too", I offered. "Also my fault."

He looked up, vaguely interested.

"The usual causes?" he asked.

"Depends on what you mean by the usual. I didn't cheat on her, if that's what you mean. I just wasn't there."

"Same as me. No cheating, no wife abuse, in fact no nothing."

"What happened?"

"Same as you, I wasn't there for them. Always away fox-hunting, chasing stories, pursuing my big career. You know the scenario."

"I know it all too well. The problem with me, Pete, was that I *was* there, but my head wasn't. Maybe my heart wasn't, either."

"Any kids?" he asked.

"Three."

"Who has custody?"

"I have the oldest two, my wife has the youngest. He was a baby when I last saw him several years ago."

"Pretty nasty."

"Yup. Leaves a hole in the heart."

"Don't I know it. My wives have custody. I don't see my kids very often. They don't like me."

"I'm sorry."

"Occupational hazard", he said.

"Yeah, occupational hazard."

This conversation was going nowhere fast. Clever lads that we were, we suddenly realized that we were indulging in convoluted thoughts as turgid as water circling a plugged bathtub drain.

Pete sat up straight and looked out at the topmost towers of the cityscape inching across his right shoulder. He drank his ale down to half empty.

"How are you doing otherwise?" I asked.

He gave me a baleful look. "Otherwise? I write my columns, I pay child support, try hard not to turn into a dead-beat dad."

"I read your articles on Africa and the Balkans. Very fine work."

He shrugged. As I watched, his hands began to tremble. Eyelids blinked too fast. Body language tightened up.

"It must have been dirty over there", I prompted.

"Understatement of the year." His voice was barely a whisper. He killed the final half of his drink, signalled to the waiter, and ordered another.

We sat in pained silence.

"It shook you up, didn't it?" I said at last.

He nodded.

I decided not to probe. I had read his accounts of the massacres, the churches full of slaughtered women and children, the torture chambers and burial pits. The man was obviously still recovering.

He cleared his throat. "Sorry", he said. "It's hard to talk about, even for an old newshound like me."

"It must be", I said.

"I'm not coping with it very well", he went on. "My doctor has me on Valium. But it's just taking the edge off. I'm not sleeping. The work is suffering."

"It doesn't show. I read your columns."

"Thanks for the encouragement, but I know where the bear crapped in the buckwheat. You don't get to be a foreign correspondent in a rag like mine by being dishonest with yourself. The fact is, my writing is slipping. If my higher brain functions keep shutting down, I won't be at my desk much longer. The publisher wants me to check into a hospital. Then after some R and R, he's going to pay for a short sabbatical. Which is generous of him."

"Not so generous. You should consider it danger pay, or compensation for shell shock in the line of duty."

He smiled sadly. "You're probably right. If I get my confidence back, I'll mention that to him."

"He knows you're worth it."

"Maybe . . ." Pete's voice trailed off. He lapsed into a prolonged stare at the horizon.

I didn't push, realizing it was better to wait for him to go on.

"There are other things happening", he said eventually.

"What kinds of things?"

He shrugged. "Nothing you could put your finger on."

"Personal things?"

"No. National things. International."

"Oh, I see, foreign affairs issues."

He shook his head. "Actually, you don't see. Nobody sees."

I pressed him for an explanation, but he wouldn't give one. Just mumbled, waved his hand dismissively. "Shadows. Bad dreams. Bogeymen in the dark. It's probably nothing."

"It doesn't sound like nothing."

He refrained from answering, stared some more, then offered the following cryptic comment:

"Nathaniel, I have nothing to go on but intuitions and a few seemingly unconnected events. None of it amounts to material that's fit for real journalism. Maybe it's all in my imagination; maybe it's just sleep deprivation or burnout."

"Then again, maybe not?"

"That's right, maybe not."

"Why are you telling me this?"

"Why did you ask?"

"I'm a newshound, too. I trust my instincts, and I've read enough of your articles to trust yours. What's happening, Pete? What shook you so much you don't trust yourself anymore?"

For a moment I thought I had lost him. His face went white, then crumpled. He stared at the tabletop, saying nothing, breathing heavily.

When he had composed himself, he looked up and said very quietly, "You haven't been through it. You don't know."

"Know what?"

"You don't know what you are. Nobody knows what he is until his world starts to fall apart."

"You've got a lot going for you, Pete. Give it time."

He looked at me as if I were from another planet. I was beginning to feel very uncomfortable. And it struck me that Peter Stanford might have gone a little way around the bend.

He read my look exactly.

"Yeah, that's right, Nathaniel, I've got a few screws loose. I'm the first to admit it. I'm doped up and drinking too much, and I'm losing it in a big way." He pointed a finger at me and said intensely, "But don't think you're immune; just don't ever think you're immune."

"Immune to what?"

He leaned forward and said bitterly, "A successful guy perceives the world in a certain way. He also thinks of himself in a certain way."

"I've had my share of failures."

"Uh-huh. You see yourself as a basically strong guy with a few flaws, don't you? I used to be like that. But when your exterior world collapses, and your interior world collapses at the same time, you wake up one morning and don't know yourself anymore. You look into the mirror, and you see a crazy man staring back at you. And you say to yourself, 'Who the hell is that?' "

"You're not crazy."

Pete snorted.

"I may or may not be on the rail line that ends at the psych ward. With a little luck I might be able to avoid that, at least my therapist tells me I might. I just don't know. But for the sake of conjecture, why don't you and I watch closely as the next few years unfold. Maybe at one of these conventions, sometime in the future, we'll go out for a drink and laugh about how good old Pete went through his psycho phase, and now everything's just peachy."

"All right, let's do it. How about next year?"

"Sure. See you next year. Same time, same place."

But it was obvious that Pete didn't think we'd be having such a conversation next year.

"If I'm wrong," he said, getting up from the table, "then we'll chalk it up to occupational hazards. If I'm right, I won't be seeing you again."

"That's a little dire, wouldn't you say?"

He threw some money on the table. "Dire? Nah, I'm probably just paranoid."

* * *

Swiftcreek. September 8

It's sure good to be back in the mountains. The Toronto trip was a total downer. Why would anyone want to live in a city? I suppose most urbanites wonder why anyone would want to live in the wilds. Bam and Ziz had a great time with Grandpa. He took them hiking up Delaney mountain and showed them the cave I used to escape to when I was a boy. The cave where I dreamed good dreams. Kids need something to dream on. Of course, it's also the place where I had that wrestling match with a mythological bear. So many years ago I had almost forgotten it.

The mind is a fragile thing, quite fragile. Pete Stanford was fairly right about that, but in his emotional state I think he was definitely blowing things out of proportion. Poor guy. He's a very intelligent man and a world-class journalist, but I guess his accumulated failures and the horror he saw in Africa and the Balkans gave him a bad scare. He'll get over it.

I've been thinking a lot about paranoia lately. There seem to be a few right-wing movements popping up here and there, screaming hysterically about Western nations moving in the direction of a "new world order", conferences on one-world government, secret meetings of international financiers. Waco, Texas. Ruby Ridge. The Oklahoma City bombing. Private militias. Conspiracy theorists crawling out of the woodwork. The lunatic fringe. All very American.

I talked this over with Woolley the other day. As usual he beat me at chess and poured me a double tumbler of Bailey's Irish Cream. Feeling mellow, we sat in easy chairs in his living room and watched the first autumn storm blow in from the north, stripping a flurry of yellow poplar leaves off the trees. He told me he lost a few lambs to wolves last week. They came right into the barn at night while he was doing rounds at the hospital. He'd forgotten to close the shed door. When he got home, he found the dog cowering under the back porch, shivering and whining hysterically.

* * *

"What do you think, Eddie," he asked me (we never seem to break our habit of using sarcastic names for each other), "why would a big bruiser like Minder fail to protect the flock? Is he a coward or a realist?"

"Well, Doc, I'd say he's probably both."

Woolley chuckled. "Good answer."

We looked down at the big lump of a dog, wheezing and snorting on a rug in front of the fireplace.

"Minder has rationalized the experience to himself", Woolley said dryly. "Just yesterday he pointed out to me that discretion is the better part of valor. In the most unctuous tone he maintained that he had saved himself for a better day. What good would have been accomplished if the flock had lost its watchdog, he asked. He's really quite clever, Minder is."

"Will he recover?"

"He'll be all right. He has nightmares, twitching paws and yelping in his dreams. But they're declining. He's almost back to his old self, though he still jumps at shadows from time to time."

"Poor fellow. Is he becoming paranoid?"

Woolley smiled sardonically. "A little. But that's natural enough."

"Paranoia is natural?"

"Sure it is. We're all paranoid when you get down to the nitty gritty. It's a matter of degree."

"Come on, now, I can't agree with that."

Woolley raised his eyebrows and peered at me. "Oh, don't you? You've just never been sufficiently traumatized."

"That's not true."

He laughed and said no more.

"Doc, you know I was in pretty bad shape when we first met. I was in the first stages of a nervous breakdown."

"A mere skirmish, old boy. A mere skirmish."

I hate it when he calls me *old boy*. When using the expression, his English accent becomes ever so slightly superior and razor-sharp.

A mere skirmish? Thinking back now, I guess my little episode wasn't as serious as I thought it was at the time. Peter Stanford, on the other hand, seemed to be having the real thing. I told Woolley about my meeting with Pete.

"Hmmmm", he said. "Now that sounds to me like a classic case. Your journalist friend gets a close-up view of how low mankind can sink, and suddenly his world of petty North American ambitions and securities falls apart. That's a first-class trauma."

"But you saw bad things when you worked in the refugee camps."

He looked out the window into the storm. "Yes, I've seen some things. I've seen burial pits and mutilated women and children. But it's all in how you deal with it afterward."

"What do you mean?"

"I mean this: At some gut level a person chooses what conclusions he makes of the horror. He can tell himself that *all* existence is horror, and then he's really going to come apart at the seams. Or, alternatively, he can say to himself, well, I just witnessed an outburst of the irrational, the primitive instincts in human nature, and now it's over. Back to business as usual. Civilization goes on."

"Wow, I'm impressed by your strength of mind. But isn't that a little cut and dried?"

He shrugged. "We choose. Sink or swim."

"Uh, yeah", I murmured.

"You know," he said in a musing tone, "this whole question of paranoia is very interesting. I've thought a lot about it. I think it's a peculiarly Western thing, late twentieth century."

"What do you mean?"

"I mean that for most of human history the dangers have been external. Out there. The tiger in the bushes, the invading barbarians, the forest fire, and the flood. The human mind is constructed in such a way that it is admirably suited to dealing with problems of a finite nature. Solid facts, real pain, hunger and cold, the immediate threat of death, et cetera. Now, civilization has arrived at a point where most of the objective dangers are largely under our control. But what does the mind then do with its root fear?"

"You're assuming that fear is fundamental to the mind. Isn't that assuming quite a lot?"

"I don't think so", he said coolly. "Have you ever met anyone who doesn't at some time or other display fear?"

I struggled to think of someone. "No, I guess not."

"So, you see, it's there in us. Existence is fundamentally dangerous. And fear is a healthy mechanism. It becomes unhealthy when the instinct becomes either frozen or inflamed."

"So how does this connect with paranoia?"

"Well, there comes a point in the evolution of mankind when the objective dangers are fairly well contained by social structures. Yet the fear-and-flight (or fear-and-fight) reflex remains. How do we act on it? What do we do with it?"

"We use reason."

"Correction: *You* use reason. Remember, old boy, generally speaking, human beings are not paragons of reasonableness. To one degree or another we wrestle with the irrational within us."

"Present company excepted, of course."

"Wrong. I admit my irrationality and adjust my life accordingly. I don't think you have reached that point yet."

"Oh, and why not?"

"Because you still think you're a rational man."

"But I am!" I protested, screwing up my face irritably. "I *am* a rational man!"

Woolley laughed outright. He poured me another drink. And laughed again.

"North America was founded on flight-or-fight", he went on. "The pioneers were fleeing the real dangers of the Old World. Persecutions, wars, famines, plagues. They wanted a clean new world, a fresh start. Generation after generation, they pressed farther and farther into the wilds, often with little more than their dreams. The imagination expanded. The dreams became objective reality. You see?"

"Uh, no, I don't think so."

"All fears were externalized: Indians, bears, wolves. There was no time to indulge in neurosis. But what happened when the westward-ho arrived at the shores of the Pacific?"

"They went fishing?"

"No, they built MGM Studios, and Paramount, and Fox, and turned the focus of the imagination inward. The inner frontier, it soon became clear, was practically limitless. And so accessible. Space travel is a bit more problematic."

"Are you saying that the film industry is paranoid?"

"Sometimes. But more importantly, it creates the illusion of space and freedom by providing an infinity of doorways through which we can walk into other worlds. It's still fright and flight. We are all—and I underline the word *all*—still trying to escape."

I chewed on it, not entirely convinced.

"It's an interesting theory", I said.

"Give it some thought, old boy. Ask yourself why urban ghettos explode into violence."

"Ghettos?"

"Uh-huh, ghettos. Isn't paranoia the ghettoization of the imagination?"

Here I am back at home, still chewing on it. The kids are asleep. I've got insomnia. I'm wondering if Woolley is right to some extent. Maybe I'm one of the really privileged ones in this country, because I was born and raised in the wilderness and have a lot more space and freedom than 95 percent of the people on this planet. Lucky me.

* * *

Swiftcreek, February 2
A year has gone by since I received the Christmas journal, and the entries are still pathetically few and far between. I had intended to leave a legacy of shining vignettes of nature, family life, illuminations of various sorts—perhaps even some intellectual insights of a sociopolitical kind. Alas, I have scratched out only a few and mixed them with my lamentations. Maybe it will mean something to the kids when they dig it out of a trunk in the attic some day, ages and ages hence.

Zizzy's gift has had the unexpected, and not entirely unwelcome, side effect of prompting my new habit of keeping mental journals. I memorize my own thoughts, hoping to solidify them some day into text. Grandpa Delaney would probably call this process an examination of conscience. Woolley would call it a biopsy. Maybe it's a biopsy of the soul.

We celebrated Zizzy's eleventh birthday on Saturday. I gave her a copy of George MacDonald's *Lilith*. Ignoring her other presents, she plunged into the book without bothering to wipe the cake crumbs from her cheeks, flipping pages, devouring passages at random.

"Oh, Poppa," she cried, surfacing for an instant, "it's even better than *Phantastes*! Listen to this: 'The business of the universe is to make such a fool of you that you will know yourself for one, and so begin to be wise.' " She laughed. "I don't know what he means, but he sure makes you think."

I know exactly what he means. *Et tu*, George.

* * *

March 1
I've been asking myself why Bam and Ziz have been so moody lately. They get off the school bus each afternoon wearing that bored, sullen look that most of their schoolmates wear. It's not like them. Bam was lippy to me this evening, which is quite out of character. Growing pains, maybe? Puberty blues? I was a bit short with him. Later we both apologized.

* * *

April 12
I am so peeved I could spit. After supper dishes, Bam slammed his homework down on the kitchen table and said, "Dad, why do we have to learn this stuff?" Then he showed me the workbooks for new programs he has to take at school. At first glance it looked like fairly reasonable material. But the course wasn't the usual academic curriculum. It was more along the line of raising social consciousness.

After the kids were in bed I sat down with the books and read through them carefully. It's social engineering in a big way—experts deciding how we all should live—but done in the most masterful pedagogical style. Nothing here to make a parent nervous, until you look close and begin to think about what it says. The content is a problem: sex, sexual orientation, "values clarification", race, religion. What bothers me most is that these are areas that rightly belong to parental authority.

* * *

April 16
I had an unpleasant encounter with Ms (which she pronounces *mizzzz*) Parsons-Sinclair, the school principal, this afternoon. I went into town to discuss with her my reservations about the new programs. One program instructs children to beware of males touching them, especially fathers, grandfathers, brothers, and uncles. The whole world is teeming with incest, according to a large number of people with doctorates in educational psychology. Another program describes the details of sexual intercourse to seven-year-olds, using diagrams that leave nothing out. Pardon me, they do overlook a few little items, like mod-

esty and dignity, and a thing called love, and another little thing called romance.

Ms P-S was professionally nice, handled me quite diplomatically, meeting my objections with perfectly timed responses. A neat exercise in public relations on her part. I was intrigued to see that she displayed no shiftiness during eye contact. Obviously this is a *righteous* PR operation. She believes in what she's doing.

When I pointed out the implications of subverting parental authority, she became tense.

* * *

"Subverting is a rather strong word", she suggested.

"You're right", I apologized. "I don't mean your intentions are wrong, just that maybe the school board isn't being as sensitive to parental responsibilities as it could be."

"We are *helping* parents", she replied primly.

"Don't you think parents should be encouraged to shoulder these responsibilities?"

Her brow furrowed. "I really think very few parents are sufficiently equipped to understand the issues we want to introduce to our students."

"*You* want?" I replied in an even tone.

"Children need to be properly informed if they are going to meet the challenges of the modern world."

"I believe it's my job to inform my kids. I want Bam and Ziz withdrawn from these courses."

She stared at me before responding.

"That is unusual. I should point out that your children will be the only ones absented."

"Really?" I said smiling pleasantly. "The only ones." I stared back until she looked away.

"Surely not the only ones?" I pressed.

"Well, now that you mention it, there is the fundamentalist family that recently moved to town. And a family that is under investigation for sexual abuse. I can't mention their name, you understand—that would be a breach of professional confidentiality."

You didn't have to be a genius to get her point. She was telling me: *Great company you keep.*

"Regardless," I said, "my children do not need such courses."

She tilted her head reflectively and, using a conciliatory tone, said, "That is your right. However, I would ask you to consider the possibility that you are depriving your children of a very valuable resource in their education."

"That's debatable—"

"If you will also permit me to say, Mr. Delaney, you are a single parent. Have you considered your daughter's needs?"

"Zizzy's needs?"

"Zöe is of an age when she needs to learn the facts of human reproduction. So many children have suffered because of insufficient knowledge—"

"My mother visits us quite often", I returned. "She is quite a wise woman, and she has been walking my daughter through the first stages of information. Also, I answer Zizzy's questions whenever they come up. We do it at our own pace and in our own style."

The woman's mouth tightened.

"I see."

"I hope you do see", I answered. We both stood up. Our conversation over, she escorted me out with a degree of cordiality that was utterly correct and absolutely cold.

That lady has an attitude problem. I would send her to the principal's office, except that she is the principal.

* * *

September 1

I missed the press association's annual convention this year. Funny thing, they didn't invite me to be keynote speaker. I wrote to Pete a few months back, just to see how he's doing, but no reply so far.

I have also written a few editorials on the issues involved in government appropriation of parental rights, with the net result of some cancelled subscriptions, a few angry letters, and one anonymous phone call.

I lost my temper this afternoon in Ms Parsons-Sinclair's office. I went down to have a meeting with her. I had learned that children withdrawn from the social engineering programs are forced to stand in the hallway during those classes. She has made it school policy.

* * *

"This is punishment", I said to her firmly.

"It most certainly is not", she replied tersely. "The children can read or do homework during those periods."

"Read and do homework while standing?"

"Then they may sit."

"On the floor?"

"We will put spare desks in the hallway tomorrow, if you insist."

"Only troublemakers are banished to the hallway, and you know it. You're sending a message loud and clear. This is political."

"*You* are being political, Mr. Delaney", she shot back. "You are being divisive!"

"Divisive?"

"Yes, you are creating unnecessary concern among some parents, especially among the uninformed and gullible. You are dividing this town."

"Oh, am I really?" I laughed in her face.

She raised her voice. I raised mine. The usual justifications were trotted out on both sides. We worked out a compromise. The kids will go to the school library during the controversial classes. This, however, does not solve the problem of the posters that are all over the walls. Diagrams of where body parts go during the marriage act. Beautiful photos of couples embracing, very much in love: man-woman, man-man, woman-woman, and so on. These couples are clothed, but who knows what next year will bring, when the frontiers are pushed back another degree. I spotted a few children's books on the recommended reading shelf in the library: *Johnny Has Two Dads* and *Tina Has Two Moms* and some occult primers for kids. Also something called *Goosebumps*, which seems to be a series that celebrates terror and gore.

All was befouled and blasted with the comings and goings of the monster came to mind. Where have I read that?

* * *

October 5
I'm beginning to get very nervous. Subscriptions are dropping. Several more cancellations. The finances aren't looking very bright. I couldn't afford to pay the insurance on *The Echo* offices this year, the first time this has ever happened. Well, they'll have to wait a few weeks for the check. I'm expecting some money for an article that I wrote poking holes in the mythopoetics of eco-spirituality—my daring attempt to break out of the ghetto. Strangely enough, it was accepted by a liberal highbrow journal, *Pacific Review.*

I told Woolley about my troubles, and he offered to lend me some money for insurance and groceries. I refused. My pride, I guess.

Then all in one week the pickup blew a gasket, threw a tie rod, and lost its muffler. I had to go back to W to beg a loan. He was gracious about it, but I was forced to swallow my damnable ego for once. The repairs cost a thousand bucks. One problem with wilderness is that you are dependent on motor vehicles and gasoline to live the rustic life. Sigh!

* * *

December 8
I'm trying my hand at some creative writing. So far the product isn't impressive, but it might be a source of income if I turn out to be any good at this. Here's something I wrote after last Sunday's skating session with the kids. It's just a first draft, a sketch of a planned longer piece. I might try working it up into a short story and send it to *Phoenix: A Quarterly Review of New Canadian Literature*. It's hard to say if my tainted name and reputation have any hope of getting past the Canlit mafia. Call me an optimist.
Tentative title: *Icarus Descending*.

* * *

ICARUS DESCENDING

Oh, that luminous day! Cranberry Swamp was just about perfectly frozen over. Snow had dusted the valley floor. Zöe and Tyler were clamoring to break in their new skates. Hers were white with teeth on the front, and pink sissy laces. Tyler's were black, molded plastic with incandescent orange laces.

The water wouldn't be firm enough to go Hans Brinker mile after mile over black glass in curious secret channels and back bays, hidden by clumps of deep swamp grass. I told them to wait. Safety first. But it's shallow, they countered. True, through the lens you could see the mucky bottom, a frozen micrology of transfixed leaf and stone over which you glide like gods until the moment you are invited to topple from a throne into reality.

The kids hung from my hammer straps and pleaded. I was building the woodshed that autumn, and the early freeze had beat me to it. I was busy. I was always busy. But they were in such earnest hunger for the winter light and the hard illusions of speed and flight. I finally gave in. They didn't know what it costs to learn to fly. Ice is a thin membrane above the void.

I ground the blades down on a sparking wheel. I got out my old brown leather creakers and ground their blades too. The kids leapt and bounced and grinned. They composed questions for the mere sake of questioning and being answered by such a clever man as I, master of fire and wheel. The answers didn't matter that day. Skates for them were not toys but instruments to free us like a horizontal Icarus. I tried to warn them. There is always a cost. It doesn't take more than a failure of the eye or a twig jutting from the ice to catapult us into pain. I told them of my own youth. My Dad took me to the swamp when I was small. These big toes are now stiff and creaking from the time I hockey-froze them long ago. I showed them the nicked bark of shin and the stitched scar where my uncle Jackie skated across my ankle by accident. It was proof that we almost never achieve what we aspire to, that we fail to be the gods we want to be. How could I tell them it is enough to be simply human.

But they took their own humanity for granted. It was good they did so. It was natural. No introspection to cloud their childhood on a winter's day. At the edge of the wide hard water, we waved and all embarked. They went into their future brashly. I went slowly, testing this film of cracks. Old bones are brittle. Let the eager beavers, light and swift, go flying over the abyss, I said to myself.

All afternoon, until the sky was a sheen of indigo blue and the first star sparked in the east, we plied our power, singing loud the great sharp bark of our humanity. My Tyler, my cavorting boy, became a form of man, and I became a form of child. My Zöe, nursing a scraped chin and bruises from her falls, was happily content to chew upon a frozen orange. Its crystals shattered in her mouth, and her cheeks flamed red, a final reflection of the dying sun.

It became night, and the moon rose high and cold over the peaks above our home. To all observers it would have seemed a Christmas card scene, complete with rosy cottage nestled under a hill and white wood-smoke going up forever. Was there a mum and a golden light in the windows? Not so. Our house was full of an absent mother and a brother they didn't get to know. It was an empty shell. Thus, we skated again, and the terror of the dark was wrapped in hot wet wool. Scarves were bunched and knotted. We sweated under our tuques. There was a mad abandon into speed; there was step and halt, turn and wheel, jig and reel. Then we were laughing together and flying, and falling, falling, falling fearless in our fear.

I remember the final cuts of the blade, carving great signatures into the silver moon-struck ice. Then we piled into our beat-up station wagon. There was only silence. My children were dazed with exhilaration. Sleep beckoned them like a mother. Oh my children, my children, so pure and blind. Their wax was melted, feathers plunged. Old Daedalus grieved for them and did not know why.

Then we tumbled into our beds to dream the deep dreams of Man. As so often happened in my life, sleep evaded me. I looked into the darkness above. I heard the scrape of steel on ice, and the woosh of flight. I saw it then, the first glimpses. Later, I forgot most of it, and at times it was completely gone. But it always came back again: I saw that we are unheeding, we are night, knowing everything except ourselves, naming everything except our own true names. I saw that we wait in darkness for words unspoken, words to shatter our unhearing. We wait for light, hoping to gaze on trees burning with green fire and to see, there upon the swamp, an expanse of water freed.
Endtext—draft one—Icarus

* * *

Well, there it is. It needs to be five times longer and less poetic. I'm inserting the first draft into the journal, in obedience to Zizzy's command to collect "good thoughts". The scribbler is becoming cluttered: newspaper clippings, used plane tickets, Zizzy's love notes, and other mementoes. A good memory was much needed today because *Pacific Review* returned my essay on ecology myths with a token "kill fee". This is especially frustrating because they have had it for almost a year, and it has yet to make it into print. Maybe they just wanted to keep it out of circulation. They offered the most excruciatingly vague excuses for not publishing it—even though they had already accepted it! "The reading public is no longer interested in this world view", the editor explained. If letters could go shifty-eyed, this one would. Are they cowards or realists? Both, I suspect. Wuff, wuff! Move over, Minder!

* * *

December 21
Maya's annual attempt at being a mother arrived in this morning's mail. A box of Christmas gifts for the kids, artistic

cards full of gooey sentiments. Nothing for me. Not a word. As usual, there was no return address on the box, though it was postmarked Vancouver. Trying to locate her would be like searching for the proverbial needle in the haystack. I would make a sincere effort at repairing the damage if she would let me. But maybe she likes her new life so much she doesn't want intrusions from her old one.

This morning Grandpa Delaney gave me his pension check, so I'll be able to buy groceries and Christmas presents. Later in the day Grandpa Tobac dropped in with a box of smoked fish and half a deer, which he helped me cut up and put into the freezer. They both offered to pray for me. Why is it, I wonder, that I have two very religious grandfathers, and none of their genes rubbed off on me?

I called Woolley and hinted at my economic straits, explaining that I have big outstanding bills from my newsprint supplier and the post office and no way to pay for them. He was really very understanding, said he wished he could help but had just locked all his money into some foreign investments. Said he felt terrible about not being able to come to the rescue. I believe him.

For some crazy reason he suddenly started talking in Donald Duck language. It was so bizarre, the absurdity of it, so unexpected that it made me guffaw. Then he rambled on in a perfect imitation of John Wayne, saying that it was a tough job being a fanatical editor, but somebody had to do it. His idiotic ploy had the intended effect of shrinking my troubles into perspective.

At the end of the conversation, he reverted to his normal accent and said soberly, "I'll try to help you, Eddie. But for the moment all I can offer is some medical advice."

"Okay. I'm all ears."

"Try to float through this. It won't last forever. Come by my house for chess next week, and I'll let you beat me. Read a spy novel. Increase your alcohol intake."

"Thanks, Doc. But I can't afford booze. Something must be going funny with my metabolism. One bottle of beer, and my brain starts to leak like a sieve. Worse, I've been hiding under the back porch. The kids tell me I whimper in my sleep. My paws twitch."

"Welcome to traumaland, Eddie."

"Gee, I didn't know paranoia could be such fun."

"In moderation", he concluded.

Good old Woolley. He's eccentric, but he does come through when you need him. A true friend.

* * *

July 23

Grandpa Delaney died suddenly in his sleep. He went peacefully in the middle of the night. It was old age. It hurts too much even to write about it.

* * *

July 28

Two days after the funeral I was slapped with a $5000 fine for "hate literature". The editorial on euthanasia, of course. I can't pay it. I'm appealing. I contacted a good lawyer in Vancouver, who is offering his services for free. He thinks the government may be making some preliminary moves in the direction of suspension of civil rights. It's highly improbable they would try such a thing, he believes, but if they do, he wants to nip it in the bud, send a warning to Ottawa.

Things are worse financially. I can't seem to get any mainline journals to accept my articles. My income is microscopic. The day before he died, Grandpa wrote out a check for $1600, which was all he had in his account. It arrived by mail the morning after his death. Pinned to the check was a note:

For my dear grandson.
A Gift.
With love and prayers,
Grandpa.

Perhaps he had a premonition that his time was short. Or he may have wanted to spare me embarrassment. The money should see us through several months. Thank heavens there's no mortgage on the house and the land taxes are paid up. We're living more simply now. The kids grumbled a bit at first but seem to be adjusting well.

I'm not so sure about their father. I've been battling insomnia for months. Bouts of depression. Woolley suggested Prozac, which is unusual, because he doesn't believe in pill-pushing unless a patient is in real trouble. I turned him down. I don't think it's that bad yet. But periodically I notice my hands shaking. Another thing has developed. I've started to weep. I haven't done that since I was a child. It's embarrassing, because even though I try to contain it until late at night when the kids are tucked into bed, I think they hear me. Grandpa's death unhinged something. Maybe it's a primitive fear of being alone. Maybe a male ego thing—fear of failure? Hell, I'm already a failure, so what's the fuss?

* * *

September 12
A really bad piece of news! I just seemed to know it was coming, an ominous feeling that began a few days ago, like a storm brewing. When the corporal from the R.C.M.P. detachment drove up the lane this afternoon I knew what had happened before he said a word. His name's McConnell, a good guy. I invited him in, and over coffee he told me that somebody had broken into the *Echo* office during the night and destroyed a lot of equipment. I drove into town with him to survey the damage.

At first it looked like plain theft and vandalism. McConnell thought it might be kids on drugs. They took the computer, he explained, because there's a brisk black-market trade in stolen computer hardware. Then it struck me that the destruction seemed curiously selective and thorough. The offset press and all the other equipment for producing the paper are beyond repair (the only thing the wreckers missed was an antique hand press I had stored in the basement). Worse than that, my data bank was all on the computer hard drive. My back-up diskettes are also missing, and my hard-copy files. Because of my recent distractions, I had forgotten to bring my back-up diskettes home. I have no other copies of the subscribers list. A *total* disaster.

And me with no insurance. Well, that's that. It's the end of the paper, unless I can send out an S.O.S. and raise some benefactors to get *The Echo* moving again. On Monday I'll see if I can remember some names and addresses. I still have contacts, people who believe in what I'm doing. They might be willing to lend me some start-up funds.

Bam and Ziz were shocked and furious over what had happened. It took me a long time to reassure them and get them to sleep. I'm more numb than anything. It doesn't seem quite real.

Ziz dropped a cup while doing the dishes after supper. My nerves were shot. I yelled at her. I've never done that before. She cried. We hugged and made up.

I've got to do some serious thinking about my life. It can't go on like this.

I'm having strange dreams. Snakes, bears, dragons, and a white stag. Symbolic, I guess. Subconscious stuff. Woolley says it's the mind's way of exteriorizing the interior fear.

Two

January 18—evening
This has got to be the strangest day of my life. We're at my grandfather's cabin, trying to assess what has happened. It began this morning.

* * *

The telephone started ringing right after breakfast, and it was driving me crazy. I hadn't slept much the night before, and my temper was short. My heart had been doing funny things, too. Palpitations.

It wasn't much weirder than any other day during the past few months. The hate mail and the crank calls had become an ordinary part of my life. Morning, noon, and night—harassers, ideopaths, and nosy neighbors. Why were they all so upset? Because I wrote such nasty criticisms about their wonderful world? Hey, journalism is democratic, isn't it? They didn't have to buy the thing, and now it's been shut down. So who or what am I threatening?

Just after lunch the telephone rang again. I rolled off the couch and found myself lying half-awake on the living-room rug. I gasped for breath, and my heart pounded wildly.

How nice, I said to myself, all I need is a heart attack to make my day perfect. Woolley told me to train the damn thing to relax. Slow down, boy, slow down!

The serpent and the white hart again. Hey, relax! It was just a nightmare. Think loose! Float!

The ringing was at the other end of the house. I stumbled along the dark hallway, groped around the desk, and found the receiver.

"Aaargh! Kreeag-bundolo!" I growled into it. "You have reached the offices of *homo sapiens complicatus*."

"Huh? Oh, hi, Mr. Delaney, this is Tracy at the pharmacy. You left some photos t'be developed. They're in."

"Thanks, Tracy. I'll pick them up later this afternoon."

"Okay. The Sears catalogue desk says to tellya that the gym socks for Tyler came in. You wanna pick them up, too?"

"Okay."

"They'll need a check for twelve ninety-five. Okay?"

"Okay."

"Seeya later."

"See you later."

Click. Click.

Funny sound, I thought. Must be line trouble.

I was snugged onto the couch and had just drifted back into semi-consciousness when it rang again.

It was a lady. I liked ladies. She informed me in a sweet, sincere tone that she was a native Canadian, a physically handicapped poetess, working her way through college. She was soliciting for an organization called Gay Women for the Advancement of the Arts. I decided on the spot that I wouldn't touch *that* subject with a ten-foot pole. I told her the truth—I was a depressed middle-aged heterosexual male, single parent, who was a borderline alcoholic, financially dysfunctional, on the verge of bankruptcy, and emotionally unstable. I explained to her also, as a safety precaution, that I was half native myself. It helped. She told me she understood.

"Take care, brother."

"You too, sister."

Click. Click.

I creaked and groaned my way down onto the couch one more time and noted that my heart was slower but no less wracked by anguish. I was worrying and grumbling about Tyler's socks because I didn't know whether or not that check was going to bounce. I think we passed our overdraft limit last week. And since he joined the track team, Tyler goes through socks the way some people go through peanuts. He also eats like a three-horned rhinoceros. I was sad. I was tired. I wanted to weep.

The bloody phone chose that moment to ring again.

"Good grief! Give me a break!" I muttered.

In a fit of perversity I lost my temper and barked into the receiver: "Whoever you are, this had better be urgent!"

"Mr. Delaney?"

"Yes!"

"This is Doctor Woolley's office. I'm sorry to bother you. But the doctor asked me to let you know he may have to cancel your chess game tonight. He has an emergency surgery at McBride, and he just left. He says if the operation goes well, the game's still on."

"Thanks. Would you ask him to phone me?"

"Sure. Sorry to disturb you."

"You didn't disturb me. I'm one of his mental patients. I'm always disturbed. I yell a lot. Sorry for the rude manners."

She replied with extreme gravity: "I know you're not one of his mental patients. I know who you are."

"Oh-oh. Even worse."

"You're one of his friends."

"Like I said, even worse than you thought."

She added in a compassionate tone: "Don't worry. We all have bad days."

"I'm having a bad year. I'm having a bad decade. I'm—"

"Okay. Well, thanks very much. I'll let him know I got the message through. Bye."

Click. Click.

Ah, how delicately she terminates those calls that threaten to become obsessive. I knew exactly how I must appear to her. Hypochondriac and paranoiac—a messy combination.

I slept a half hour before it rang again. They were coming in like dive bombers.

Faking an answering machine tone, I said: "Hello! You have reached the House of Bliss. If you wish to speak to one of our counselors, please press *one* now. If you wish to speak with one of our spiritual guides, please press *two*. If you would like to make a donation to our foundation, please remain on the line and one of our financial facilitators will answer your call. If you wish to leave a voice memo, please press *three* and give your message after you hear the word *Peace!* . . ."

"*Peace*, Eddie. Talk to me, Eddie."

"Doc, is that you?"

"'Tis myself. Congratulations on the recorded message. Very creative. You sounded just like a machine."

"Thanks."

"*Vita artem imitatur*. Life imitates art. Brilliant."

"Whatever. Don't tell me you drove all the way to McBride and performed brain surgery in just under an hour."

"False alarm. The ruptured appendix turned out to be a tummy ache. Mrs. Zosky's little grandson, Ryan—you know, the toddler from hell—he ate too many cookies."

"Where are you calling from?"

"Car phone. I'm halfway back to Swiftcreek."

"You still want to be trounced tonight?"

"Feeling a little overconfident, are we, O Presumptuous One?"

"You've lost three games this year, Woolley. Who's the presumptuous one?"

"My attention wandered from boredom, that's all", he said in his thickest fake-Scottish brogue. "You merely took advantage of a momentary weakness."

"I'll try to make it more interesting for you, then."

"Got any rye? I'm out of everything except brandy."

"I'll bring some. I've got a half-bottle I've been saving for the Great Depression."

"The economy collapsed long ago, old boy", said Woolley. "Let's drink it."

He sighed.

"You sound weary, Doc."

"It's been a long week."

He sounded genuinely tired, as tired as I am all the time.

"You sure you want a game tonight? Why don't you get some rest?"

"I need diversion", he said.

"The radio says a storm's coming."

"You have four-wheel drive. Don't let a bit of snow checkmate us."

"Okay. I didn't know it meant so much to you", I said.

"Don't get sentimental. I enjoy our little get-togethers. Who else have I got to talk to except decrepit editors of antediluvian rags? Right?"

"Right. And who else would put up with you? Right?"

"You're so tolerant, Eddie."

"You're so sensitive, Doc. What would I do without a friend like you?"

"You'd take to drink."

"I already have. And what would happen to you, old boy?"

"Oh, I'd just keep myself busy saving humanity."

"Gee, that's great. Maybe I shouldn't waste your time."

"Just kidding, just kidding. Even geniuses like me need to waste a little time. It keeps our brains supple."

"I'm glad I'm so useful to you."

"Me, too", he said in a Dracula voice. Then he hung up with a Transylvanian monster laugh.

Good old Woolley. My one remaining friend. He's almost as crazy as I am. He's really quite good at fake accents.

I phoned his home and got the answering machine. Perfect!

"Hello", I wailed into it after the beep. "This is Nathaniel Delaney. Look, I can't come to the chess game tonight, after all.

I'm getting really depressed. I'm not feeling very well. I'm having suicidal thoughts."

I picked up Tyler's starter pistol from the desk. I'd been planning this for weeks.

"I need to talk to you", I cried into the receiver. "I need to talk to someone—anyone. But all I ever get is an answering machine. I've left messages everywhere for days and days, and no one calls back. Please, please, help me! Please!"

I gave a three-second pause for effect. Then I fired the pistol into the receiver. I gurgled and hung up.

I rolled all over the couch, laughing hysterically, hugging my sides. It was really too funny. This was just too, too perfect. I knew it was sick. Sick, sick, sick. This kind of humor was so pitch black that Woolley wouldn't be able to go me one better.

I was still giggling when the phone rang again.

"If you say my name, I'll instantly hang up", said a voice that was strangely thin, metallic. It sounded filtered.

"Oooh, mysterious!" I laughed.

"This conversation will never have happened."

"Oooh, mysterious and scary!"

"Listen to me."

"Pretty good, Doc. You never tried this voice before. Darth Vader the soprano!"

I waited for his repartee, but none was forthcoming. The silence was a masterful dramatic touch. He's good at this.

"Doc? Is dat you?"

"*I that was a child, my tongue's use sleeping . . .*"

There was an ancient sadness in the voice. I knew those lines, because my grandmother had taught them to me when I'd barely learned to read. A series of connections went off in my mind, and I began to suspect this was not my friend Woolley.

"There is very little time", the voice said.

"Who is this?"

He didn't answer.

Gradually, a subtle and strange feeling came in through the wires, a feeling that made my skin crawl.

"Tell me who this is," I said, "or I'll hang up."

Pause.

"We knew each other once", the voice said.

"Yeah? Like when?"

"When you were a child. By the canoe."

Suddenly I knew his identity. My journalist's instincts told me to obey him. I didn't say his name. If he had a good reason to remain anonymous, who was I to question?

"Listen carefully", he went on. "Your line is monitored, but it will take them a minute to get a geo-track on this. I'm at a phone booth. I'll call you when I find a different line. I'm going to hang up."

The line clicked but didn't immediately buzz. Then there was another click, and the ordinary tone took over.

I was wide awake now, and a sense of foreboding was growing. The mystery man was no less than a very high apparatchik in that new state security agency. OIS, they called it, internal security, or something like that. His name was Maurice L'Oraison. It was a name that no longer appeared in the media, which meant he was becoming very important indeed. He was at least a subminister in the government. He had been born in our village and attended my grandmother's one-room school, where he memorized the poem she taught to three generations of children. He left Swiftcreek while still a young man, became a lawyer, and rose steadily through the strata of power.

I felt a wave of anger against him. His department had helped to shoot me out of the water last year. Under the new laws, a court declared me to be a purveyor of "hate literature". Heavy fines were levied. I couldn't pay them. I appealed but lost. Some benefactors came forward and offered enough funding to keep the presses running for a few more months, as I disseminated my hateful ideas about personal responsibility in the just society.

Next, the postal system refused to accept the *Echo*'s bulk-mailing bags, so I sent them by courier to reliable friends in various cities, people who were willing to distribute an illegal publication on foot. It was then that I learned about the courage still left in the land. Our subscription numbers had never been very high, but many of the readers were key figures in the world of culture and politics, what remains of it. At one point a diva from the national opera and an old non-conformist who just happened to be a federal senator delivered our final issue door to door. I received so many calls congratulating me on the quality of our dissent that I was lulled into a false sense of security.

Then the thugs broke in and destroyed my presses. Who did it? We'll never know, but I'm pretty sure they weren't doped-up vandals. They had to be political. Probably OIS types or some other agency of the Department of Justice. Nice people, these federal employees. Of course, the government declared *ad nauseam* that the new statutes were designed to eliminate precisely this kind of violence. Nevertheless, all dissent was now safely submerged beneath the surface of the artificial culture. The presses of the land were exulting over "peace, peace, peace". It had been a mean century, and everyone was desperate for peace, including myself. But I had balked at a false peace, a social order purchased by the erosion of fundamental human rights. I was just repeating some hackneyed words, some very old stuff, but it was the stuff that healthy societies are built upon. Few people wanted to hear about it any longer. Obviously someone took notice. I should have known my articles on the new world order would touch a sensitive nerve.

I sat at the kitchen table and gazed out the window at the forest on the mountain. I was pretty tired. Yesterday the kids heard things on the school bus. More than the usual ragging about their criminal father. Someone threw a punch at Bam, and someone else spit in Zizzy's face. It enraged me at first, because I knew those kids had got it from their parents, my oh-so-polite neighbors. Anger had given way to bitterness, then a deep, sleepless angst began gnawing at my soul. I debated about sending them off to school this morning, but they were perky and full of bravado, and I thought it better for them to learn now: You can't start running in this life, or you'll never stop.

Before the first phone call I'd been trying to reclaim the lost sleep, and in it there was another of those dragon-snake-bear-white stag dreams: the world was in chaos, and legions of gray men and gray ladies were trying to fix it. In measured tones they assured us that, if we killed all the "dysfunctional" children and the geriatrics, it would make everything right again. I was arguing with them, but it didn't make the slightest difference. They were absolutely convinced that they were saving humanity. The more I argued, the nicer they became, but it was a strained gentility, a professional veneer designed to keep us powerless until the leopard-bear-dragon arrived. When it finally came, I realized that I'd always known it would come. But I hadn't suspected the appearance of the stag, who bounded between the beast and me. An unfinished dream.

I was still exhausted and trying to rub some sense back into my face with the heels of my hands. Real coffee was perking on the stove. An admirer had sent it. I drank one cup. Then another. Addict! Typical journalist!

But what had happened to Maurice that would prompt him to make such a politically compromising call? Obviously he didn't want his colleagues to know about it. What was brewing in the halls of the capital?

The phone rang. I didn't say a word, merely listened to the sound of city traffic coming through the wires. If he was calling from the capital, it was nightfall there—three time zones away. It was two o'clock in the afternoon here.

"You know who I am?" He spoke slowly and carefully.

"Yes."

"Good. We don't have much time. When I tell you what I have

to tell you, they'll respond very quickly. They're listening right now, or at least someone will hear a recording of this within the hour. Then they'll be coming for you."

"Quit the mystery! What's going on?"

"Try to understand that I couldn't hold them back. For thirty years I've climbed with them because I thought they would make a better world. But it looks like they're going to go too far."

"So why are you helping them?"

"I'm too far in to get out. Besides . . . despite everything I've done, there's still a chance I can slow down the process a little. Not much, you understand."

"What do you mean you can't get out? Anyone can quit a job."

This was followed by a few seconds of silence.

"You understand nothing. Listen. I'm wasting precious time discussing this. We're both in danger at the moment, but for different reasons. I'll call again."

Click. Then the second click. Then the tone. Probably an automatic recorder that an anonymous clerk was checking periodically somewhere in a distant city.

He rang again about fifteen minutes later. By that time I'd had a hot shower and another cup of coffee, and a sense of reality was creeping into the afternoon's confusion. Curiously, I no longer felt depressed. Time had been long on my hands during the past few months, and it struck me that a real mystery could provide some escape from the ghettoization of my imagination.

There was the noise of a supper club in the background, with a chanteuse and the roar of muffled conversation. A piano. Glasses clinking. Electronic beeping from a cash register.

"You must understand that I had no final say. It's a higher decision. Your name and that of two other editors and a network owner came up at a Privy Council meeting. You're each to be taken into custody for the good of the—"

"Arrested? On what charges?"

"No charges. There isn't any need for charges, or warrants. There won't be a public trial. It's permanent."

I turned the word over and over in my mind. *Permanent?* It was still turning when the line clicked twice.

"What do you mean permanent?" I said quietly when he rang again.

"There is simply no legal apparatus any more that would keep you from disappearing indefinitely into civilian internment camps or other subterranean mazes. They wish to know everything, you see. There are new sciences that will extract everything there is to know. We now employ these sciences."

We? They? What is the guy talking about? What do I know that they don't?

"This is absolutely certain. Within twenty-four hours you and your children will cease to be citizens. To all intents and purposes, you will no longer exist, though perhaps for a very long time you will remain alive. You would find it the greater of evils, believe me."

"What about my wife?"

"Your wife left you eight years ago. She is the sort of person who completely sympathizes with our position without knowing it. She is of no interest to us."

"And Arrow? What about him?"

"He was too young to be contaminated by your ideology. He is of no interest to us."

"Where are they?" I couldn't hide the intensity in my voice.

"Don't be alarmed. They are living a perfectly normal counterculture life, I assure you." Here Maurice's voice became ironic, "She thinks she is a revolutionary. She lives with the boy in a rural commune on the coast. She is convinced that she is hidden and anonymous. You see, we know everything."

Click. Click. Buzz.

Ten minutes later it rang again.

I yelled into the receiver: "Not everything, dammit! If that were true, you wouldn't need to apply your *sciences*."

"This is taking far too much time. I merely phoned to give you the information. If you wish to remain at liberty, I suggest you move within the hour to some safe place, and take your children with you."

"Look, I don't buy it! If they can record this call, then why can't they trace it back to you?"

"The electronic distorter I'm using confuses voice prints. The monitor still records everything we say, however, which is why I don't want my name mentioned. They will know only that, during the twenty-four-hour period before they come to take you into custody, someone made a series of short calls to you. The problem is, if they catch you and apply the science, I too may become a non-citizen."

"If they catch me?"

"It would be most unfortunate for you. You see, for the sake of preserving my work, I would be forced to silence you before you betrayed me."

"Silence me? What the hell do you mean by that?"

No answer.

"What happened to you? What are you?"

"What am I? I'm a man who is trying to save your life and the lives of your children."

"But what for? You and your friends are trying to destroy everything that makes life worth living."

"I didn't start out this way", he said after a pause.

"But answer me—*why?* How come you're letting a virus like me loose in your system? I'll destroy your beloved program, if I can."

"You won't be able to destroy it."

"I'm going to give it a good try!"

"To answer your question: I want to see if you're right about things, or if we're right. The problem interests me. And it won't have a chance to be argued fairly if we eliminate all other possibilities, you see."

"I'm not sure I do. I thought you worked for them. Why are you telling me this?"

"Because the problem interests me."

"Which problem, precisely?"

"The dialectic between individual freedom and social order."

"How noble of you! I'm really impressed by your ethics."

Ignoring my slighting tone, he went on. "The dialectic alone would not have prompted me to try to save you. There are other questions. Your grandmother planted a doubt I can't resolve. It's not something I can discuss now, but let me just say there's a small possibility we're wrong about things, and if so I want to leave a seed for an alternative future. Your grandmother is responsible for this reprieve. She's dead. Her grandson I can help. You can accept my help, or you can refuse it. But I tell you with absolute certainty, unless you go now, you'll cease to exist, one way or another."

Click. Click. Buzz.

I stared at the receiver.

Wait a minute! Wait a minute! I said to myself. This has got to be Doc!

Maybe it was his most elaborate joke ever. I deserved it after my suicide prank this afternoon. I entertained that possibility for about thirty seconds. I even laughed—a strained little laugh. But then I realized he couldn't have concocted all this in a few minutes. I knew he was smart, but he wasn't that smart. Moreover, I was fairly certain he wouldn't know the poem Grandma taught me.

Was it really happening?

I felt a flash of anger. C'mon, Maurice, what game are you playing? What are you? Some kind of virtuous mole who burrowed under a tyrant's skin? Or are you a bad guy having second thoughts?

It was too schizoid. First he tells me that he's out to destroy what I stand for, but he wants to save me. Then he implies that he might have to do something drastic to me if I'm caught, but what I stand for may be the truth, so he wants to give it a chance. Just a little bit of a chance, mind you. Is this guy confused or what? Maybe he's crazy, a split personality.

The skeptic in me raised other objections: They had assumed a lot of power in the past few months, but they couldn't go that far. There was still a conscience in the nation. There was still a legal system. People believed in freedom and the due course of law. Though into my mind flashed an old photograph of judges of the Supreme Court of Germany raising their arms in the Hitler salute. A civilized nation before things went wrong.

Maybe he wasn't so crazy. This could be their indirect way of making me run. Give me a good scare, banish the opposition without so much as the rattling of a handcuff. Clever. It would be just like them.

Now I was convinced that this was the real situation. Plans started humming in my mind for another issue of the paper. I decided I would uncrate Grandma's old pony press in the basement of *The Echo.* The wreckers missed that. Then I would print a new issue that would sting their hides and rouse the populace! It was time to call their bluff! Lately I had been toying with the idea of selling the house and moving to the city; maybe finding a lowly job at some daily newspaper in Vancouver, burrowing deep into the system and living anonymously for a while. It would be such a relief not to fight any more. But I usually rejected this as escapism, as cowardice.

Just this morning I had said to Bam and Zizzy, "You can't run from trouble, kids. If you start running away, you'll never stop."

I got up off the couch, went over to the window, and looked out across the valley. There was a black storm boiling over the crest of Canoe mountain, a front moving in from the north.

I sat down at the kitchen table and drank two more cups of

strong coffee. I lit my pipe and hacked and coughed. Then another cup.

By that time it was 3:10 P.M. I didn't want Bam and Zizzy to have to go through another nasty bus ride. Let things cool down a bit, I thought. I decided to drive into the village and pick them up.

While I was buttoning my parka in the kitchen, I stared at the venison stew bubbling on the back burner of the wood stove. The kids eat a lot of that stuff—I'm not the most imaginative chef in the world. Forget the venison stew! I said. We'll get a frozen pizza at the supermarket and a video at Pino's Videoflix (I think I've still got credit at both places). I'll make popcorn. Fun night at the gloom house! They're great kids, but it isn't easy living with their old man way out on the edges of the lunatic fringe.

It was a dark gray afternoon. The overcast rolled overhead, and snow began to drop out of it. The pickup didn't want to start at first, and the button that engages the plow merely grunted. But I put it into four-wheel drive and chugged down the lane in first gear. Even the Canoe Road hadn't been sanded yet, and I had to take it carefully. There was country music on the local radio channel, beamed in by satellite. A cowboy in the deepest slough of despond wailed, "*It don't matter nohow . . .*", but he didn't elaborate on what *it* is. We all know anyway: *Luv*!

It was a slow ride, and I arrived at the schoolyard none too soon, just as the kids were piling onto the bus. But Bam and Zizzy were nowhere to be seen. The driver didn't know where they were. I asked some of the other kids, but they just shrugged. One of them said he saw Bam talking to Ms Parsons-Sinclair.

I left the truck idling in the street and went into the school. Hustling down the hallway, I narrowly missed Bill the janitor. He gave me the oddest look I have ever had from a human being. Normally a taciturn individual, he grabbed me by the coat sleeve and whispered into my ear.

"I don't believe it, Mr. Delaney, and I won't never believe it. You're a good guy, and I know you'd never do nothin' like that t'yer kids. Or t'anybody's kids!"

"What are you talking about, Bill?"

"Well, they says I'm to give a shout if I see y'comin, but you sailed in real unexpected like. So I ain't seen you, right?"

"Uh, right."

Bill speaks a form of hillbilly that doesn't exist anywhere else in the world. It's not his native tongue. It's an entirely invented dialect that he has cultivated over thirty years of janitoring. I'm convinced he does it to protect himself. It's his way of being considered of no account in the eyes of local people. This leaves him considerable freedom to read and to think. I know for a fact that he is an intelligent man because I surprised him reading a Dickens novel in the furnace room late one afternoon when I was in the eighth grade. And in recent years I've cornered him variously with More's *Utopia* and something by Solzhenitsyn. He is always terribly embarrassed when caught in such acts, not because I surprise him reading on school-board time, but because his cover is once again blown. Bill is, I think, the only really educated man in town. Still, he plays his role to the bitter end, and I play the part he has assigned me, that of the bright young "master" who has gone on to great things, greater than Poor Bill's ol' noggin can understand. So, I'm forced into a democratic pose, pretending the breezy condescending equality of the socially superior, when in fact I'm his inferior. He knows it, and I know it, but for perverse and complicated reasons, we long ago agreed to leave it that way.

The principal's suite was next on the left down the hall. Bill nodded toward it. There was a light behind the big glass window that covers the reception counter. I knocked at the wicket.

The secretary came and gave me a look. This look was quite different from the janitor's. I analyzed it and recognized the elements of fear and control. Those eyes despised me. They had never done so before. They had always been, until today, quite friendly. I was father of the two best students in the school, descendant of the valley's first settler. Mister Editor and all that. The usual garbage. It had been nice being respected.

"Hi, Marty. Have you seen Bam and Zizzy? The road's bad, and I think I'd better drive them home myself."

Her face was an icy wall. A strangulated "no" and a swift glance down at some paperwork.

I stared at her. What? No interest, no concern, no advice for the worried father? Curiouser and curiouser, as Alice would say.

Then a child's voice came faintly from the inner office, followed by a woman's interrogation. Then silence.

I stared at the closed door. The secretary looked at it, too, then down at her papers again. I suddenly knew that my children were in there and that I was being lied to.

I walked through the dutch door into the secretary's office, then swiftly opened the door into the next office. Behind me Marty's excited voice protested loudly. In front of me I found Bam and Zizzy sitting on a bench looking frightened. Over them towered the principal. Anger flashed on her face when she saw me. The children flew across the room and hugged me.

"I told you—" she fired at the secretary.

"I'm sorry, Ms Parsons-Sinclair. He just seemed to know, and then he—"

"What's going on here?" I demanded.

"Under the law, Mr. Delaney, we do not owe you any explanations. I request that you leave immediately, and you will be contacted shortly by the Ministry of Social Development." She paused, and her face hardened. "And by the police."

"What are you talking about? Ziz, Bam, button your coats, we're going home."

"Zöe and Tyler are not going anywhere, Mr. Delaney. Under the law we are not required to release them into your custody until the investigation has been completed."

"What investigation?"

She gave me a withering look.

"Within the past half hour we have received instructions by telephone that your children are to be kept here until Ministry employees arrive from Prince George."

"What Ministry?"

"Social Development. Also Child Welfare. And also . . ."

Her face struggled with itself.

"I don't know what kind of a man you are!" she declared in a furious little voice. "Even the Office of State Security seems to be involved. What have you done? And what have you involved these children in?"

"What in hell are you talking about?"

A lump of cold fear beat its way upward from my stomach to my throat.

"The police have been called and will be here also." She shot a look at Marty, who slipped back into the outer office and began to tap on a digital phone.

"I believe there is a difficulty regarding your sexual practices, Mr. Delaney. There has been a complaint to the Ministry on behalf of your children. Under the new law we are required to protect the children until your . . . innocence . . . has been established."

She grimaced over the word innocence.

"Do these look like abused kids?" I growled at her.

"You needn't take that tone with me", she said, drawing up her chest to full authority. "That kind of emotional violence is also a form of abuse, and I shall not tolerate it."

"Wait a minute here! I am not guilty of anything. In fact, in any sane society, a man is considered innocent until proven guilty."

She paused only momentarily.

"Nevertheless, I shall ask you to leave quietly, and your children will be well cared for. The process of the law will facilitate a just solution."

The jargon decided it for me. The use of the word *facilitate* is the sure sign of an infected brain. I don't know how or why, or from where it came (maybe the phone calls earlier that afternoon), but through my mind flashed a complex scenario of what could happen if we were swallowed whole and digested in the bowels of this régime. In any other situation I might pity the man who panicked and did what I was about to do. But I saw with an awful clarity and a quite uncharacteristic stillness of vision that it was the only solution. I grabbed one of Zizzy's arms and one of Bam's, and we made haste for the doorway.

Ms. Parsons-Sinclair screeched and pulled at my parka tails. It might have been funny in a Chaplinesque way had it not been for the dread that filled the office like poisoned gas. The secretary yelled into the phone. I pulled free from the principal and bolted from the office. We did the one thing I had cautioned the children against doing that very morning. We ran. We stampeded down the polished hallways, scattering dustbane and children's mittens left and right.

The yard was empty under the black overcast, and I found my truck still idling out on the street. We tumbled in, and I gunned the engine. With a lurch we were a block away before I saw in the rearview mirror the car of the village R.C.M.P. constable squeal into the school parking lot. I was fairly certain that McConnell hadn't seen us. We were soon out on the Canoe Road heading south into the wild old barren valley in which our family has lived for four generations.

The weather was getting bad and would slow all traffic down. I heartily blessed the snow.

* * *

"Why am I doing this", I asked myself. "I have to think. Think, Nathaniel, think!"

We had been given a grace period in which to plan what to do next, but it would probably be a short one. As we rumbled along in the dark, my pulse slowed, but my hands gripped the wheel ferociously. The kids were confused, excited, and scared.

"Dad," said Tyler, "what's going on?" He used his I'm-no-longer-a-child voice, and I saw in a glance that his face was a mask of bravery.

"I'm not exactly sure, Son. But I think it has something to do with the newspaper. They want it destroyed."

"But it's already closed down, and the machines are wrecked."

"Yes, but I'm not wrecked, and they're afraid of that."

"But what was Mrs. Parsons asking all those sick questions for?"

"What sick questions?" I said in a steady voice.

"You know", he shrugged. "Like warpo. Sicko stuff."

"Warpo? Sicko?"

"Yeah, she kept askin' Zizzy if you ever did . . . well . . . like *stuff* t'her. Course she didn't even know what Mrs. Parsons was talkin' about. But after she asked about twenty times if you ever make us sleep in the same bed with you or pet us in weird ways . . . Well, I kind of got what she was gettin' at. So I told her that was all crap and you were the best dad in the world and would never do stuff like that."

I felt a surge of gratitude for the boy and rage against that vicious, stupid woman. The next time I saw her she might very well become the victim of a certain amount of verbal abuse.

"Then old Parsnips turns to Marty and says, 'You see, victims are often loyal to the very people who abuse them. They try to protect them.' She looked at us real pitiful and then started all over again. She got Zizzy really confused, and instead of shaking her head after each question Ziz nodded once or twice 'cause she didn't understand the questions. When she did that, Parsnips got really excited and said, 'Now the truth is coming out.' And she got all sweet to Ziz and told her not to be afraid and that she'd never let you do those things to her again. I tried to tell her that you never did anything to us, and Ziz tried to tell her, too, but she wouldn't listen. That's when you came in."

Zizzy pulled her thumb out of her mouth and turned to me with an indignant, righteous look in her eyes, on the verge of tears, and said, "She looked madder and madder every time I shook my head, so I thought I'd nod yes just once t'make her happy. I didn't understand what she was talkin' about, Dad. But I knew you'd explain it all to her when you came, so it didn't matter if I said yes or no."

"Except it did matter", Bam murmured, looking grumpily at his sister. "We're all in hot water now 'cause you didn't have the guts t'stand up to old Parsnips!"

"I did so", she cried, and they commenced word-to-word combat.

"Quiet, kids", I said, "I've got to think."

Both of them fell into sullen silence, and I could see that the younger one was controlling her sobs. The thumb was corked back in the mouth, and the boy looked away disgusted. She was awfully old to be still sucking her thumb.

Five minutes later the gateposts leaped out of the darkness, and the red eyes of the reflector tabs marked the turn. Another five minutes of tortuous driving, slow and swimming on the unplowed lane, and we were home.

Everything seemed perfectly normal. Never had the kitchen looked so good. I lit every lamp in the house. The coffee was still steaming, as narcotic as it had been earlier. The radio was muttering weakly in the background. The venison stew simmered. It looked pretty darn good at this point. Too bad about the pizza.

Zizzy hugged me and said in a small voice, "Sorry, Poppa."

"Don't worry about it, Honey. You didn't do anything wrong."

"But why was she asking us all those stupid questions?"

"I think she wanted to find out if I'm a mean dad. If I hit you kids or do cruel things like make you eat liver and spinach."

She laughed.

"Well," she said primly, "you do make us eat liver and spinach, and I think that's very cruel!"

We both laughed. Only this child can make me laugh in the middle of a crisis.

I love her to the point of distraction. I've tried not to spoil her. She has my wife's extraordinary beauty, but her eyes are full of character, a trait she inherited from my grandmother.

Ziz was in the bathroom, blowing her nose, when the phone rang.

"Mr. D? This is Bill at the school. Like I said, I don't got nothin' against you, and I don't got much sympathy for Mrs. Par, Mrs. Parson-Sin, Mrs. Parson-Sink . . ."

"Righto, Bill. Look, I'm sorry about your hallway. I'm afraid we made a mess of it in our departure."

Bill cackled.

"I saw the whole damn thing, Mr. D, and I enjoyed every bit of it. But I'm callin' bout somethin' else. There's a string o' cars just got here from Prince, and they're full of some mighty funny lookin' fellas. It don't smell quite right t'me, even if they are govermint. Seems t'me I heard one of 'em say they'd best be droppin' out your way t'visit with you. Mrs. Pars, Mrs. Parsni, Mrs. Parson-Sin . . . hell, she and McConnell told 'em where you live, and I think the constable may be even leadin' the pack t' your gate. They went out the door less'n a minute ago."

"Thank you, Bill. Thank you from the bottom of my heart."

"T's nothin'."

Click.

Then another click. Then buzz.

I ran to the woodshed and scrounged three cardboard boxes, then yelled at Bam to fill them with everything edible. He stared at me.

"Canned soup, dried rice, oatmeal, sugar, tea! Quickly!" I barked.

"Huh?" he said puzzled, but proceeded to obey.

I raced through the house and found three sleeping bags, warm winter socks, anything that struck my eye in passing. I threw it all into the cab of the truck. Then I literally shoved the kids in after it. As a last thought, I ran back inside and found a big thermos jug, filled it with the stew, and ran back out the door. Four minutes might have elapsed since Bill's call. The truck engine was still warm, and it started instantly. I had to control my impulse to speed down the lane. After what seemed an infinitely long ride, we made it out onto the dark road. There were no headlights showing yet from the direction of town. I turned left, away from it, and drove with all speed toward the south, deep into the valley that was drowning in the blessed darkness and storm.

* * *

"Where are we goin', Dad?" Bam asked. We were hurtling into a white-out, and, despite the comforting throb of the engine and the soft lights from the dashboard, there was a tone in his voice that worried me. He wasn't sure he trusted my judgment.

It's fascinating the way the human mind can leap across several relays to a proper solution. It was completely without rational process that I arrived by such flight at the answer.

"Grandpa's", I said with a serene voice, adding just the right amount of firmness for emphasis. This was a voice to trust.

"Oh", he said.

My heart was racing hard, but I smiled calmly, wondering too late if this looked macabre.

The whole affair must have seemed very strange to them. Their father's behavior this afternoon was unprecedented, bizarre, to say the least. Only madmen act like this, and they knew it. We were fleeing from the very figures of authority who had played the greatest role in their lives, after their father, and . . . well, after their absent mother. Now we were transgressing normal relations with the natural world as well, flinging ourselves onto its mercies at the very moment when it was most irrational. There was a rising wind, and a thick snow falling, falling through an empty universe in which all bearings were lost.

Poor kids.

Ziz took her thumb out long enough to ask, "You mean our grandpa in Prince George? Aren't we goin' the wrong way, Poppa?"

"No, *my* grandpa. My dad's dad."

"But he's dead!" she said.

I looked at them. They were really worried now.

"I know he's dead. We're going to his place. The old cabin."

"Oh." She resumed sucking her thumb.

"Why are we doin' this, Dad?" Bam mumbled, the anxious tone increasing.

"I . . . I'll explain later, Bam."

The anguish of doubt began. It was an ancient weakness of mine, a willingness to disbelieve in oneself, engendered now by the quite understandable doubts of my offspring. A bad pain for a father. There are worse pains, of course, but this one was strong. God, I love them, but I've never been enough for them. I was suddenly pierced by a terrible fear. Could I be the victim of my own paranoia? Perhaps this flight from an ordered society was simply a late-blooming neurotic reaction to my wife's departure and other crises, such as the demolition of my career and a hell of a pile of stress. I could see the headlines:

SINGLE FATHER GOES BERSERK
KIDNAPS OWN KIDS

Captured and consigned to mental institution for psychiatric observation! Yup, it happens every day. Why not to me?

But I kept driving. Mental illness has its own logic, I suppose.

This useless self-doubt did the double disservice of making me miss the big bend before the crossing at Canoe River, just before it swings south toward the great lake. The right-hand tires hit the soft shoulder, and we careened at a wild angle down the embankment. The kids were screaming. I yelled, "Hang on, hang on", and we miraculously sailed past dozens of big Douglas fir trees and white mounds, which hid the rocks. We bounced hard, and my head hit the roof a few times. Finally, after what seemed five minutes of free fall, we thumped to a halt in a huge drift by the river. We were buried up to the headlights. All three of us were still yelling. The engine died.

"You all right? Ziz, Bam?"

"Yeah, we're okay—I think", Bam grumbled.

Ziz was crying loudly, which meant she was unharmed. I hugged her and whispered comforts.

"Now what do we do?" said Bam, disgusted.

"We walk. It can't be far."

Ziz tried valiantly to dry her tears.

"This may be a blessing in disguise", I said with an optimistic note in my voice. "You know, they probably would've followed our tire tracks right to Grandpa's house. I never thought about that till just now. Crazy. Thank God for that bend in the road!"

Both children looked at me, puzzled.

"Who's *they*, Dad?" Bam asked in a low voice.

I didn't answer.

"Who's they?" he insisted.

"We'll talk about it later, Bam", I answered firmly. "Come on, let's get out of here."

The doors were locked in deep snow. We struggled out through the windows and pulled the luggage after us. Bam unloaded some things from the back of the truck: the toboggan and the two sets of snowshoes he must have got from the garage. These snowshoes are made for deep-bush logging. They are small, gray wonders made of rubber web and aluminium tubing, much more efficient than the beautiful Alaska trail shoes.

"Good boy", I thumped him on the shoulder. "I'm glad you thought of those."

He looked at me tentatively, still worried, still assessing me. Then some undercurrent of trust must have thawed and flowed, because he suddenly grinned—an orange grin illuminated by the fading cab light.

"Be prepared", he said. "That's what the Boy Scouts say, Pa."

He piled a couple of boxes onto the toboggan, tied them with rope, then battened down an axe, sleeping bags, and, unceremoniously, his little sister. Her feet were snugged under the curved bow and her mitts clung to the side ropes.

While I fiddled on the dashboard to shut off the running lights, I heard Bam say, "Hold on tight, Ziz, we're going to have a real adventure."

Good boy.

I killed the lights, and we looked around blindly. The night was a wall of unseeing. Bam flicked a switch, and his pocket flashlight sent a beam in the direction of the river. We found ourselves standing only a dozen yards from it. Lucky we had stopped where we did, for the ice was too thin to bear a pickup truck, though probably we would have no trouble on foot. The boy slogged off toward it, and I pulled the toboggan after him.

"Careful, Bam, there could be weak spots on that ice. The snow hides everything, even holes."

"Okay, Dad."

The snow was only an inch deep over a good three inches of ice, more than enough to support us. A hard wind blew up the lake, and the river mouth caught it like a funnel about a mile south of us. It was clearing off the ice quickly. Up on the road where the wind was lighter, snow was falling heavily, filling in and drifting over our tracks. We couldn't have asked for a better night to be chased by our government. Perfect. As Bam said, a real adventure.

I caught up to him at the riverbank.

"Here's the plan, Son. We have to avoid tracks at all costs. As soon as this storm is over, they could have hell-cops flying up and down the valley looking for any trails or unusual signs of movement. We need to strike a path down the river to the mouth. We'll stay on the ice along the shore where the wind will blow away any marks we leave. Just before the river meets the lake, Grandpa's creek comes in on the left. We'll climb up the creek bed, go through the culvert where it cuts under the road, and keep going on up to the field. It's not likely anyone'll spot us."

"Okay", he said, laughing ruefully at the weirdness of it all. I could almost see the rising blood in his face, the quickened pulse, the breath coming fast in frozen clouds. He was enjoying it. I was grateful for this: he could have been resenting it mightily. He could have been hankering after pizza and videos. Good boy, I said again silently, good, good boy. Nothing like a crisis for bringing out the hidden contours of a character. It relieved the ache I had felt only moments before up on the road. I still didn't know what we were going to do, but I now knew that I wasn't hauling dead weight. Bam, at least, and possibly Ziz, too, would help me carry it. It was that emotional weight, not the baggage, that had most concerned me.

We were about a half hour's slow pull along the ice when above us on the high road we saw a flashing blue light and heard the roar of a heavy machine. Its tire chains sang loudly. It was the town snowplow heading south to the end of habitation, the Van Thu house down on the lake. That was the plow's turnaround point, the end of the road in winter and the end of the power and phone lines. Beyond that were two hundred miles of wilderness and absolute solitude. Not a human habitation until one reached the big dams on the Columbia River.

"Great news, Bam", I said. "The plow has wiped out all signs of our tire tracks. He didn't see them."

"Hurray! Hurray!" the kids cheered.

Another ten minutes and the toboggan was no longer scraping. It hushed suddenly into a whisper as we left the ice for the soft, silent snow by Grandpa's creek. The narrow ravine was choked with drifts. It was deep and dark, and no one, I hoped, would look into it in search of fugitives. We headed up into it, to the east, gaining height with each step. The going was harder, and the boy and I hauled together on the rope that pulled Ziz and the baggage.

"Wheee, I feel like a snow queen", she cried delightedly. "This is a real adventure!"

"Yeah", gasped Bam. He caught my eye and smiled.

I realized suddenly that we had caught each other's eyes by some light other than his flashlight. Above us a pale moon struggled out of the heavy clouds. The snowfall was thinning. The flanks of the ravine had contours now, and when the moon burst out in full silver, the world was suddenly brilliant. Trees cast long shadows. The sky was a tumbling sea. The last few flakes of snow settled on our parkas, and we could see each crystal shine like mica.

"You can hear the snow falling", said Bam.

We held our breaths to hear it. Minutes passed.

"Time to go", I said at last, old practical father.

Another ten minutes climbing, and we arrived at the jaws of the culvert. It was six feet in diameter, and only father was forced to bend a little. Inside we skidded on the frozen creek. It was dark except for the moon-hole at the other side. There was too much magic for claustrophobia, but I was worried about the loud scraping of the toboggan over sticks and rocks frozen in the surface. What if there were a car sitting up there, parked, silent, watching for any movement on the road? Zizzy walked for the first time. Bam and I carried the toboggan with its full load between us. On the other side, the creek continued upward as before. The toboggan appeared to wipe out most of our snowshoe trail, and it was highly unlikely that anyone passing would gaze down into a ravine. Would they? I hoped not. But even if they did, they would have to strain their eyes to find anything.

Twenty minutes later we reached the place where the creek passed through the field below my grandfather's cabin. I crawled up the banks to spy out the situation. It was dark and still, and the house was just as it had been left months ago when he died. No lights. A black square against the moonlit clouds. A box full of memories. I felt a rush of joy.

"We're here", I whispered loudly.

"Hurray, hurray", they whispered back.

The field was a sheet of white paper without a single letter written on it.

The key was still on its nail under the back steps.

The door creaked, and we went inside, safe in the sanctuary of our past. Our boots were loud on the floorboards. The kitchen smelled of pipe tobacco. A great smell. The windows were patches of blue light. Our lives were anchored again. An island universe wheeling faithfully in the waters of the abyss.

"I'm cold", said Ziz.

I drew the blinds on every window and pulled the curtains tight for good measure. There was a quarter mile of thick pine forest between the house and the road, and the lane bent in several places, so we were completely hidden from view. But best not to take any chances. Luckily, there had been no plowing since Grandpa died. No vehicle could get up that lane until spring. But I worried that our pursuers might put two and two together and send someone out to check. Unlikely, though, because they would probably still think I was travelling by pickup, and they would be on the lookout for tire tracks. Nothing led up to or away from this house except the vaguest of toboggan marks deep in a ravine. Perhaps we were safe.

I lit the oil lamps.

"*Furtive shadows fled from the approach of their torches fluttering in the draughts*", Zizzy whispered.

The tiny house was full of peace. I was struck again by the way houses without electricity had that peculiar, delicious stillness. Wood heat, too, was different from electric baseboards or the blast of an oil furnace. Grandpa was always a great man for firewood. He faithfully cut the fifteen cords of birch that he consumed each winter, three years in advance of burning. An organized man.

Behind the cookstove there was an apple crate full of cedar splints for kindling, and I felt almost as if he had split it just before dawn this morning. He would come in from the shed in five minutes or so, after having repaired some implement in an ingenious manner. He would light the fire, and then he would rock meditatively on his chair for maybe half an hour, with a cat and a Bible on his knees, reading and stroking, reading and stroking, as the tea kettle slowly boiled. Only memory was possible for us now. But there was presence in the absence.

The big woodbox was full of seasoned birch logs, his last signature before departure. Bam stuffed paper and matches through the fire door, then the kindling crackled, and the light hurt and healed at the same time. Warmth was spreading. We all smiled. The picture of the grinning apple-cheeked child on the crate appeared less crazed. Life was semi-normal again. We were back to a world where people did indeed grin from ear to ear as they bit succulent chunks out of ruby red apples.

The radio battery was dead. There wasn't a single TV set in the place, thank God. Yup, Grandpa was definitely counterculture. There were a half dozen log cabins along the road to town, some with broken-down pickups in the lane, several with horses out back in the corral, homesteads that looked as if they came from the last century. But each one of them had a satellite dish in the front yard. The national plague. No, international. No, *cosmic*!

Three

January 18—8 P.M.
After we arrived, Zizzy whipped my journal out of her knapsack and handed it to me. I put it on the countertop and stared at it. Considering our current state of affairs, I'm in no mood for journaling. I'll try to make a few brief entries, in order to keep track of the chronology, but it's hard to concentrate. Mostly I'm writing it in my mind, engraving it in gray matter as it happens. Will I retain it all?

I'm having difficulty believing this is actually happening.

Keep writing, keep writing. Translate the liquid of memory into the solid form of letters on a page. If it's in print, it happened, right? (A debatable idea, but I'll try to think more about this later.)

I'm switching to the present tense, so that when I reread this some day I'll be able to recall the sense of immediacy. The present is tense indeed.

I have to leave the journal for a few hours and get the kids fed.

* * *

Everything is especially good here. The stew is savory, the tea we find in a ceramic jar is still potent. Canned milk is not half bad. There is even a tin box of hardtack biscuits that the mice haven't broken into. Raspberry jam from a pot sealed with wax. Why is it the best meal we've had for years? We've been injected with a marvellous elixir by the thrill of escape, the heightened sense of life, and an awareness of its transience. Did its unspeakable beauty finally get through to our dim, pampered interiors, the sluggish soul of *gotterdammerung*-man?

Ziz bustles out of the bedroom with a big hardbound volume in her hands.

"Dad, Dad, it's *The Lord of the Rings*!"

She is excited beyond containment. This is her favorite book, *our* favorite book. They love Lewis' *Narnia* series too. And Carroll's *Alice* books. And George MacDonald's *Curdie* stories. But Tolkien is the master. Grandpa read it to them one summer when she was six and her brother eight. Some of the theology and the Oxonian witticisms went right over their heads, but they got the thrill of the quest, and the terror of Orcs raiding in the hills of the peaceful Shire. Black Riders made the hair on the backs of their necks tingle. There were heroes and traitors, a hidden king, wizards, martyrs, brave men and women, creatures of every sort. The final climax made them tearful. By the end they longed to know real elves, the beautiful, beautiful elves, half man, half angel. For a brief moment they were in love with the inexhaustible splendor of the imagination, until they went off to school again that autumn and it all faded away under the onslaught of the drab men without chests, as Lewis called them.

The school board provided teachers and literature that informed the children about the correct attitudes a responsible citizen must take toward the role of men and women, toward other sexual orientations, world religions, and nonwhite races. I had no problem with the latter two. We were already an oppressed minority on two counts, being Catholics and me part native. And a third count if you include the male heterosexual.

My mother is a mixture of Shushwap-Slavey-Dogrib, though, forgive me, those three peoples would not have considered themselves a unit. Time blurs even the best of distinctions. The family gene pool had come from, in part, a nonwhite race, and for a while this guaranteed some immunity from the massing forces of social reconstruction. Not that we cared much. We just continued on being odd as we always had, oddest of all because of those characteristics that could never be assessed by color of skin or chosen rituals. It was in the heart and in the eye.

Nevertheless, the ideological conditioning at school had its effects even on Bam and Ziz. They began to question everything I asked them to do. They became sour and smirking and bored, something they had never been before. I began to hate the jaded little pout on their faces when they stepped off the school bus each afternoon, a clone-image of all the other faces pressed to the dull glass. It took most of every weekend for them to return to normal, to find out again who they really were. I didn't realize it, but they were being indoctrinated against "value judgments", against homophobia and witchophobia, and who knows what else-o-phobia, before they had properly learned the goodness of unwarped being and the dangers of the perverse. At the time I was too stupid to see it, too engrossed in fighting a titanic malignancy, the growth of Statism. The newspaper consumed all my time and energy. I failed to see how thoroughly the nonviolent revolution had already invaded a small backwoods town in the Rocky Mountains. Indeed, it had invaded my home, and I discovered this not a moment too soon.

When things finally began to break down, and my little controversy with Mizz Scylla-Charybdis erupted, I became very upset. I raved against the system to any and all who would listen. I made presentations to stony-faced school trustees. There was not an insincere person among them. They were saving humanity by educating away the undesirable elements in the human condition. Admirable, idealistic, and colossally naïve. I wrote editorials about the phenomenon. Nothing came of it but a series of dull thuds. I harangued across kitchen tables and office desks, and unfortunately the kids overheard a lot of it. They began to cringe when certain subjects arose in conversation. I wasn't sensitive to the natural trust that children have in figures of authority such as teachers and textbooks. Nor did I understand that somewhere along the line they had learned no longer to trust completely the word of their father. Granted, my words were far too intense and the principles too complex for them to grasp. I merely unsettled them. It took me a long time to cool down, to begin to think on my feet, and to win them back again.

I know now that Tolkien taught them better than all my pedantic, despairing diatribes against the follies of this century. I read the trilogy to them again last year. Tolkien had the charm. He could manifest the thrilling drama of reality through his "sub-creation", as he called it. The kids were soon rehooked on this bracing vision and eventually returned to their own world with clearer eyes and with hearts full of true things. They never did like school much after that. They had learned that we are not cells in a vast organism or numbers in a collective. Not that they had the words to express this, but I observed how they had the truth of it deep down; you could tell by their questions and their revised likes and dislikes. They were human persons in a community of persons now, and if most members of that community had lost their sense of personhood and had opted for herd law, this in no way negated Bam and Zizzy's right to the real thing.

Tonight I don't comment on any of this but merely acknowledge Zizzy's discovery by raising my eyebrows in delight, smiling at the sheer embarrassment of riches. Little did we know what the day would hold when we arose this morning. We've been plunged into a drama for sure, though I'm not so sure the thrill is worth it.

She's lost in the book now, curled up on the love seat beside the wood stove. A quilt that my grandmother made is wrapped around her. Stacked beside her like touchstones are *Alice in Wonderland*, *Through the Looking Glass*, *The Voyage of the Dawn Treader*, and *The Princess and Curdie*. She has read each of them three or four times over the years. She can't possibly read them all tonight. She just wants them with her. She sighs. She is once again rooted to the more real world. She has a local habitation and a name.

Oh, Maya, if only you could see your daughter now. You would love this bright woman-child. And you would hate me all the more for taking her into danger, wouldn't you?

Some years ago Maya and I suffered through a week of near sleeplessness. Several times a night Bam awakened us with a repeated nightmare in which the central character was a malevolent reptile. I think the boy was then about five years old. Numerous remedies were applied: hours of consoling hugs, warm milk, even rational argument. Grandpa Delaney suggested prayers and holy water. I tried it. All to no avail. This puzzled me, because Bam was a jolly, secure little fellow. In his short life he had been fed on gentle stories, exposed to no television and no monster imagery. Wracked with fatigue, I grew increasingly frustrated and made the decision to forbid him further entry to our bed. He would now have to survive in his own little room, which was brightly lit and surrounded by a loving family. We would conquer the irrational, I thought, with an exercise of firm will.

That night, after the decision, I fell into an exhausted sleep. And dreamed. In the dream I walked on a deserted beach beside an ocean. With me was a prince, a man about the same age as I. We were discussing philosophy when, suddenly, an enormous reptile rose out of the water at our sides. This aquatic Tyrannosaurus Rex was at least two houses high, and its eyes glittered with a fervid, evil intelligence. It paid no attention to me but instead spoke to my companion in a low, rumbling voice. Its words were like soft thunder, flattering and seducing the prince, while my whole being was filled with horror. The presence of evil was so palpable that even in my dream I knew it was more than a dream. "Run!" I shouted to the prince, but he couldn't hear. At this point I awoke to find myself in a state of unspeakable terror. From then on I never again refused a child entry to our bed.

Maya was into Jung at the time, and in desperation she suggested that Tyler needed to "swallow his shadow", as she called it.

Something about the idea repelled me. I didn't know much about Jung's theories, but around that time the herd was stampeding off to bookstores in search of everything he'd written. The sound of hoofbeats always makes me nervous, and Maya was galloping pretty fast. She put on a puppet show for our son, complete with a homemade dragon. Her aim was to make the boy befriend it. We would tame the "demonized symbol", she said, and have no more problems. The puppet was made of green and yellow felt with zany button eyes and wooden fangs that clattered. It was so cute it made you nauseous. Maya acted it out for Bam.

"Hi, Tye, I'm Smoggy!" she exclaimed in an ingratiating tone. "I'm lonely. Can I be your friend?"

At the point where Bam was supposed to take it and hug its cuddly little fangs and scales, he surprised us both by grabbing the thing, tearing it to pieces, and running for the fireplace. He hurled the bits into the flames and stood there with his chest heaving and a happy look on his face. After that he had no more nightmares. Maya was supremely irritated. A five-year-old boy simply cannot demolish the ideas of Doctor Jung in one fell swoop.

Shortly after that I began to read him fairy tales. Later, when Zöe advanced beyond baby-English, she joined our nightly story sessions. I rummaged through attics in search of as much old literature as I could find. I have haunted used-book stores in most of the big cities of the world. I found *The Hobbit* in a stall in New Delhi, of all places, and *The Blue Fairy Book* in an antique shop in Cairo. Children's classics were disappearing fast from North American libraries and were being replaced by a tidal wave of books written by people who appeared to be social engineers instead of storytellers. The new wave wasn't as much fun as the old, but the writers threw in enough perks and twists to bait adolescents. There was a lot of preoccupation with the occult. Perceptions of good and evil seemed confused. At least in the old days dragons looked and acted like dragons, which, if you ask me, is a lot more interesting. Life in a landscape with dragons is seldom boring.

My cousin Tara gave me a tongue-lashing about all of this. She's a likable person. She lives in Vancouver and is a "famous artist". The National Gallery recently bought one of her paintings, and she has an important show coming up in Venice. She scolded me for prejudicing the children (especially Zöe) against serpents and dragons. For Christmas one year she gave us a signed print of one of her paintings, titled *Icon 2*. The "icon" turned out to be a portrait of a woman with dozens of snakes wriggling in her womb. It was beautiful and horrible, technically a work of genius. It was a self-portrait, she explained. Judeo-Christianity, she went on to say, had unjustly maligned the serpent. And in order to rehabilitate this symbol, it was necessary to take the serpent into her womb, to gestate it, and eventually bear it into the world as a sacred feminine icon.

I looked at her as if she had swallowed a goofy-pill.

"A sacred feminine icon?" I said. "Come on, Tara!"

She gave me a compassionate look. "That's right, Cuzzie", she replied. "Symbols are arbitrary mental constructs. And your half of the species has had its version for a long time—too long. It's done a lot of damage to women. Now it's our turn."

"It's your turn, and you want *snakes*?"

"No, not *snakes*, not nasty little slitherers in the grass. I'm talking about sacred archetypes."

"I'm not very religious, Tara," I said, "but I'm not stupid."

She countered with a pitying smile.

I tried to argue that there are fundamental symbols in the human mind and heart; to tamper with them is dangerous. We can't arbitrarily rearrange them like so much furniture in the living room of the psyche. They are a language about the nature of good and evil; furthermore, they are points of contact with these two realities. But my arguments made no difference. She had heard a more interesting tale from a famous theologian: There is no absolute good and no absolute evil, he said. Conflicts are based on illusion, the products of dogmatism! All is ultimate mellow! I'm okay, you're okay, dragons are okay!

Of course I didn't want the kids to grow up believing in the literal presence of dragons. The well-nourished imagination knows that the dragon-serpent isn't frightening because of fangs, scales, and smoke pouring from its nostrils. The natural imagination knows that it's a metaphor of malice and deceit, of evil knowledge, and of power without conscience. If dragons do exist, it's not in the form of green steam engines or painted Chinese masks or lizards with weight problems. The dragon that takes no visible form is the worst of all. Call it a mental construct, call it a snake or a serpent, a theology or an ideology—call it whatever you like, but I'd rather it not prowl around these hills that I call home. Most of all I don't want it infesting my children's minds. I don't want it befriending them, either, or swallowing their fears and perhaps in the process taking possession of their very selves.

Bam took one look at the "icon" on Christmas morning and screwed up his face.

"Warpo, Dad, sicko", he muttered.

"Snake in the manger!" I growled.

Zizzy looked at it carefully, her intelligent eyes analyzing. She liked my cousin Tara very much.

"The colors are pretty", she said at last, then hurried off to find the cloth doll my mother had made for her.

I burned Tara's thoughtful little Christmas present that night, on a pile of snow in the back yard, when the kids were asleep.

"So long, *Icon 2!*" I waved as it went up in flames. "Thanks, but no thanks."

As I kicked away the ashes, I accused myself of ingratitude, insensitivity, defensiveness, patriarchy, prejudice, ruthlessness, and maybe even a subconscious degeneration into Nazi book-burning, the latter the most horrible accusation of all, because I was by temperament a pseudo-liberal. I felt a little guilty. Most of all I felt relieved.

Traditional fairy stories confirmed my feeling that I had done the right thing. As we developed into a bookish family, I noticed a change in my children's play. They acted out the fundamental dramas of the cosmic struggle, embellished upon them, revised, edited, and composed with startling ingenuity. I saw that the purpose of dragons and fairies in literature isn't to breed superstition but to defend the mind against superstition. The children would gallop over our mountain in the sunny autumn afternoons, on a yellow carpet of birch leaves, stalking the shadows lurking in the forests and caves. They were armed with homemade bows and arrows, willow rods bent to the breaking point by baling twine, and wobbly shafts outfitted with chicken feathers and armed with arrowheads they had chipped from stone. Swords were cut from branches, and silver shields were borrowed from the tops of our garbage cans. It was good that they feared dragons, for in the fearing they learned to overcome fear with courage. Dragons cannot be tamed, and it is fatal to enter into dialogue with them.

The old stories taught our children this. By contrast, the new stories were definitely in favor of the civil rights of dragons and encouraged perceptions that were in fact a form of ancient newspeak. It is still a puzzle to me how Bam and Ziz recognized that insidious tongue for what it was. I suspect it was because the truer old tales had already informed their hearts, leaving no room for invasion and plunder.

Once, when Ziz was around six years old and Bam eight, I read a book to them about a magic kingdom in the sea. In this tale two children were fishing from a rowboat off the shore of their land, while on the horizon a volcanic island spewed lava into the sky. A swarm of flying dragons circled above the cone. One of the monsters spotted the children, separated itself from the rest, sped across the water, and hovered a few feet above the waves, by their side.

Although the two children in the story were frightened at first, the dragon spoke to them in honeyed tones, using something called the Ancient Tongue. Softly, softly, the beast won their confidence and offered itself as a flying steed.

"Come, ride on me", it said. "I am your servant."

I could see that Bam was utterly entranced by this exciting one-time-only offer. But Ziz, raising a finger of warning, piped: "Careful, Tye, dragons are liars. They *always* lie!"

Bam shook himself and grinned. "Yeah", he said, the spell broken.

It was interesting to see how other children were drawn so magnetically to my young tale-bearers. Those poor town-kids had been stuffed full of the new television fantasy and had been robbed of their own imagination. The native powers of the mind were numbed and replaced by toys that were cartoon spinoffs. It wasn't a sub-created world but an ersatz world, generated by the commercial world's desire for profit. That world seized a child's imagination and fed on its life, sapping vital energies and replacing them with an addict's appetite for visceral stimuli. I was delighted, then, when these children came to play and abandoned the sinister and the idiotic plastic toys one by one at our gate. I noted carefully the hunger in their eyes. A community of questers was born on ordinary afternoons. For brief burning moments they knew that nothing is ordinary, least of all themselves.

* * *

Bam steps outside to peer at the moon. He pulls the door shut behind him, reducing the wailing wind to low moans. I throw another birch log onto the fire.

Is it my imagination, or did that rocking chair beg to creak again, just like the old days? It beckons me. I submit. I'm sitting and rocking, sitting and rocking, and if I had a Bible and a cat, I would read and stroke into the bargain.

It's ten o'clock. Ziz is forcing her eyelids open in an effort to follow Frodo's passage through the night woods. On his little hobbit feet, he's going away from safety into the unknown. He understands the perils of the journey, not least of which is the temptation to power. He would be about her size and not unlike her in disposition.

"Even hobbits have to sleep", I tell her.

She nods and closes the pages with a dreamy smile, then drags herself off to the little cot beside the old double bed on which many of the Delaneys were conceived and born. When my grandmother was alive, we kids used to take turns sleeping on that cot. We loved rising early to start the morning fires for the old folks and their slow joints. We hopped around on the cold floor while the stove warmed the house. As the years passed, our own children came and spent many nights here, listening to stories and to snoring and the wind under the eaves and the crackle in the wood stove. A restful symphony, impossible to resist during the last moments of consciousness. You always fell asleep. Ziz is asleep in less than a minute, and I tuck the quilt tightly around her.

Bam is back in. He's making his voice deeper than usual. He's tall and serious now, and his shoulders are wider than they rightly should be.

"Dad, I went down through the pines to spy out the road. Nothing went by except Mr. Thu's wreck goin' home."

Right on time, Matthew Hoàng Van Thu returning from the Chinese restaurant in town. He drives a car that's so beyond roadworthy that it has ceased altogether to be considered a motor vehicle. But it musters the guts to make the eight miles there and back each day. Matthew is lowest cook on the totem pole, and he supports his wife and six children by this trade. He's Vietnamese. He's our friend.

"He didn't see you?"

"No."

"Good."

Better to be safe, I think. Catching myself, I check my paranoia-meter and find that it's registering a little low-grade activity. Still, after the events of the day, I wonder if any man can be trusted.

"Where are we gonna go?" asks the boy.

"I don't know for sure. We can't go home. And we can't stay here."

He doesn't understand why we just can't go back and explain everything.

"If they don't believe us," he protests, "we could take lie detector tests and ink blots and all that!"

Ah, *homo sapiens psychologus.* The school did a good job on him, they did. It may take years to undo what they've managed to do in such a miserably short time.

I explain the situation in detail, and he listens carefully. He's growing up, this boy, and I'm grateful for it. He is startled by the details about the agents of State Security, which is an early indication that he has begun to think. I debate about telling him Maurice's name. In the end I decide not to tell him, because who knows what will happen in this screwy century? I explain, however, that a high government official has warned me that our lives are in danger for political, not sexual, reasons. The sexual accusation was a ruse to detain the children until we could all be scooped up in their net.

Bam looks relieved. Better to be shot for your ideas, he thinks, than for being, what did he call it, *warpo, sicko*. That would be horribly embarrassing. When you're a teenager, death is preferable to embarrassment.

Eventually he sleeps on the big old bed. And I'm left wide awake, rocking and rocking, and staring at various forms of muted light. The world is growing dark.

* * *

January 18—11 P.M.

The cabin is quiet. Time to think—but my brain is a mess.

What is happening to the world? You live in it on different levels. Physical, intellectual, emotional, social. It can get so bloody confusing. You're plunked down into the sea of being and asked to make sense of it. You swim around in the riptides from birth to death and never really catch sight of solid land. Most of us give up trying to find it. The media supply the answers and relieve us of so many burdens, don't they? Only the criminals, the power-mongers, and the saints persist. They ask the real questions and come up with opposing answers. Where does that leave people like me? Well, from time to time people like me drown. We choke quietly on the sewage, and then we sink without a word of protest.

All right, Tan, it's time. No more treading water. You'd better do some fast paddling, because something cruising out there in the abyss doesn't like you. It wants to eat you. It wants to eat Bam and Zizzy.

I'm struck again by the absurdity of the situation. Should I believe this is happening?

Yup, it's really happening.

* * *

I put down my pen and rub my face.

The whole afternoon was insane. Millions of ordinary folks out there are plugged into their TVs and think everything's just fine. A guy like me sinks beneath the surface, and nobody wonders why. People sink beneath the waves all the time, they say to themselves, so what's one more. Right? Besides, I'm a sociopath.

I feel scared.

I'm exhausted. I need sleep. But keeping a record helps to keep panic at bay. Analyzing and articulating situations provides the illusion that one is, in a sense, transcending the chaos. I pick up my pen again. Now, what shall I call these scratchings?

A Mnemonic Journal? Nah, nobody can ever remember the meaning of that word or pronounce it.

Combat Notes for the Culture Wars? A bit pretentious.

Samizdat West? Also pretentious.

An Examination of Conscience? A trifle religious.

The Paranoia Gazette? Accurate but unflattering.

The Metaphysics of Flatland: An Oxymoronic Quest? Hmmm, tempting.

Plague Journal?

Hey, I like the sound of that. Yes, a journal of the plague year! A sociopolitical plague recorded for posterity in 3-D stream of consciousness. I'll be a modern-day Defoe.

Maybe I could embellish it with one of those fustian English subtitles:

> *Plague Journal: A Cautionary Tale*, chronicling Extraordinary Events occurring at the end of an age, including a mosaic of notes, letters, newspaper clippings, airplane tickets, didactic dialogues, confessions, poems, humorous sallies, and laments—in short, Thoughts both edifying and disedifying, for the purpose of Self-Examination.

And on the back of the dust jacket, a publisher's disclaimer:

> The Incidental Reader and the Accidental Reader may discover items of some interest within the covers of this slender volume, though not all entries are of equal merit, for it is a compendium of purely private matters and certain epidemiological concerns pertinent to the scholar and the specialist. Although it clearly owes a debt to its great forebear, Defoe's *A Journal of the Plague Year*, so admired by the author of this journal, it makes no pretension to either stylistic coherence or literary permanence. It was written in haste and in conditions of stress. Indeed, evidence of the author's confusion can be seen in the several provisional titles with which he experimented. Although they have now been discarded for obvious reasons, they are included here in the interest of archival precision.

Scribble on, dear fellow. It doesn't have to be fancy or well edited. You'll have lots of time later to axe the dangling participles, stitch together the split infinitives, and make the possessives consistent. Whatever eventually fills these pages will be sloppy. But that's all right. When the dust settles I can retool the text and restore myself (and the hypothetical reader) to a sense of the author's dignity. Such as it is.

I hope.

I keep replaying the past year in my mind, looking for clues. The small entries in the journal offer at best only circumstantial evidence that something nasty is afoot. Come on, gray matter, cough up! And while you're at it, keep imprinting every detail of what's happening. Memorize, save, store it away for the day when fight-or-flight have run their course and I will have time to compose a closely reasoned tome of social criticism.

I hope.

In the meantime, I'm wondering if this fight-or-flight will make me a better man. Or will I, as Peter Stanford suggested, look into a mirror some day and see a stranger staring back at me? I hope not. The fight-or-flight reflex is a pressure valve, a way of avoiding interior collapse, but it can do things to one's personality. Unpleasant things.

Old Stephen, my Irish grandfather, came to this valley just after the turn of the century. He was fleeing some troubles in Ireland. "I killed a man once", he told me. In his old age he urged us to call him Stiofain, his real name, the name he had been given as a child. He was married to Annie, my grandmother, a suffragette with a quester's heart and a longing for true things, beautiful things, and adventure. She, too, had been an exile, a soul in flight from the tame England of her childhood. She had been raised in an enlightened New Age family, Fabians, Liberals, cultured revolutionaries without a revolution. She had early on recognized the stifling air of their own peculiar form of social romance and fled. During the last world war she purchased *The Echo* and remained its editor for more than thirty years. She was always a loner, an intellectual with no one to talk to except in the words that could be translated to Stiofain. He was as deep as she, perhaps deeper, but he was no rationalist. He was mystical and cultured after the ancient Irish way, and he was the sort of Catholic who goes to the gallows rather than step on a crucifix. He died in the bed where Bam is now sleeping. He was in his nineties when he went, and most people thought him a half-wit. But I knew better. I spent many an hour asking him questions about everything from the cosmos to horseshoes, and he had answers. But he had to be asked. Grandma, on the other hand, was always ready with a perceptive analysis, whether you asked for it or not. They had a very odd marriage that somehow worked.

They were like two eyes, these strange old exiles. Between their two ways of seeing, they gave me a vision of the world. Gradually I came to see that most people have only one eye. The person with one eye and the person with two can describe the same object word for word, but the invisible dimension of depth is lost to the former, and it is the latter whom I would prefer to see driving a car down a busy city street.

Oh, for five minutes with those two strangers and sojourners! Oh, for a Bible and a cat! I throw another log on the fire.

I prowl around, poking into drawers and cupboards, craving a whiff of their presence. When I open the broom closet I find a yellowing sheet of newspaper scotch-taped to the inside of the door. It's one of my scratchings from *The Echo*. Grandpa must have saved it. He must have thought it was pretty good. Egomaniac me.

Hail to the Brave New Culture!

by Nathaniel Delaney

(from "Curmudgeon's Corner" column in *The Swiftcreek Echo*)

I wish to applaud the efforts of the art department of Swiftcreek Regional High School for sponsoring this week's exhibit, "Art for the New Age", which, I am told, presents the work of students from the entire valley. I found it most interesting to see the range of interests current among our young people. I counted thirteen representations of rock stars, five cartoon characters, six occult symbols, eight scenes from well-known horror films, four portraits of the new state security helicopters in action (laboriously executed by boys), eleven posters warning against ecology abuse, seventeen surreal and abstract works, and finally a rather fetching portrait of four galloping horses. The latter was painted by a grade-nine girl, and I thought it deserved the first, second, and third prizes respectively. I was disappointed that it did not receive even an honorable mention. All of which has prompted me to express a few thoughts on the matter of culture.

We are familiar with the grotesque scenes of repression common to tyrannies—the times have been awash in them: images of KGB bulldozers crushing a free exhibit of painting in a Moscow park. Or a poet mumbling at his show-trial, his mind deranged by drugs courtesy of a state hospital prison. One thinks of book burnings in Hitler's Berlin or the humiliation and expulsion of Solzhenitsyn. The list is endless, yet it pales against the background of a century of unprecedented brutality. In the West we have almost reached the point of satiation, a certain numbness instilled by the passive observation of constant streams of horror on television. Electronic vision has given us immediate knowledge of distant events, but its price is a schizophrenic relationship with the world and a cumulative apathy. Crisis is now art form; above all, it is entertainment.

The flood of refugees to the West from the former Communist régimes of Eastern Europe, however, has recalled us to the reality of suffering. The deranged poet is not merely a tragic character in some vague ideological drama. He is a brother found weeping and bleeding on our doorstep. Many victims escaped through the net, arriving in the land of freedom in a state of euphoria, talking about their suffering as if it were real, in a language barely comprehensible to Western man. They exulted that now perhaps they would not die but would live and give birth to their gifts. It is astounding, therefore, that shortly after their arrival so many of them experience radical disillusionment. The several refugee artists whom I know have all expressed dismay over the condition of their new home.

"In Moscow we were suffering", one painter said. "We were dying and starving, but we loved each other, we artists. We looked at each other's work, and we understood it."

"I hate your country", said another. "There, they kill us, but here they kill the heart. You are already dead. You are a dead people!"

This, from a former professor at the Moscow Art Institute, a man hounded by the KGB, with half of his friends dead or missing. A violent, complex emotion was released in these harsh words, a reaction that we ignore at our own risk. He gave voice to what is felt by most expatriate artists in my acquaintance: they feel that the people of the West have by and large become unable to understand what is being said to them. We listen without hearing, look without seeing. It is not that the emigré artist produces imagery too esoteric for comprehension or limited by a provincial experience. On the contrary, his suffering has allowed him to break through to perception of universal truths, the perennial object and language of art. The modern North American simply has no time, inclination, or apparatus to read correctly the face of reality.

In February of last year your beloved editor was fortunate to find himself in Paris on a writing assignment. There I attended a fascinating exhibit comprised of some five hundred works of art (and several artists) brought from the former East Germany to Paris by the French Ministry of Culture. In one typical work a live woman was covered in cattle blood and her male counterpart enacted a mock castration with a chainsaw. Nudity and butchery were everywhere, and though the exhibit was hair-raising and nauseating, it was not the most extreme art event that has occurred in recent years. It was advertised widely, however, as a sociopolitical message of profound implications:

"No one in the West can understand what we've lived through", stated action-artist Heidi Haftmann. "There's a lot of butchery in our past, and we've internalized it", she explained. "Now is the time for catharsis. This is vomit-art! This is zeitgeist purgation!"

The overwhelmingly pessimistic themes of the exhibit did succeed in mirroring the desolation of modern man. The preoccupation with style over content, the use of horror as primary medium, the self-conscious obsession with destruction of artistic norms, all point to the long-term effects of suppression. The persecution of "degenerate art" by a degenerate state has merely legitimized and heroized the cultural degeneracy. One form of revolution has been exchanged for another, and the degeneracy itself has become the establishment.

It is important to note that preoccupation with absurdity, violence, and death is not peculiar to artists oppressed by their governments. It is endemic to all postwar Western societies. With the fall or decline of overt tyrannies we must not assume that man will now right himself and produce works of art restored to a sense of beauty, truth, and goodness. The opposite may occur, if the East German exhibit is an accurate barometer. The locus of the revolution may be shifting from the exterior political sphere and plunging into the interior, riding on the vehicle of culture. In this way it can penetrate to the soul of man in a way that violent régimes never can, for they alienate their citizens, rendering them perpetually on guard. The most effective revolution is the one that appears as liberation. The culture of negation, which took forty years to germinate and produce its fruit under the severe pressure of dictators, has evolved smoothly and efficiently in the democracies, where there has been little public violence to alert us to the fact that the worst is indeed happening. The enemy, we find to our surprise and disbelief, is not so much this or that tyranny as it is a concept of man that has become well-nigh universal.

As a result of the flattening effect in the new global culture, Western (and now Eastern) man is cut loose from submission to both tyranny *and* legitimate authority. He must now stagger about his existential landscape, his apparently "real" world, in search of his own lost face. In reality, every aspect of his existence is reduced to the level of accident and absurdity. He must more and more grasp at power in order to reassure himself that he is real. Thinking himself to be free, he is in reality the most tragic victim of the spirit of global totalitarianism.

This new man yearns for the decadence of the West as if our toys and drugs are icons of freedom. Has he been liberated from an austere and perversely moralistic communism just to become like us? Amoral, dedicated to our appetites, and barely able to produce a lasting work of art or literature?

[*Note: This is the one and only time I intend to pop into Delaney's journal. I thought I should let you know that this article caused more bad feeling in the valley than any other the guy ever wrote. People were really insulted. You had to use a bloody dictionary just to get through his stuff. Ridiculous in a small-town paper like* The Echo. *Most folks didn't get it, and I guess neither did I. Our oldest girl, Tanya, painted the picture of the galloping horses. It was the best thing in the show. He was right about that. — Frank McConnell*]

I insert the clipping into the plague journal for further meditation. Nothing like meditating on your own meditations to stimulate a classic case of hubris, eh? Sigh.

I keep prowling. Eventually I discover Grandpa's tattered copy of *The Imitation of Christ*. What an archaeological dig this place is! I flip through the book, and, lo and behold a letter falls out and flutters to the floor.

It's from me to ol' Stiofain, dated about eight years ago. I can't even recall writing it. I guess I'll clip the dang thing in here with all the other memorabilia.

Dear Grandpa,

Thanks for dropping by last night. Your words of encouragement meant a lot. I appreciate what you said about praying for me and Maya. But look, I think it's silly of you to "offer up" stuff for us. And no more nonsense about fasting. Don't you dare go missing any meals for our sakes. Not at your age. Not for us.

I'll grant you, it's a mess. A real mess. Yes, I'm worried, but not that worried. Maya's mad as hell at me, and who can blame her. She'll call eventually and tell me where she and the baby are. I'm sure they're all right. She always knew how to look after herself. I miss Arrow like crazy. The kids are still upset. They keep trying to get me to pray, but I've lost the taste for it completely. Damn it, but where is God when you need him? Sorry to hurt your feelings, Grampa, but sometimes I wonder if the whole religion thing isn't just some kind of placebo. [Written on the margin in my grandfather's shaky handwriting is a dictionary definition of *placebo*.]

To answer your loaded question: Yes, I've stopped going to Mass. To answer your second question: Yes, you're welcome to pick up the kids on Sunday morning and take them to church, as long as they want to keep going. I asked Paul Blackwell to weld that cracked axle on your buggy. I paid him forty bucks in advance, so don't let him cajole you into forking over any more. Hey, Gramps, when are you going to learn to drive a car!

I know it's bothering you, me backsliding, me turning into a bad Catholic. But maybe I always was a bad Catholic. Try not to worry about me. It'll turn out all right in the end. I talk with God. I do, I really do.

This morning Bam came into my bed and told me he had had a dream. In the dream he is climbing a steep mountain, between rivers swollen with molten lava on either side of him. The way is growing steeper and steeper, when he sees above him, standing on the peak, his favorite pal, the stuffed monkey named Captain Coco. Coco is waving at him and telling him that it's easy, he can do it, keep climbing. But he falls, falls (Bam, that is, not Coco), falls down toward the lava river. Bam tells me with great joy that he woke up before he struck the molten river.

I'm not sure if I'm more worried about the bad dream or about the joy.

After he left on the school bus, I had to babysit Zizzy all day because the sitter has the flu. I put the stereo on—Celtic music by the Chieftains (you would approve). Very fast, very intoxicating. Zizzy drags me up to my feet and in her toddler talk commands me to dance. Dad in his pyjamas and girl in her nightie, dragging a caboose of loaded diaper, start dancing up a storm. We laugh together like we never have before. Her face radiates pure joy. She's a good little dancer, music in the blood—your Irish genes, no doubt. I'm boogeying around the living room, when it hits me that her tiny body is so packed full of codes that maybe she's a kind of word. Maybe a word from God. Maybe this is the only liturgy I can handle right now. She's so strong and so happy, despite her world crumbling around her, that I can only gaze in awe. She leaps into the air, giving shape to the music that reposes in all matter, just waiting to be released. She lands solidly on her fat little feet, then leaps again. She liberates the music and, in her innocence, cannot know what she has done and thereby is all the stronger. Is God speaking to this tired old heart? Is he saying, "Look, stupid, don't you get it? She's as marvellous as a galaxy. You have nothing to fear. If I can call her into being, there's nothing I can't do. Now dance", he says. "Dance!"

So we dance and laugh together. As I sit writing to you, I am aware that you are rocking beside your stove only a few miles down the road. It's easier for me to put things down on paper. It's after 8:30 P.M. Bam's doing picture puzzles at the dining-room table with a toothbrush hanging out of his foaming mouth. Zizzy's asleep in her crib. I sit here trying to capture this little theophany so I can send it to you. I know it's a futile attempt. Foolish me, an incurable devotee of the cult of prose. Words always fail, darkness pulls the quilt over our weary minds, and we fall from our mountain into a troubled sleep. Only to awake to a new day.

I'm still waiting for the joy part. Can you come to supper on Sunday?

Love you,

Tan

I read it, then read it again. It's painful. Ghost of Christmas past. Foolish me.

There are other artifacts lying about the house. Boxes of Anne's journals, Stiofain's trapping notes, prayer books. And the stone cross. The uncles and aunts have agreed to leave the place unplundered until next summer's family reunion. Then we'll divide the spoils. There's little to dispense that has real value. The land is poor. The house is homemade and contains only one bedroom, a kitchen-sitting room, and a pantry. There's a blunderbuss hanging on pegs over the door that looks like it fought in the battle of Culloden, but is actually a .303 with "George V Rex" engraved in its hardware. It has killed deer and Germans and possibly Irishmen, for it's English army surplus, which my grandfather bought in the 1930s as a protection against bears.

The stone cross is the one thing in the house that I covet. Years ago, during the great fire that scoured the valley, I took shelter in a cave on this very mountain. There was something with me in the cave that night, and I wrestled with it until morning. It nearly devoured me. It had no form that would permit a battling of flesh by flesh. It was a beast of some kind, but a clever beast without shape, though capable of talking into my mind. It nearly destroyed me. Just before my climb I had rescued some things from the fire. My grandfather's house, the dwelling that stood here before this present one, was about to be burned. I thrust the cross and the journals and some books into a knapsack. Later that night I found my hand upon the stone thing while wrestling with the presence in the cave. Only when I raised the cross against it like a sword did it retreat and did I find the courage to renounce its suggestions.

The cross had been dug from the soil of a cave in Ireland on another bad night in the chronicles of the century. Family lore said that it had been carved by a saint during the lost years and buried for a millennium. My great-grandfather dug it up and bled upon it the day he was shot by a British soldier. He gave it as an inheritance to my grandfather Stiofain, who cherished it. But his son, my own father, refused it, being neither sentimental nor an antiquarian nor a believer. I am all three of those things. I held it in my hands on the night of fire, and, not long after, I returned it to Stiofain, its rightful owner. But he didn't measure the passage of time or count his mortality as significant. Thus, he left no will, and I didn't have the greed or gumption to beg for the piece of stone that meant so much to me.

I take it off the wall where it has hung for years above the maudlin prints of saints. It's not in the least sentimental, like these pseudo-religious images from the eighteen hundreds that, for all their mediocrity, could still move Stiofain's heart. No, this cross has a visible form that's true to its message—austere, dark, and beautiful. A paradox inscribed into history. It's a marvel to look upon, for the one who carved it was gifted with art as well as faith. It's scored, pitted, and stained with memories. Engraved around the Celtic wheel is the Latin word *Veritas*. Truth.

I rock some more. O bad Catholic me. Stupid me. An ache bursts inside. I try not to cry. I hold the carving in my hands and gaze at it. It's a word uttered across the centuries, connecting the one who spoke it and the one who now hears. How many generations have looked upon this object, held it, blessed it, blessed with it, worshipped before it, or made promises before it? Will the family care if I borrow it for our flight? I think not.

Stiofain, father of my spirit, what do I do? I am hunted by my own nation. I have become an enemy of the people. Where do I go? Who can be trusted? Where is there a soul who isn't infected with the atmospheric lie?

Speak to me, Grandfather! Oh, speak out of the ocean of your silence.

The stove spits and cracks. The wind curves around the corners of the house. Silence. I am alone at the end of an era.

"You mustn't hate them", he said to me once when I was a boy and raging against injustice. Yes, I was an early rager.

"Tan," he said, "you aren't just angry with their foolish ideas, you're angry with them. Be careful, lad, or you'll end by hating them."

"I do hate them, Grandpa. I hate their stupid, deceiving guts!"

How grieved the old man had been on that day. His eyes had filled with tears.

"If you hate them, you'll become like them, and maybe worse than them, no matter how many things you get straight in your mind."

I had sloughed off the words of a man I considered to be worn out and too kind for valor. Forgetting that Stiofain had learned his lessons the hard way. He had seen his own father murdered, and he had killed. I, too, had to learn many of my own lessons the hard way. I know some things now that I didn't know then.

Tomorrow I'll think of practicalities. Tonight I'm trying to see clearly. And what I see is this: there is no room left in the world. It's an increasingly narrow place. They either bend us out of our true shape or force us to make fantastic leaps as we attempt to escape. They mustn't make me leap without thought, without remembering who I am.

Tomorrow I'll try to reach my father by phone. He's not sympathetic to me or to my newspaper and what it stood for, but I'm his son. He'll help us, or at least hide us. If I can get to the Thu place and call him, maybe Dad will drive down from Prince George and get us out of here. There must be a million places they haven't yet computerized or monitored. We'll find one and sit out the storm.

I sleep.

In the garden stands an ancient tree. The children sleep beneath it. The white hart circles the children, protecting them.

The serpent bellows and coils to strike. The children awake and cry out. The hart stands firm as the beast weaves back and forth, tearing the air with its claws. It lunges forward to deliver a killing blow.

The hart intercepts it, though his white hide is now raked with red. He is bleeding heavily. His eyes are golden. They are full of fire. He rears his rack of antlers and strikes an unexpected blow in return. The beast reels backward, and its malice smolders.

Everything is mine, says the beast. *These, too, are mine. I will have them.*

"Nothing is yours", replies the hart, fending it off with thrusts of its horn. "Nothing is yours because you wanted to possess all, to be master of all, to destroy what you willed."

It is my art, says the beast.

"You create nothing", replies the hart. "You have learned only to break, to corrupt, and to ruin."

I teach them to break and corrupt and ruin and I make them think they are creating. That is my highest skill. I go where I will, doing as I please.

"Only for a brief time."

In devouring them, I shall destroy you.

"You will not", says the white hart.

I wake, sweating heavily, panting from the dream. I wish to weep, but I can't. I am a grown man. The children are still sleeping.

Night is almost over.

I am afraid.

Four

January 19—early morning
The kids are still sleeping. Reason and unreason are circling each other in this shopworn psyche of mine. I found a ream of foolscap paper in a box in the closet. Grandma's, no doubt, left over from her days as editor of *The Echo*. I add some to the plague journal. Last night I tried to copy into this journal the contents of a fast-growing mental file titled "Delaney's Great Adventure". The material is there, all right, tucked away in the subconscious, but I was too exhausted to get much of it out. All I can manage at the moment are a few running entries. When all this is over, I'm going to go into deep file-recover. How many gigabytes are in the average human brain? I'll try to get it onto paper and publish it some day, or at least get it circulating in manuscript form if publishing is no longer possible. If the Conditioners succeed in wiping out every authentic account of history (in the Orwellian sense), then they'll be able to recreate the world in their own stunted image. I must leave a trace. If a thousand fugitives leave enough fragments, there may come a time in the future when the world will be reconstructed.

* * *

I get up at dawn, opening blinds and drawing back curtains. A golden light breaks in through the glass. Rest has restored my spirits a little. Outside, the field looks as if nothing has walked across it since Indian summer. Our tracks have been obliterated.

Night fire is a slow story told by an old man in whispers, drowsing off into sleep. It is meditation. Morning fire is young, crisp, and earnest, busy about the tasks of cooking, warming a chilled house, and reassuring all occupants about the virtues of rising. It bustles noisily in the stove.

I find a tin of bacon in the larder and a box of powdered eggs. There are dried onions too. Within minutes I have an omelette simmering and coffee perking. It's my one remaining vice, this sense of exotic smell. That and my tendency to preach, of course.

Ziz is still sleeping after her late-night plunge into quest. It's nine o'clock. We've all slept in. Time is elastic and lazy as we awake. Bam is stretching his muscles in long johns, bending and looking out the window.

He suddenly stiffens and beckons me over beside him.

"Dad, I think they've found us."

Sure enough, there, crossing the upper field is a figure carrying something that looks like a gun. He has just stopped in mid-stride and is gazing down at the house. The smoke from the chimney! We pull back from the window.

Strange. If they were searching for us, would they cross an open field at its most visible point?

Bam dares to look again.

"Yahoo!" he shouts. While I'm peering cautiously around the window frame, he slips his boots on and is out the front door in a flash.

"Bam, come back here, right now!"

But it's too late. The boy is shouting to whoever is out there, and the visitor is waving back, brandishing his gun. They meet halfway up the hill. I watch them pounding each other's backs and making loud conversation. Too loud.

"Get down here right now", I yell angrily.

The two figures come down fast, laughing.

It's Hoàng Van Thu's eldest son, Anthony. He grins from ear to ear and his eyes are sparkling black agate. He's seventeen years old, as handsome as an elf-prince.

"Mister Natano, Tie-lore is get too cold. He should come inside. He gots no clothes on."

"Quite right, Anthony."

We sit around the kitchen table, joking and drinking coffee. Anthony eats a bird's breakfast with us. Then Ziz is awake, dragging her feet out of the bedroom, rubbing her eyes. She slept in her clothes and looks rumpled. She slumps her body down and nods at the elf-prince.

"Hi, Anthony."

"Hi, Zoo-ee."

Anthony finds everything hilarious, but he's reverent about manners. He pronounces our names with care, if not precision. He's always good-natured and a very hard worker. He long ago popped my prejudice that all teenagers are lazy. On occasion I pay him to help Tyler split firewood or cut back the encroaching bush behind our house. I just don't have the time to do it myself. I hire him mostly for the good example he gives to my son.

Ziz is not much shorter than Anthony. She has a preadolescent crush on him—most of the time. Today she's still busy waking up. She eats a trucker's meal. Bam eats even more. I make do with coffee and some hardtack with jam. Another famous repast. It tastes great, and the light coming through the window is a marvel. I light my pipe and sigh back in the rocker. We should try to be fugitives every month or so.

"Why are you out so early?" I ask our visitor. His face becomes impeccably polite.

"I am hunting rabbits, Mister Natano. I think maybe this is a good place to find some. I see many cars on road last night and this morning."

"Cars?"

"Yes, cars."

"What kind of cars?"

"Gray cars with green circle on it."

Police cars are piebald, and the other ministries have bright colors. This one is new to me. State Security possibly.

"Two men, they stop at our house and ask my dad and my mum some questions."

Anthony looks at me very seriously. With great significance in his voice, he says, "They want to find *you*, Mister Natano."

Conversations with the Thu family are usually elaborate oriental creations, full of beauty and form. Exquisite. Emerging from an entirely different concept and experience of time.

"These men talk very nice to us. But my mum look in their eyes. She say these are bad men."

"They're probably a type of police", I say.

"My mum see into people's souls, Mister Natano. Nobody fool her. God give her this gift. We try to fool my mum lots. One time my dad he show her a picture of boss of Communists. My mum never read papers. She not know this guy. In this picture this guy look like very nice man. He is talking to Pope. My dad say to my mum, this man is friend of Pope. He try to fool her."

Anthony laughs.

"Oh, my mum, she is so smart. She look close at picture, then she say, No, Matthew, this is very evil man. She look at Pope's eyes, and she say, Matthew, the Pope knows he is evil, but he want to bring him to God. My dad laugh hard. Nobody fool my mum."

With his mother's credentials more than assured, he falls silent.

"Anthony, did the men who came to ask questions go away?"

"Yes. Last night. But come again this morning. They say you make very bad crime. They say you go to jail and then have fair trial. They gone now. My Dad say to me, Anthony, you go to ol' Mister Delaney's field, and you hunt for rabbits this day. I don't understand my dad, but now I understand him."

I understand him also. Thank you, Matthew. Thank you, Anthony.

The boy is sipping coffee with his head nearly touching the table. An Eastern custom, perhaps. His back is a bent bow. He's only an inch or two taller than Bam, but he's a diminutive man, perfectly proportioned. The ratio of height to width is fully developed, whereas Bam is still mostly child. Bam's shoulders usually slump unless he's engaged in a moment of bravery or is trying to impress. But Anthony is always set firmly in his essential form. He never slumps. Though when occasionally he bows, he's a valiant little warrior pausing in a humble gesture. The gun is still strapped across his back. It's a relatively harmless .22. How is it that I know he would use it on an enemy?

"What does your mother think of me?" I ask him.

He becomes thoughtful.

"My mum say you a good man. She like you. She say you a very, very smart man, too. If you want, you could be rich. But you not wanna be rich . . ."

"I'm not so sure about that, Anthony."

"My mum never wrong. She say you stay here keep paper going. She say you got trouble, and you got no money because you wanna say what it is true in your paper. Right?"

"Your mum's a great lady, Anthony. And your dad, too, he's a great man."

"Thank you, Mister Natano."

"You can call me Nathaniel."

"Thank you, Natano."

Bam says, "Dad what are we going to do? If hell-cops go over, they'll see the smoke. And they'll see footprints too."

"My dad say to me, if you see Mister Natano, you tell him he is safe at our place. He come and have supper with us. He come and sleep with us."

While I've been soaking in the ambience of the country kitchen and the sleepy morning light, these two have snapped right to the central issue: how to escape detection. I have always been too philosophical, and usually at the worst possible moments.

"That's a great idea, boys. We'll do it."

Bam is jumping into his pants and jackshirt, Ziz is scurrying around looking for socks and *The Lord of the Rings*, while I collect boxes and sleeping bags by the door. I add two eiderdown bags that belonged to my grandfather. I take his big gun from over the door and a pair of willow and rawhide snowshoes. Anthony straps it all onto the toboggan on the kitchen floor.

I take one last sweet draw from a jug of water from the kitchen pump. It tastes like no other water in the world. Stiofain dug a good well. I use the rest to kill the fire.

Then, all of us are ready by the open door. After a search of the sky, we're out onto the field and running for the south woods. The boys are pulling the toboggan. We make it in three minutes flat. We're puffing hard. The skies are still silent. Lucky. There is usually little warning of an approaching hell-cop now that they use whisper jets.

Five minutes into the bush we pick up Anthony's trail.

"Here I am this morning", he says. "Now we go fast to my place on this feet prints. No one see us."

Sure enough, he has hugged the sides of cliffs and kept always under the canopy of spruce and cedar. It's doubtful that a *feetprint* is visible from above. We make good progress, and as we trot along, I give the boy a thumbnail sketch of why the secret police are interested in me. He seems to understand right away. Half an hour's steady trek, and we're abreast of the lake. Thu's is not far. Blue jays are scolding happily. The world appears normal. Though it's cold, trees are beginning to drip under the waves of the sun. The snow is thinner here, and there must have been a melt recently, followed by a deep freeze during the night, because the surface is like rock for most of the way. Down toward the road it gets softer underfoot, and close to the embankment at road's-end Ziz is sinking deeper with each step. We put her on the toboggan. Bam and I have the logger's shoes, and Anthony has the long willow trail-shoes.

He crawls up the huge snowbanks made by the plow and peers over the edge. He stands and waves at us. All clear.

The road is empty. The sky is silent. We can see Thu's little compound down on the edge of the lake, with a thread of silver going up from the chimney. The last homely house, as Frodo would have called it.

* * *

I use the word *house* advisedly. It was once a boat. In the seventies it had been used to corral the millions of square feet of logs and trash that floated to the surface when the valley was flooded. The prevailing winds had blown most of it up the long arm of Canoe Lake until it all jammed at the northernmost end, precisely over the drowned fields and the ruined cabin in which my father was born. That was the year Stiofain and Annie moved to the place where the kids and I spent last night. Then during the great fire everything in the valley was scourged and purified. The town was eventually rebuilt. Stiofain's little cabin was put up again the following spring. The insurance paid for new machinery for *The Echo*. My father and mother moved to Prince George. Many old people died of grief. But here and there small grace notes lay scattered throughout the valley. One of them was the big iron barge that lay abandoned down on the shore of the lake. Most of its deckhouse was intact, though blistered by the intense heat it had endured. It sat out the fire just offshore in shallow water, with an inferno of forest on one side and ten square miles of floating logs blazing not a hundred yards away toward the head of the lake. "The Lake of Fire", Stiofain called it. The big boat was one of the few items to emerge intact from the conflagration. The logging company let it go as a tax write-off.

That was the year of the last Vietnamese boat people. Matthew Thu arrived in Swiftcreek with haunted eyes, a wife, and three boys. They lived in a local church rectory for three months while Matthew worked at the restaurant and saved enough to put a down payment on something for them to live in. I gave them food and any spare change I had, but there was precious little of that. Then they found the boat. It had drifted onto the muddy banks of the lake and listed. Matthew hired a bulldozer to pull the thing up above high-water mark. He managed to buy the ten acres of land that surrounded it. The family moved out to the new property in the spring and took up temporary residence in a tattered white camp-tent. Every day Matthew travelled the eight miles to and from work by bicycle. On weekends he cut poles and braced the old scow so that it would withstand a mighty earthquake.

"You're like Noah", I said to him when I went down for the first time to drop off some moose meat that Thaddaeus Tobac had given us. When Anthony translated, Matthew laughed—a little hysterically. Jeanne, his wife, smiled. They invited us to stay for supper, which turned out to be a fish soup. That summer they were eating wild berries and pulling lots of graylings and dolly vardens out of the lake. Sometimes whitefish. The chowder they concocted from the abundant catch was their daily fare, but it was so heavily spiced it nearly tore the flesh off the insides of my mouth. Still, the friendship tasted very sweet. I needed that friendship badly, because the entire town, as small communities do, had taken sides over the issue of my departing wife, and my wife's position had won the field. I wasn't terribly popular to begin with, because of my editorials. Most of my subscribers lived far away in big cities, and the few copies purchased at the local supermarket only fueled the prevailing unpopularity of the editor. I provided something for them to disapprove of, I suppose, which is a form of entertainment common to isolated, ingrown communities. It was a case of local boy makes bad.

When my mouth caught fire that first time, Matthew suppressed an immense mirth behind his Charlie Chan coke-bottle glasses, then burst. We all laughed till the tears spilled from our eyes, everyone from the exhausted, discouraged, and self-pitying editor to the littlest Thu. Matthew drowned my fire with a bottle of cold beer pulled up by string from the lake bottom. And from then on we were friends in a curiously formal friendship that crossed all cultural and language barriers. Over the ensuing years, we discovered that we had a great deal in common: we are both about the same age, we are male, we are husbands and fathers, we are Catholics, and we are relatively sane, and have managed to be so in an era that encourages none of those things. In order to last, however, friendship must have a bond of conversation. Most of our conversations are still conducted in pidgin English, enriched with an extravagance of hand and facial gestures and, on occasion, when abstractions enter into the talk, with painstaking translation through the boys. It's strained discourse at times, but always worth it. I go home after an evening at Thu's feeling, well, . . . feeling joy.

Three little girls have been born since their arrival, and they all speak like perfect North Americans. School has done that, school and a battery-operated radio that brings in the C.B.C. northern service. The older boys retain a thick bondage in their tongues. They are fiercely proud of their family and of their home. The boat is a house now, after a fashion. They painted the hull fire-engine red and the pilot house a Kelly green. Outdoor Christmas tree lights are strung along the mast wires and burn brightly all year round, powered by a small wind generator and batteries. No power lines lead to the ship, but a ratty looking phone line drapes across several pine branches from the last pole out on the road. Matthew and the lads have added a woodshed on the port side and a large storage area and smokehouse to starboard. That's where they cure most of the fish they catch. There are various other appendages at odd angles. A small log barn has been built across the yard and contains several impolite goats; there is a chicken shed, too, a pig house and a run, and a noisy black and white mongrel dog barking in the front yard.

It raises a terrible ruckus now as we dash across the end of the road and through the yard toward the front porch. This structure leads to a covered stairway that zigzags up the exterior side of the hull. The tall caucasian is forced to bend his neck a little to get to the deck. The only entrance to the dwelling is up top through the pilot's cabin. Rather unsafe, a real firetrap, but it does make it something of a fortress. As we climb, Anthony shouts ahead of us in Vietnamese. From below there comes a torrent of noise, the stomping of many feet, and we're met on the deck by the first wave of the family. Within seconds everyone has emerged, even Jeanne with the baby, and her mother, a very ancient, shrivelled, woman whose eyes are, I suspect, the genetic source of the family radiance. Jeanne smiles at me politely and bows her head a little. She pats my arm.

"Nice, nice", she says.

Matthew hugs me. Children are jumping around clamoring for answers to questions. Bam and Ziz love it, but they are somewhat embarrassed by the exuberance of the attention.

Why are these faces so rare? Why do they shine so? Why are the faces of most people in our society so burdened or blank or sour?

"You come inside, please, Natano, in my house", says Matthew. Anthony and the other teenage boys are exchanging rapid-fire conversation. Anthony is doing most of the talking. Everyone looks suddenly serious.

"What did you say to them?" I ask.

"I tell them about my visit to you. I tell them why police looking for you. I tell them be careful watch out for car or hell-cop."

The younger boys scatter across the deck to various look-out nests. They are adrift on the China Sea, watching for pirates.

We negotiate the narrow stairway that descends into the dark interior of the hull. The smell of fish and sweat and woodsmoke always hits me like a wave. It's pungent but not offensive. It's the universal smell of humanity. We are down in the main part of the hull now. It's divided into three rooms. The large central one must be twenty or more feet long and is about fourteen feet wide from port to starboard at its midriff. It's filled with a homemade plywood table, covered with oil-cloth and surrounded by ten chairs, plus a highchair for the baby. Along the walls are two sets of bunk beds, closets, a couch, an armchair.

On one wall is a shrine with a crucifix, a small porcelain madonna, a framed print of several Oriental martyrs, plus a yellow oleograph of Saint Joan of Arc—the latter an inheritance from the colonial days of French Indochina (Jeanne's full name, in fact, is Jeanne d'Arc Thu). A hanging vigil lamp burns red beside the shrine. Grandma sits down on a bench beneath it and fingers a rosary. She arrived last month. Matthew and Jeanne paid ten thousand dollars ransom to the Vietnamese to let her go. They took out a mortgage on their land and the boat to raise the money. The bank grudgingly admitted that the acreage was worth at least that much. Grandma flew in an airplane for the first time in her life. She has had more bizarre experiences during the past month than in her previous eighty years. The sight of a six-foot-one-inch man running away from home is possibly one of them. She's staring at me.

At the end of the room, right under the pilot's cabin, is a chipped, enamelled wood-burning cookstove on which Jeanne makes meals. At both ends of the room are doors into the fore and aft cabins. Each of these two chambers measures roughly ten feet long by eight feet at its widest, dwindling to a sharp apex at the bow and a curve at the stern. Along the body of the boat there are small portholes letting in circles of daylight, but the interior is mostly lit by kerosene lanterns and a single dim light bulb (powered by the homemade wind generator). We sit around the table now, this heart of the family's life. Here is the place where meals, homework, sewing, and debates occur.

Anthony explains to his parents what has happened. I think it's a translation of my earlier thumbnail sketch, minus some details about the politics of my predicament.

Once again, everyone looks very serious.

"Not too good. Not too good", says Matthew.

He's thinking hard. "What you do, Natano? Where you go?" he asks.

Jeanne speaks rapidly in her language.

"My wife say you stay here with us. You eat, you sleep. She think maybe police not come back."

"Thank you," I say, meeting their eyes, but unable to hide the moisture in mine.

Jeanne suddenly begins to chide me by way of distraction.

"Look at Zoo-ee! Look at Tie-lore!" she cries. "They hungry. You bad daddy. Children too skinny. You should make them fat!"

Everyone knows what she's doing, and we all enjoy it immensely. She's playing the scold, and by doing this, she tells us that we're one of the family, and at the same time she shakes off the looming paralysis. Jeanne hands her own skinny baby to Matthew to hold, dishes up three bowls of fish stew and sets them in front of us. Tyler and Zöe stare down into the depths with looks of suppressed horror. They think they're about to be burned.

Every Vietnamese face in the boat laughs uproariously. They understand perfectly.

"No worry", says Jeanne. "No hot in this. No fish sauce in soup. Just fish. Noodle. Salt. Try! Eat!"

It's a marvellous chowder. I still can't grasp why everything tastes and smells so intensely. Sounds, too, are becoming clearer, flushed with meaning.

"Hey," I say, "why aren't the kids at school?"

They all look suddenly mysterious. There's a discussion.

Anthony explains, "My mum know you coming today. She know we gonna look after you. She had a dream."

Not only does she read souls, she dreams of events before they occur.

"My mum say your kids play with our kids. So our kids stay home. We phone school, tell principal we sick."

He coughs. They all begin to cough on signal. Eight people coughing very fabricated coughs. Even the baby joins in.

"It not a lie", explains Anthony. "We sick of school."

"Very sick", adds Matthew for emphasis.

* * *

Later in the day I'm chatting with Matthew and Anthony on the deck.

"Thank you so much for making me and my children welcome here, Matthew."

"You stay?" he replies.

"I'm afraid we can't stay. You'd be harboring a fugitive from justice, and then you'd be in trouble too."

He smiles. "We play dumb Vietnamese people. They not bother us."

"They would, though, you know. They'll bother you very much if they ever find out we were here."

The thought of the forms that the "bothering" would take makes me cringe.

"No, I have to go. First I need to telephone someone. I'm pretty sure he'll drive down to get us. Then, when we get out of this pressure cooker, we'll go away into the bush and live anonymously for awhile."

"A-non-ee-muss?"

"It means hidden. Like we'd have no name; no one would knows us. We'd be nobodies."

"Like Hoàng Van Thu family", he remarks in a voice that's unusual for him. It's a distinctly ironic tone, accompanied by an odd little smile. I'd like to pursue this further, but first:

"I should phone."

"Yes, yes, Natano, you come phone now." Matthew points into the pilot house.

Suddenly, without warning, Anthony shouts, "Go below fast!" and pushes me to the forward hatch. I stare at him, more surprised than affronted by this departure from manners, until seconds later I hear the hum. My heels have just disappeared down the gangway as the hell-cop zings by overhead. It's no more than ten feet above the treetops. It doesn't stop.

The whole family, with the exception of Grandma and the baby, is quickly out on deck. Zöe and Tyler don't appear. It's late winter afternoon, a leaden twilight settling in under high overcast with a smear of red horizon over the Cariboo range in the west. The colors around us are still discernible.

"Hell-cop", says Matthew. "Very fast, very quiet. Police."

"What color?" I ask.

"Gray with green on it", says Anthony.

It's a tiny wasp now, zigzagging down the lake in a search pattern. Anthony points out a second one on the other side of the lake. I hadn't seen that one. The boy's eyes are good.

Everyone returns to his own tasks.

"You phone now?" Matthew asks.

I'm still shaken by the speed with which these infernal machines appear out of nowhere. I take three deep breaths.

"Okay, I guess I'd better make that call."

Matthew goes below and hands the phone up on a long extension cord through a hole in the floor. Usually it sits on a shelf down in the main room. He returns to the pilot house and stands beside me. I ask for privacy. Matthew looks hurt for a moment until I remind him that the police may return, and it's better if his family knows nothing of my plans. The police, I tell him, have a new science for extracting everything there is to know. He understands. He has met that kind of policeman in his own past.

When I'm alone, I dial the number. There's an answer after the second ring.

"Hello."

"It's me, Dad."

"Tan, where are you?"

"I'm in really big trouble. I can't tell you where I am just yet."

No reply.

"I need your help. I need it badly."

"I know. It's on the news. TV, radio, the papers."

"What are they saying about me?"

"They say you're mentally ill, possibly armed and dangerous. They say there's a warrant for your arrest on charges of sexual assault against your children and possibly other children . . ."

I groan. "Oh, God, this is horrible. It's not true, Dad."

There's a silence on the other end, and volumes are spoken in it. I feel dread rising.

"Dad, it isn't true!" I say intensely.

"Look, Son, you've been under a lot of stress since Maya left. And I know you're discouraged about the closing of the newspaper. But you can't make Tyler and Zöe suffer for it."

"I'm not. They're happy. Want to talk with them?"

Pause. "Yes. In a minute."

I slowly and carefully explain to him what has happened. I mention Maurice's phone call this morning without using his name. My father can guess whom I mean.

"That would have been fairly convincing, except for all the evidence they've found. Tan, I want to believe you, but don't you think kidnapping the children is a little extreme?"

"Dad! Listen to yourself. Kidnapping my own kids? They're *my* kids, dammit! I don't have to kidnap them. The State is supposed to justify to me anything they propose doing with my children, not the other way around. It's all been turned upside down, don't you see? Until recently it was the parents who let the government educate them for six hours a day, on loan, on trust. Now they think we have to justify our parenting to them, and they loan the kids back to us, on trust."

My father is a retired principal of the high school in Prince George. He prides himself on being a reasonable man. He's an atheist. He is not fond of the new social engineering, but he dislikes the old world view even more. My world view. The measured, tolerant note he strives always to maintain has been profoundly disrupted. He's upset and perhaps a little frightened. Not for himself, of course, because he's personally fearless. For his grandchildren.

"It's totally screwed, Dad!" I'm close to shouting.

"Calm down. I'm willing to listen. But the violence, Tan, the violence. Old Bill never hurt you."

"Old Bill?"

"Maybe it was an accident. Maybe you didn't mean to hit him so hard. He was only trying to stop you. Why did you—?"

"Dad, what's happened to Bill?"

"He's dead. He died in emergency at McBride Hospital about an hour ago. That's the other thing they want you for."

Bill dead? My heart starts pounding too fast.

"Dad. I'm telling you with every ounce of conviction I have in me, and I swear on everything I hold sacred, that I just do not know what happened to Bill. The last time I talked to him he was fine. He phoned to warn me that . . ."

Then it hits me.

I am stunned into silence. I sit down on the floor of the pilot house, shaking my head, trying to think. This can't be happening.

After a long pause, my father goes on.

"Tan. You're in crisis. It can happen to anyone. There are people here who'll help you."

I had forgotten how completely my father places his faith in psychology and sociology. It's his religion. It never bothered him that the expanding constellations of theory in those disciplines are continually at odds with each other. More than that, the theories are always being demolished and reconstructed. Yet my father invests an extraordinary trust in them. He believes they are sciences.

This is especially puzzling because I know that he's quite an intelligent man. He's also an honest man. It has been more and more confusing for me in recent years to hear him mouth the new popular myths. He does it in a unique style, of course, intellectually correct and all that. He'll never cease to be the quintessential rugged individualist. But he no longer seems able to admit the contradictions in the world materializing around us. What has happened to him? Has he breathed too deeply of the ideological gas that's spreading everywhere? Has he become a creature of impressions like everyone else, or almost everyone else? Has he abandoned his lonely quest for Truth? That's the prize he always maintained he was searching for. Where did it go?

I'm dismayed by what is now coming out of this great mind. I can only stammer, "Did you just simply believe what they told you?"

"Well, it seems pretty evident—"

"What? What evidence has led you to judge me and find me guilty? Just the fact that they say I am? In the old days you questioned everything, you didn't take anything at face value."

"There's the evidence of a dead man, Nathaniel. And two missing children."

"Did you consider that there might be another explanation? Maybe somebody else killed Bill. Maybe Bill knew something or refused to tell them something."

"But it's the police and the media who supplied the information—"

"I rest my case."

"What do you mean by that? You *are* paranoid. Get a hold of yourself, Tan. Turn yourself in."

"Hand myself over to the very people who probably arranged Bill's death?"

"Look, I've read a great deal about psychosis, and the mind is capable of blocking out painful memories. In all probability you had a moment of panic and extreme rage that erupted in murderous emotions. You did it. But you also have a moralistic temperament. You just couldn't function with the duality. You submerged it. In therapy you'll be able to look at the experience and integrate it into your personality."

"Where does that leave Bill?" I murmur.

And where does that leave me? If I'm lucky, I'll take up residence in a cage, and mental vivisection will become my way of life. They'll demolish and reconstruct my personality according to the latest theory. I'll believe anything horrible they tell me about myself.

"The radio stations have been playing a recording of a message you left on an answering machine yesterday, around the time of the murder. It's your voice, Tan. You sounded pretty off the wall, and there was a gun shot."

"A gun shot? What are you talking about?"

"You kept crying, 'Help me, please.' They've been broadcasting it every hour on the hour. A dozen times now I've listened to that gun shot, and I wonder each time if I'm hearing the sound of my son killing himself. Or killing another human being. Do you know what that does to a father?"

His voice shakes.

"This isn't happening", I say. "This is unreal."

"Your mother is very upset. She doesn't believe it's true. But, it's true. You know it, and I know it, and you're going to have to face up to this mess if you're ever going to be well again."

"Well again?"

I still don't understand what he's telling me. Then, with a horrid, sinking feeling I remember my recorded message to Woolley.

"Dad! It was a joke."

"A joke?"

"That's a thing Doc Woolley and I do for fun", I plead. "It's our weird sense of humor. We're always laughing at death. It's a joke."

"It's not very funny."

"Look, it was a dumb exercise in black humor, that's all. In very bad taste. I repent of it in dust and ashes. I should never try to be funny."

He doesn't answer.

"You don't believe me."

"Look, where are you? I'll drive down and get you. We'll go to the authorities, and I'll be with you, Son. Don't worry."

Why do I not feel reassured?

I'm weeping silently now. But I'm able to get a few words into the receiver.

"It's okay, Dad. I'll figure something else out."

"Where are you?"

"It's better you don't know."

A long pause.

"I want you to know that I love you, Nathaniel."

He has never said that before. My father.

"Do you remember, Pa, the time a few years back when we went out fishing? The last time. Do you remember what we talked about?"

"Vaguely."

"That was the most important conversation we ever had. I'm going to ask you to try to remember it, all of it, after I hang up. Then compare it to this conversation. Will you do that?"

"I'll try. What did we talk about?"

"We talked about truth. We talked about how governments are afraid of the stuff. I tried to convince you that totalitarianism was already here. Then you said my arguments were groundless because no journalists were being arrested for writing the truth."

"That's still the case."

"It's not. That world's gone, Dad."

"You're being sought by the police for what you've done."

"No. I'm being sought for thought-crime."

He doesn't answer.

"I love you, Dad."

"Yes." His voice is choking.

"And I'm innocent."

Silence. Then he hangs up.

I'm busy wiping my eyes and forget momentarily to hang up the receiver. There is no second click. Obviously they haven't got around to bugging Dad's line yet. Lucky for us, because if there was a monitor on his line, the Thu family might find itself in deep trouble.

He didn't get to talk with Bam and Ziz. It's better this way. He might have dug a comment out of them that would give the Thu family away. He wouldn't for an instant believe in the bother this would cause them.

Dad, I say to him in my mind, I had hoped for something different from you. Father, my father. I had been confident that you would believe my word, a word I've always sacrificed a great deal to keep. Didn't you notice that? Or have you always wanted me to be proven wrong in the end? All these years, have you been gathering an enormous indictment against my religion? You considered it an antiquated system that produces repressed and repressive individuals. Did you ever wonder if perhaps it was necessary for you to believe that? Neat, isn't it, Pa, the way the State has provided the perfect evidence to support your favorite myths. What can I say against a myth that masquerades as a science? Nothing. It's a closed system. A very dangerous mental construct it is, too, because it classifies dissent, not so much as heresy (for heresy enjoys a mystique of romantic revolution), but as sickness. And who would ever want to be sick, right? Right, Pa?

Pride, it'll get you in the end every time. My pride lay in thinking I could save the world single-handedly. Your pride lay in a terror of being caught in the act of blowing your liberal credentials. You didn't even know it. You couldn't admit your addiction to politically correct opinions. You scoffed at the reality of dragons, and as a result they pinned you to the ground as you loudly denied their existence. You thought that by your skepticism you had escaped mythology, and all the while a myth was eating you alive.

Try to remember that last conversation, Pa. Try.

* * *

It was a hot August afternoon, and the lake was spattered with molten silver. The sun fractured into a million pieces off the butt of the little flat-bottom fisher I had named *Bobabout*.

We had built it together, Dad and I, when I was a boy. After years of affectionate abuse, *Bob* was chipped and split and shipped water, but that was part of its charm. We made a point of never taking care of it until it had sunk in shallow water, our sign that it needed another dry dock. It was painted three times in its life. But on that day, somewhere between number two and three, it was still relatively seaworthy. Dad had finished off two beers. I was drinking coffee from a thermos. The scent of blistering green enamel and old fish was intoxication enough for me. Mnemonic to say the least. We hadn't caught a thing all day, but that was never the point, anyway.

I don't now recall how we got onto the subject. I think he asked me a question about the newspaper. I answered. He asked me another. I answered that one, too. Innocuous queries. But I sensed he was bothered about *The Echo*.

"Dad, you're chewing on something. Come on, out with it."

"I'm worried, Tan."

"About what? About me? About the paper?"

"About both, really."

He let me digest that.

"Anything in particular?"

"Well, I suppose I could say the tone of your recent articles."

"Oh? What tone is that?"

"Things are basically very good in the country, the economy

is humming along nicely. But under everything you write there seems to be a deep reservoir of . . ."

There he paused, and I could tell he was still thinking his way through to an insight he wasn't sure of.

Eventually he said, "I guess you could call it a pool of anxiety underlying everything. I just don't understand why you're so unhappy."

"I'm not unhappy. Are you unhappy?"

He flashed me a look.

"Hell, no!"

By which I learned that my father was indeed unhappy. I wondered why. He was loved by my mother, a good and wise woman. He was in excellent health. He owned land and had established himself as a figure commanding respect in education circles throughout the province. He would soon retire. I saw also that he didn't want me to know he was unhappy. Victims of the reactionary religion to which I belonged shouldn't be allowed to suspect the profound misery of the enlightened. He was a liberated man, and he wished me to be one too. But it was I who was grateful to be alive, and he who remained unconvinced of the goodness of being.

It was this existential pain, I believe, that forced him to take the opiate of politics. I observed that world with a journalist's eye, as a critical bystander. Dad wanted to hurl himself into it full force. He never did, of course, because his own skeptical nature wouldn't permit such a complete activism. He wasn't overly fond of politicians, but he did believe in a new world order and called it that long before the term became fashionable. He worked hard in our riding to support Maurice L'Oraison's campaign for a seat in the provincial legislature, and later to the federal parliament. He and Maurice thought alike. Maurice, he said, was an idealist, a humanist, a man of vision, incorruptible. Furthermore, he was rising in the ranks of the one party that showed promise of ushering in a global economy. World government was inevitable, he said, and we had better work for it as quickly as possible if we wished to avoid the disasters brought upon us by nationalism. History had provided us with a number of nationalist monsters who showed us the alternative.

And so, on the afternoon of our last fishing trip, with Maurice L'Oraison recently appointed whip of the official opposition in the federal parliament, my father should have been content. His dissatisfaction, I saw, was with me.

"Your last editorial was a bit extreme", he went on. "I mean, simply because Maurice is exploring ways of networking globalists is not a sign of an international conspiracy."

"I never said conspiracy."

"No, but you said something that implied—"

"I used the words *symptoms of collectivist thinking*, if I recall correctly."

"Well, there you are."

"You misunderstood me. To say that certain ways of thinking about society are the seedbeds of conspiracies against mankind isn't the same thing as saying there *is* a conspiracy. Not the same thing at all."

"But it did cast a shadow on the reputation of a fine man, Tan. Possibly a great man."

"Maurice, a great man, Dad? I'd say a *dedicated* man."

"He invited you to work with him once. It's too bad you turned him down. You might have got to know him. You'd be taking a better view of his ideas right now, I think."

"Would I? Look, I know he's got some useful ideas. Some of them might even be good for the country. It's, well, it's just that I'm not sure about him. Grandma didn't trust him, you know, even though I think she loved him a little. But more than that, I smell whiffs of something in the air whenever he's around."

"Like what?"

"I don't know. Call it a sense."

"I think you dislike him because he supported the Columbia

power project that made this lake. You never forgave him for making it possible for the farm to disappear."

"Maybe. Maybe that's when I first got uneasy with your fine idealist. A subtle but very real principle went under during that project."

He snorted. "I think your grandmother poisoned you against the whole thing. Her editorials at the time were really extreme, as if there were ultimate, philosophical questions in building a dam, of all things!"

I leaned over and plunged my right hand into the lake, index finger pointing down, down, down—crown prosecutor that I am.

"Dad, right there, forty feet below, is the bed you were born on."

"Please, spare me the nostalgia! Hospitals are much better places to be born in."

"And over there, look at that mountain they're stripping off. That mountain was a place in my mind when I was a boy. It stood for something."

"For what?"

"I don't know. Maybe it stood for perceptions there aren't any words for. Even now I can't find the words."

"I agree they shouldn't be stripping these mountains, and when people like Maurice come to power, they'll put a stop to it."

"Maybe. But in exchange, will they strip away other things that make this a human world? Maybe we'll be so grateful that they saved our forests we'll let them kill some of our people."

Here my father looked at me with disgust.

"That's exactly the attitude I mean", he said, raising his voice. "Dammit, Tan, don't you see how negative you're becoming? A few more years of this type of thinking, and you'll be like those nuts who say the Holocaust never happened. Next, you'll be absolving the Nazis of their war crimes!"

That year a German Canadian high-school teacher in Toronto

had been dismissed for teaching a bizarre form of revisionist history, claiming that the Holocaust was nothing more than a Jewish propaganda ploy. It had never happened, he said. Genocide, what genocide? He had sued the school board, and the ensuing legal fracas had been a hot news item throughout the country.

The teacher was either demented, unspeakably ignorant, or a cynic of epic proportions. But equally troubling were the knee-jerk reactions that had exploded in every direction. People were falling into the trap of thinking they had only two choices: you either become a liberal, or you become a Nazi.

Getting a little hot under the collar, I replied in a low voice, "It's because the Holocaust *did* happen, Dad, it's because it's so important to our history, that I write the things I write. What I said in those editorials is that it can happen here."

"If anything of the sort happens here, it will come from the right-wingers. Just the sort of people who take a great deal of comfort from your kind of writing."

"I used to think that, too. And I understand perfectly why you think it's a danger. But I know for a fact that it isn't a danger. Because they're noisy and crazy doesn't make them a big threat. But the left-wingers are a whole different matter. They're growing so fast because they've taken over the communications media and education, and they've erected a straw man of the conservative monster as a danger to the people."

"But it is. Look at Hitler—"

"Yes, look at Hitler. What you see at first glance is jackboots and book-burnings and Auschwitz. But look carefully at his policies. What you're forgetting is that for more than a decade as the National Socialists jockeyed for power in Germany, they looked like a party that would 'save' the people. The Germans were so bruised by the negative events in their recent history that they were mortally scared of negativity. They tried to concentrate on Hitler's positive promises and hoped that when he came to power he'd leave his more unpleasant ideas behind. They became desperate optimists."

"That's a theory."

"A bit more than a theory. You know, every time I scratch beneath the surface of an optimist, I find somebody wrestling with despair."

"According to your theory, then, what's a pessimist?"

"Same thing, just another form of thinly disguised despair."

"So what are you, Tan?"

"A realist."

I remember the sardonic look on his face, which is his mechanism for retreat. He made another cast and squinted into the sun as if the line of conversation had used itself up. But I, of course, fool that I am, went on. Not a pretty scene: self-righteous son lecturing father. The irony of it escaped me at the time. I wasn't impressed by the fact that when he was already a full-grown man, I was nothing more than an enthusiastic little package of chromosomes. Nor did I recall at that moment just how many of my diapers he had changed, nor did I count the meals for which he had paid and which I had consumed unheedingly into my twenties. To this day I believe that I am right about the matters we spoke of, and I believe him to be wrong, but there remains the question of discretion. When does one speak, and when keep quiet?

That day I hadn't yet begun to learn silence. I was a noisy firecracker exploding with a rage so deep that I failed to see how it darkened the light of my words. People don't listen much to angry men who vent their anger. By contrast, an angry man who controls his rage and forges it into cool thought is an estimable force in society. But I hadn't yet learned this primal lesson. I thought words were all you needed. I believed that everyone would be convinced if I just explained things properly. I didn't suspect for a moment that they weren't quite as desperate for the truth as I was. In the process I lost an important truth.

He pulled up a five-pound whitefish, and I helped him net it. Together we brought its silver glory flapping and gasping into *Bobabout*, and together we gazed down on it with sheer pleasure. Not a word passed between us. Re-communion was established. This, combined with the flush of his victory, permitted him to engage me in debate.

"Let's get back to the subject of nationalism", he said gravely. "For instance, your recent editorial on globalism."

Aha! I had questioned a fundamental doctrine of his religion, and he couldn't let it go unanswered. I searched my mental files for the text. What had I written in that piece? Something like the following, probably:

> Contemporary Western nations would do well to study the cultural state of Germany during its descent into totalitarianism. Hegel and Nietzsche had exercised a powerful influence on dramatists, journalists, and visual artists of their own time and the ensuing generations. By the 1920s and 1930s the German people had been prepared to accept political philosophies that would have been unthinkable in a Christian nation a short century before. Spiritually divided by the Reformation, grown indifferent to papal warnings about National Socialism, saturated in artistic decadence, and undermined by post-enlightenment philosophies that set man adrift in a flattened cosmos, they were ready for a secular messiah. The similarities between their culture and ours do not end there: at root is a gnawing angst, a camouflaged despair. And man in despair becomes capable of any outrage. He becomes willing to elevate clearly evil personalities into positions of absolute power as long as the new rulers promise a secular redemption. If God is in fact dead, then it is permissible and even logical to do so. If there is no absolute good or evil, then why should we not employ evil men and evil means to bring about a perceived good—meaning, of course, any social good of which the collective mind is convinced. A reading of the culture of prewar Germany offers astounding evidence of just how swiftly and extensively the collective mind can be convinced. Add to these similarities the almost limitless powers of the modern media, and there emerges the potential for a complete deformation of man's sense of reality.

The Echo was not then or ever after a radical paper. I firmly held it to the moderate centrist position that is despised by all ideologues. But I lost my credentials utterly with that editorial. Using the word *God* with some respect blew my cover. Several people whom I admired cancelled their subscriptions.

My father didn't cancel his subscription, but only because of family loyalty. He believed that, with the decline of nationalism, a new age had become possible. Science, properly applied, would make it happen, a kind of mystical science that was more a cosmology or a philosophy than an application of knowledge. Maurice's party was the vanguard of this philosophy. It was a minority in parliament, but it was growing. The leader had recently published a book called *Unitas: A Vision for the Third Millennium*, in which he warned about something he called "paradigm dysfunction and limits to growth" and outlined a corrective proposal for radical economic and social restructuring.

My father was an optimist. He saw the modern world as a place that had progressed, needing only some fine-tuning. I agreed with him that the Hitlers had been defeated, the atom had indeed been split, the sound barrier broken, and smallpox wiped out, but I maintained that not a dent had been made in the fundamental human condition. If anything, it was worse than ever. Its surface appearance remained in a steady state of development, astounding us with signs and wonders, but it had created a world in which evil no longer looked like evil. A brave new schizophrenic world.

"Dad," I said, "do you really believe we're about to make a utopia here?"

"I don't know about utopia, but I think it now lies within our power to make a decent world, where children don't go to bed hungry or afraid."

Actually, he was defending the new quality-of-life laws. He didn't especially like the murder of children, but he thought every parent should have the right to do it. He had absolutized rights and radically devalued life. A weird cosmos, if you ask me. He even supported a party that would one day force us to pay for it through taxes.

"By eliminating children, you do indeed eliminate a great deal of hunger and fear", I said.

He gave me one of his patient looks, but he had no reply.

"Dad, even your fellow atheists can see the shape of the future. Huxley's *Brave New World* was a warning to the West in the thirties. They ignored it. They ignored Orwell, too. By the late fifties, Huxley said that the totalitarianism he had foreseen in 1931 was materializing at a much faster rate than he had thought possible. He predicted a society in which literature, religion, and the family would be neutered and all conflicts eliminated by genetic engineering. He portrayed a perfect synthesis of technology and paganism. In *Brave New World Revisited*, he had come to believe that the totalitarianism of the immediate future would be less visibly violent than that of the Hitlers and the Stalins, but it would create a society that was 'painlessly regimented by a corps of highly trained social engineers'."

"Are you finished, Tan?"

"Not quite."

"That's quite a lecture you've just given me. Don't you ever get tired of that tone of voice?"

He was right. I was using my didactic voice. Unpleasant, to say the least.

"Sorry. But just hear me out, please? A couple of minutes' indulgence, okay? I don't like the way I'm talking, either, but maybe you could try to listen to the substance of what I'm saying? Too much depends on it."

He laughed.

"I think you take yourself a bit too seriously, Son."

"That's probably true, but just let me finish. I'm staking my future on these ideas. They aren't just mere abstractions. Ideas have life-and-death consequences, as the events of this century have proven all too often."

So my father indulged me and listened.

"Huxley maintained that, in the future, democracy and freedom would be the subject of every broadcast and editorial, but the underlying substance would be a seemingly benign totalitarianism. It has been pointed out by a few sane men that this kind of totalitarianism is the worst of all, the most inhumane, impossible to throw off because it can always argue that it's not in fact what it is."

"All right, for the sake of argument, let's say that the world he predicted is here. Can you explain to me why you're still writing your editorials and not going to jail for it? People buy your words, read them, and spread them all over the country. Maurice says that you're regarded with some grudging respect in Ottawa and Victoria."

"Granted, it's not in full swing yet. But all the technological apparatus is in place. The Prime Minister's Order in Council last year provided for the construction of concentration camps. Sorry, *civilian internment camps*, I think they called it. Merely a precaution in case of civil unrest, they said. Parliament didn't vote on it. No ordinary citizen had a say on the question, and the government has smoke-screened it by providing a good budget for the first time in a decade and doubling the rhetoric about freedom and democracy."

"You're defeating your own argument. The party that's done this is supposedly the most democratic body in the nation, according to your definition. They're capitalists. My party would make every effort to—"

"Don't you remember, Dad, when the government passed those statutes, your party made a few unhappy grunting noises for a day or two, but then they got awfully quiet about it. Why is that? Could it be they foresaw a time when internment camps just might come in handy, if they ever got power?"

"That's nonsense."

"Is it? What *is* the difference between the capitalists and the socialists? They're both materialists, after all."

"Let's get back to the plan that's going to reshape the world in a few years from now. Most of the world's poverty is caused by imbalances in the global economic systems. People like Maurice are going to do something positive about it for the first time in history. Did you hear the C.B.C. series on the cashless society?"

"I heard it. It gave me the creeps. Theoretically, it may bring a certain semblance of peace and social justice, but it would be built upon a denial of basic rights. Sure, if you eliminate the economic motives for war, then you might get a peaceful planet for a while. But in the process you could bring about another kind of destruction of man."

Dad wasn't convinced. "All it will entail is the giving of credits and debits to every person in a global computer bank. Everyone on earth will have a number. You'll walk into the drugstore and present a single card, the computer will scan it and deduct your purchase automatically from your account. It eliminates massive amounts of duplicated labor and wasted time. It's a perfect system. So what's wrong with that?"

"All kinds of things. But let's look at just one of them. You neglected to mention that one of those experts, an economist, if I remember correctly, said that the card was only temporary. Because cards can be stolen and lost, that still leaves room for crime. The final step is to imprint everyone on earth with his own personal code. Laser technology can burn it painlessly under the skin. A scanner can read it, even though it's invisible. They're discussing a miniature chip, too, injected under the skin."

My father grunted. "Sounds like science fiction to me."

"They're talking about the right hand or the forehead. Ever read the Bible, Dad?"

"God, Tan! Please don't tell me you've become a fundamentalist!"

"We'll leave that question for another fishing trip. Let's get back to tattoos. You say you hate the Hitlers in this world. Yet you propose to do exactly what he did to the Jews and the gypsies and a lot of Christians, too. He tattooed them, and then he used them as slave labor, or he disposed of them en masse. He was saving his people."

"We are not fascists."

"No, but you're talking totalitarianism with a human face . . . just as Huxley said. Sounds utopian in theory. But in practice something far more ominous is going to happen. No one, simply no one, will be permitted to be exempt from the program. How would they pay fines, for heaven's sake? How would they pay taxes? One government economist went so far as to say that people who try to opt out would be destructive of the public good. They'll face imprisonment. You call that freedom?"

"I . . . I call it a reasonable method of ensuring social order. I—"

"Is the social order worth preserving if it reduces the human person to a component in a State machine?"

"You're overstating the case. It's for their own good."

"Is it? Invasion of privacy? Undermining of family rights? Forced 'free' participation? Imprisonment for refusing to cooperate?"

He pointed a finger at me and said sharply, "What about keeping families well fed and the streets safe?"

I smiled. I had lured him into my mouse trap.

"Dad, are you aware that your arguments are the very ones used by Hitler to justify the destruction of civil rights in Germany?"

He looked supremely irritated but said nothing.

"Oh, by the way, the European Union has already developed a pilot program for numbering all the people on the planet, and the code they developed is three groups of six digits. Those eighteen figures will store essential information about an individual. Any cop or supermarket checkout clerk will scan it from your hand or forehead, and so on."

"So what's the problem?"

"Take a look at the Book of Daniel and the Apocalypse, Dad. It makes for some very disturbing reading."

He shook his head, his face wrestling with disbelief and pity.

"I thought you were a lapsed Catholic. Don't tell me you've become a true believer again."

"I guess I've never lost faith in what the Bible teaches. I just haven't lived it very well."

"Then why so fervent about this hysterical end-times myth?"

"I'm not so sure it's hysterical. More than that, if the Bible's right on this subject, and if our generation is the time it was talking about, then people like Mum and my grandfathers and a lot of other people you and I care about are going to be in big trouble."

"Are you telling me that you believe—seriously believe—that a big nasty devil is going to swoop down and force the twenty-five million citizens of a democratic nation to be tattooed, tortured, thrown into concentration camps, and eventually murdered?"

"Of course not. All I'm saying is, it *could* happen. If it does, the number of victims will probably be fairly low. Even so, it'll take ten or twenty years to get the country used to the idea."

"Get used to the idea of concentration camps? Rather far-fetched, I'd say."

"It wouldn't be that complicated, really. Most people would see it as a good policy, especially if we're struggling to recover from a crash. The small number of people who don't like the devil's economics would seem like genuine crazies, wouldn't they? If the crazies were arrested, the average Joe would tell himself, well, it's really for their own good; they'll just have a little holiday in a rehabilitation center."

My father laughed. "You've been reading too many fairy stories."

I shrugged. "Maybe."

"Snap out of it, Son. You're going to start seeing devils under every bed."

I looked at him, wondering if he was right. He shook his head again, his scarred mouth twisting at an odd angle. His was a tormented face. He had been badly ripped up by a bear when he was a boy, just over there on the mountain that rises above the old homestead. All my life I had seen my father's scars and considered them normal. I had learned to read his gnarled smiles and inoperative nerve reflexes fairly well. But this look was entirely new. It struck me for the first time that perhaps my father did not like me.

I tried to stammer a counterargument, but stopped in mid-sentence. I cleared my throat. In a flash of intuition I caught a glimpse of how he must see me at the moment: A young idealist enamored by the nauseating sound of his own voice? Master Bombast on the *Bobabout*? Captain of the battleship *Didactica*?

It hurt. It hurt badly.

"All right, you have a point", I admitted. "We do have to be careful about seeing devils under every bed."

"Good. You see that."

"Yes, it's a danger."

He nodded, and his face relaxed a little. We lapsed into an uneasy silence, during which I nursed my own scars. We cast our lines again.

"Want a beer, Tan?"

"No, thanks."

"Did I hurt your feelings?"

"Nah."

"I thought this was an academic discussion. Looks to me like you took it personally."

I shrugged, produced a fake smile. "Just a flesh wound."

He laughed, not unkindly, and thumped me on the shoulder.

"Tell you what, if you ever get into trouble with the devil, I'll go to bat for you."

"Ha! You don't believe in devils!" I scoffed.

"Sure I do. The two-legged kind."

"Seen any under your bed lately?"

He chuckled.

"We're getting off the topic again", he said in a conciliatory tone.

"No, Dad, the two topics are connected. In fact—"

"Whatever. But let's just say, for the sake of argument, that your worst case scenario is a possibility. If so, tell me how it's going to come about when the weight of opinion in this country is moving in the opposite direction, in the direction of a global perspective? Most thinking people are universal humanists, radically opposed to the things you're afraid of. Can't you see that it's nationalism that breeds fascism and the destruction of human rights?"

Okay, I said to myself, *if you want another round, let's go for it!*

I came out swinging. "You're half right", I said in my lecturing tone. "Fascist totalitarianism is evil, moral chaos, and pain. It's a great big bogeyman striding across the stage of history. Only a fool would want it. Totalitarianism in its nationalist form gets into power by seducing a people with illusions of security or glory or progress. It feeds on legitimate patriotic feelings and then perverts them to its own ends. Globalist tyrannies, on the other hand, attempt to sweep away or submerge the national, religious, and racial loyalties of various peoples in an effort to create homogeneous masses, more easily subdued and reeducated. But they do it in the name of a universal generic mankind. To accomplish this, they must invade culture, which is the sanctuary of a people's identity."

"Racial loyalties, huh?"

I gave him a dirty look. "I am not a racist, and you know it",

I huffed. "Hell, I'm twice as brown as you are, so don't try pulling that trick on me!"

He laughed. "Okay, okay. Take it easy."

"I'm not talking race here. I'm talking about what happens to *everyone* when some super-state or artificial super-culture destroys the unique genius of various peoples and small communities. I'm talking culture war—*your* culture war."

"Tan, I'll grant you that the arts and education are getting pretty thin lately, and no amount of money seems able to pump them up again. But you're simply taking one tendency in a highly complex society to an extreme. There are all kinds of forces at work, good and bad. Given the right opportunity, we'll be able to do something constructive about the bad ones."

"Sounds terrific."

"When we reeducate—"

"When you reeducate! Listen to yourself. Who gave you and your pals the right to do that? Why do you assume that *you* can educate away flaws in human nature? That's incredibly naïve. Incredibly dangerous, too."

It was his turn to take offense. "Dangerous? Why do you think that?"

"Because you're tinkering in the innards of a rather mysterious creature, the human person. The witch doctors have convinced you that their theories about how a human being works are facts. Of course some of it *is* simply fact. But their overall theorizing is really a kind of mythology. Some of the myths may be proven true one day, and some proven untrue. But they undeniably function as faith systems, with their own sacred texts and rituals and shamans and the works. It's a cult that's taken over an entire culture in one or two generations. It gets away with it by claiming that its dogmas are sciences. Everyone treats them as such. That's how myth functions in any given culture, primitive or sophisticated."

"Of course you're referring to your pet hate, psychology."

"And sociology, and anthropology. I don't hate the sciences. I just refuse to be manipulated."

"I knew it! Scratch a true believer, and you find an anti-intellectual every time!"

"That hurts, Pa! It's a damn lie, too." Now I was good and angry: "It's because I do believe in the intellect that I hate like hell to see real thinking replaced by mythologies. Liberalism is a religion. And *secular* liberalism is your version of dogmatic orthodoxy."

"That's nonsense. We're objective."

"You're the most subjective people on the planet."

"And what are you? You're a conservative, that's what, but you can't bring yourself to admit it."

"I'm not sure what a conservative is any more. But if it means someone who believes you shouldn't dismantle the structure of the universe, then I guess I am one."

He snorted. "My, my, aren't we grandiose!"

"Grandiose? Tell me who's grandiose? Aren't your social engineers busying themselves about the grandest project of all?"

"We have our experts, and you have yours", he said coldly.

"So, where does that leave us? An ugly little power struggle is where it leaves us. The difference between your experts and our experts is that yours want to save collective humanity, and ours want to save each human being. You'd turn them into a number in a computer bank—for their own good, of course. We want to restore your so-called masses to a sense of their individual personhood. That's the only way a real community, a real nation, and a sane world come about. By freeing people to be what they truly are, one by one, person by person."

"That's the slow method."

"It's the sure one."

Five

January 19—6 P.M.
We have found temporary refuge with the Thu family in their boat on the shore of Canoe Lake. How grateful I am for this wonderful family. Matthew has gone off to town in his mobile wreckage. He has the night shift at the restaurant. The Thu boys are showing Tyler their vast hockey card collection. Zöe is reading aloud from *The Lord of the Rings* to the Thu girls. I doubt they understand much of it, but they are sitting beside her on the couch, their black eyes wide with rapture.

I called my father earlier today, but he doesn't believe my side of the story. I thought that he of all people would give me the benefit of the doubt. But I guess he couldn't bring himself to escape from the liberal ghetto. This is a source of real pain. I don't know what we're going to do next.

* * *

"You look sad, Natano", says Anthony.

I put my pen down and nod. "Yes, I guess I am sad."

"Because of your friend on phone?"

"Yes."

"He no believe you?"

"He no believe me."

How does a seventeen-year-old understand things so well? He's not an especially brilliant boy, though he is perceptive. The whole family is that way. Are we large, crude, open books easily read by these people?

He gives me a sympathetic look but says no more.

After supper Tyler and Zöe and I wash up the dishes in a galvanized tub. The littlest Thus are getting into pyjamas in the stern cabin. Grandma went off with the baby to the forward cabin a few minutes ago and is just now returning. The baby, we hope, is asleep for the night. Jeanne is issuing commands, and even the biggest boys humbly obey her. She wants the main room spruced up after the day's mayhem.

Then we're commanded to kneel around the kitchen table—all of us. The family immediately obeys as if this is perfectly normal. It's quite a culture shock for us to be on our knees in a crowd of Oriental Christians. Tyler and Zöe look at me, I nod, and we obey. We do pray at home—usually at Christmas and Easter and funerals—but nothing like this, for we're lazy sprawlers, late Western Catholics. Now, to our surprise, we are immersed in stillness. It enwraps everyone except the youngest girls. They wiggle a little, as any children would, but there is a basic attention.

Grandma begins to pray with closed eyes. The words are Vietnamese, but the fervor has a universal quality, remarkably similar to the tone and expression of faces I've seen in Rome, in a basement in Kiev, at a Coptic church in Egypt, at a shrine in Portugal, and at a secret jungle Mass in Central America. I've been all over the world in the course of my work as a journalist. I've been to many beautiful places and witnessed fabulous ceremonies. Never before have I experienced what is happening here.

The old woman falls silent, then she flips open a book and passes it to Anthony. He reads in his gentle language. It soothes our spirits. In my mind I can almost see pictures of the events the sounds represent. Is this what happened so long ago at Pentecost, when people of many nations and languages understood what the apostles were proclaiming? Something like it, I would guess. This is good news, glorious good news. Almost without knowing it, I'm filled with the sweetest peace and an interior stillness so reassuring that I feel at last I can face anything, even hell-cops. I mutter the words of prayers in the unedifying style of the North American bad Catholic. Bad, not because I am an outrageous profligate whose sins are scarlet, but bad because I'm a hypocrite. I do not love my enemies as my Lord told me to. I loathe what they've done to my family and to my world. They've ruined everything, and I hate their guts. But I'm also a bad Catholic because I've been neither hot nor cold in matters of faith. I've been simply mediocre for too many years.

Our era desperately needed conviction and the words of a true hope. I had believed in the power of my insights; I thought I could salvage the world by my intellect and my pen. I learned too late that most people aren't interested. They don't think. They make their decisions about practically everything according to their feelings, their subjective impressions of reality. I had assumed that my father, who is a cool rationalist, would be immune to the impressionism that has invaded everything. In the end even he proved vulnerable to its seductions. I know that it was right to keep the paper going and to fight the erosion of civilization as long as I could. At the same time, I have trusted far too much in my own ability to convince others. I have not prayed as I ought. Is this my own share in the guilt?

Now the rosary begins, each decade led by one of the children. It's a sing-song chant, and with it come mental pictures of the mysteries. Half an hour goes by, and we're still on our knees. Mine are a little sore, but somehow nothing seems to matter except staying in this unexplainable, timeless peace.

Then it's over, and everyone is shouting, teasing, laughing, and brushing teeth at the tiny galley sink. Grandma turns down the gas light, and there are kisses all round. Jeanne is a very beautiful woman, and the children are fortunate to have inherited her looks, but the family shine is more than a physical legacy. It has a great deal to do with the spirit of love pervading everything in this home.

Where will we sleep? Jeanne points to the empty bunks. The two little girls who usually sleep there have gone forward to squeeze in for the night with Grandma and the baby. The two younger boys double up on one of the lower bunks. Zöe will have the upper bunk. Tyler will have the upper on the second set of bunks; I will have the lower, which is Anthony's bed. Anthony smilingly tells us he will sleep on the floor. I protest and insist that it is I who must sleep on the floor. I don't want to inconvenience anyone. Jeanne, Anthony, and the younger brothers look at me, shocked. This would be *not good*, they say. Anthony, who is especially adept at wheedling, makes me feel guilty for wanting to take the poorest place. With carefully poised facial expression, he uses a masterful diplomacy on me. In the end, I simply have no choice: Anthony sleep on floor in sleeping bag and honored guests on bunks. They all smile with victory as I accept defeat.

Later, when everyone is abed except Anthony, I check the green luminescent dial of my watch. Nine-thirty. I want to turn on the radio to hear what they're saying about me. Then I realize that I don't want to hear it. No, not at all. This room is reality: Anthony is reading by a small kerosene lamp, which must throw the equivalent of ten watts of light. The vigil candle flickers under the icons. There are sighs and snores from various directions. Tyler is totally unconscious, with his mouth open, breathing heavily and muttering in a dream, his big, socked feet sticking out over the end of the bed. Zöe is restless but might be asleep. The baby squeaks for a few minutes and is quieted by soothing words. The fire crackles. Anthony blows out his lamp and rolls over on the floor. Now the interior is lit only by the soft glow of the metaphysical heart.

I lie awake for a long time listening to these sounds, savoring the light. I dare not articulate it even to my own mind, for fear of trapping it and thus losing its essential form, its power, and perhaps even its life.

In this era so many good things are fading, fading without a cry of protest, with hardly a whisper to tell that something substantial was once there. I think of the many unique souls who populated my family, my town, and my world. So many people of that quality will never be seen again. I think of Bill, and I want to yell into the face of the darkness: "Why? Why did you have to kill him, you bastards?" He never harmed anyone in his life. He just loved books and handed them on to kids, swept up after the little brats, and went home to a shack where he ate out of cans, did crossword puzzles, and listened to the radio. Or Turid L'Oraison, that fake tyrant, who died last year of pneumonia—she kept the town honest for sixty years with her earthy wit. And Jan Tarnowski, who passed away ten winters ago, in a coma, after a long, silent battle with cancer.

I grieved for him especially, for he was my friend. He was a man who had suffered under fascists and marxists alike and who was endlessly surprised to find yet another kind of suffering in the free West. He was, as they say around here, slightly out to lunch. But sane, too. Rock bottom, absolute sane, because he had grasped the essentials rightly. For years spanning my childhood and youth, I had helped him to build a spire full of gears, bells, and trumpets, which he called the *enduvdevorldkluk*. He knew, in the way that only crazy men and prophets *know*, that he had a vocation to warn and to protect, and because he was alienated from neighbors by his tortuous English, he chose the only form of language left to a mute genius: he invented a word that would shatter the deafness of our people. It was a sign of contradiction—a tower containing bells that would ring for fires and foes, and a set of trumpets that would blow on the day of "de end uv de end", as he called it. I often found him sitting up there in the cupola, just watching. Faithfully, year in, year out, the bell rang at three o'clock. But the trumpets never blew. They never have blown in my lifetime. Not yet.

It burned in the great fire, of course, and the last few years of Jan's life were occupied in rebuilding it, a monumental task with which I helped him from time to time. What a joy it was to labor on that impossible, useless, scandalous machine. And how freeing. It reminded me that when the normal folk are doing insane things and justifying them with rational arguments, the madman might be the fellow with a firmer grasp upon reality.

After Jan died, there was no legal will and no one to inherit. The house and property were put on the auction block for back taxes, but who was interested in buying a place that was moldering into ruins and had a reputation for the irrational? I ached with longing to buy the *enduvdevorldkluk*, but *The Echo* was teetering on the edge of bankruptcy at the time. If there had been any money, I would have paid off the taxes, dismantled the tower, and moved it out to my place. But not every wild scheme in life is destined to be fulfilled. To this day the *kluk* lies abandoned in the complex ruins of Jan's back lot.

I'm almost asleep when I hear the roar of Matthew's car returning. He comes in a few minutes later, puttering around quietly. He dishes up a bowl of noodles from a pot warming on the stove. Jeanne left it out for him. He eats soundlessly.

"Matthew", I whisper.

"Ah, Natano!"

"Everything okay? You have any trouble in town?"

"No trouble", he hesitates. "No trouble for me. But police stop my car. Stop every car. Make me open trunk. They nice guys, talk very nice, but they have gun in hand."

Not so good. Not so good at all. Is it a blessing in disguise that my father didn't drive down to rescue us? Almost surely we would have been apprehended.

"Natano, we go upstairs. Talk."

We don parkas and boots and climb out onto the deck, closing the door softly behind us. The overcast has drawn back. The sky is full of stars. We can see the Milky Way. A satellite is going over high in the southwest. For a few minutes we say nothing. It's cold but windless, and there's a little heat radiating from the deck under our feet. We stand side by side near the stern, which offers a panoramic view of the lake and of Canoe Mountain on the far shore. An almost-full moon is floating above the crest.

There's a total illusion that we are at sea and the deck is heaving. I breathe the fresh air deeply. I get my pipe burning and the warm bowl of cherrywood provides some ballast. The ember and the aroma remind me that human beings were created for better things than rootlessness. I'm a hobbit at heart. I love my pint and pipe and a merry hearth. I clutch the bowl just a little too desperately. It's a mobile hearth for nomads.

Then Matthew snaps a cap off something that goes fizz, then another snap and fizz, and I realize that all three of my wishes have been granted.

He chuckles.

"This my home brew, Natano. You like?"

I draw on the quart bottle. The beer is green and weak and tastes of ginger. But it's good.

"I like it very much."

We watch the stars.

"You scared?" he asks.

"Not so much any more."

"You no be scared. Everything okay in end."

"I hope so. I do hope so." I take another pull on the bottle.

"I see news at restaurant. Boss-cook have TV in kitchen. We see picture. You and Tie-lore and Zoo-ee and . . . dead man."

"Dead man?"

"Bill from school."

So he knows.

"What did they say?"

"You kill Bill."

Perhaps it's his poor grammar. My panic returns momentarily as I wonder if he's making a statement. Does he mean: "You killed Bill!"

"You believe them?" I ask in a barely audible voice.

Under the wash of starlight I can see just enough to know that he has turned suddenly toward me. His face is probably as stricken as his voice.

"I believe *you*, Natano! I know you! I know you!"

I'm ashamed. I hug him sideways round the shoulders. He pats my arm reassuringly, small pitterpats from a miniature hand.

"You no worry! I know this kind of peoples. One time, before we leave Vietnam, I am like you. I run. I hide. I in big trouble. If they catch me, I dead. First torture. Then dead."

"Tell me about it?"

"Ah, too long time. I forget it too much."

"Please, tell me, Matthew."

He turns to me. He's a stubby little man with thick glasses and thicker accent, a nobody in the eyes of the world. He's not especially good to look at. His teeth are bad. His work contains no prestige. He's a kind of slave, the only kind of slave that is socially acceptable in a capitalist democracy—ex-democracy, that is. If you had to draw a portrait of a loser, Matthew would match it comfortably. But he's not what he appears to be. He is, as I soon find out, the farthest thing from a slave that one can find in the modern era.

It's a long story, and by the end of the telling I'm shivering and the moon has risen and crossed over a quarter of the sky. We've killed another bottle of the brew apiece and don't feel the passage of time. Never have I spent a night like it before. This Lilliputian tells a strange tale on the deck of a ridiculous ark, beached on the edge of a frozen lake in a cold northern land, on the far, far edges of a cruel century. Just before the very end of an age, I have found a true man.

* * *

I won't try to tell his tale in his dialect, because it would take considerable skill to make sense of the cross-references, back-flashes, the side excursions into his philosophy of life and death, and his analysis of the subtle tactics in the war between good and evil. Add to this his anger at both North American materialism and marxist materialism. (He's one of the few people who knows that in essence they're the same thing.) We spend a long time on that subject. But there is also a great deal of bad grammar, and key passages are rendered unusable by his curious vocabulary. I have quite a task splicing the pieces together into an intelligible whole.

It began with the fall of South Vietnam to the Communist North in 1975. Matthew and Jeanne lived in a small town named Nam Binh ("Place of Peace"), one hundred kilometers southeast of Saigon. They ran a food shop that specialized in noodles, dried fish, a few canned goods, the Saigon newspapers, cigars, and cigarettes. It was one tiny room fronting on a dusty street in which banty roosters strutted and children played without fear of being run down by the motor scooters that did occasionally purr through on their way to other places. The center of the town's life was the village church. There were Buddhists there, too, but most of the population was Catholic, descendants of the people who were converted by French missionaries during the eighteen hundreds. One of Jeanne's great-great uncles was martyred under a Confucian emperor. Her ancestor refused to recant his profession of faith and was dismembered and fried in a giant wok in the square of the provincial capital. He is now a canonized saint of the Roman Catholic Church.

The faith in these villages was strong. Prayer and sacraments marked the passing of time, and the young were severely adjured to avoid the big cities of Saigon and Danang, because those places were corrupt. The family, the Church, and the village were everything, in that order. When the North Vietnamese came, they arrested any former employees of the Saigon government who could be found, and they shot on the spot anyone who had been a member of the South Vietnamese special forces. An army detachment and an office of the political police, the Cong An, were established in the town. Informers developed a brisk trade that kept the populace subdued. People disappeared from time to time, but not many. There were interrogations and beatings, but not so many as to make the new régime appear to be the monster that had lurked in the public imagination since the battle of Dien Bien Phu. All monstrosities occurred in discreet places. No one was fried publicly in woks.

I flew into Saigon the year after its fall to the Communists. To be a Canadian journalist at the time was to enjoy a position of privilege that allowed me liberties an American could never have. We had made a lot of sympathetic noises during the war. As a result, I was able to walk the streets of Ho Chi Minh City and use my camera without attracting much attention. I wanted to find out about the condition of the common people. I had a "shadow", of course, a "tourist guide", who ensured that I saw what the régime wished me to see. I tried to be as clever as a serpent and harmless as a dove, and in due course I found out that there were food shortages and political trials and large numbers of orphaned children. Some of them had been orphaned by the purges that came after the war. Though there was a certain business-as-usual feeling in the air, you could see signs that the foundations of an entire culture were being shifted. The family as the heart of everything was being usurped by a vision of man as a pawn in someone's ideological game. Little did I know that only a few miles away lived a young family who one day would save my life.

I flew home and wrote editorials and feature articles about the schizophrenia of nations. They were rather good pieces, I thought. I pointed out that totalitarianism is essentially a spiritual condition, and it might take overt forms in our own country some day, just as it had in undeveloped nations and in Eastern Europe. My mind is still cluttered with those old news clippings. I wrote something like:

> The average citizen strolling down an average street in a totalitarian state does not experience his world in terms of continuous, absolute madness. However distressed it may be, the passage

of months and years gives to even the most extreme of situations a certain semblance of normality. That is a dynamic easily observed in someone else's country. But what of our own? The image we have of our society is an unreal mental construct. It is no longer the home of the free but a landscape of secret nightmare, where countless children are murdered annually, discreetly, hygienically in the clinics and hospitals of our land. Legalized murder, loss of the transcendent vision in culture, and the death of art are each in themselves key symptoms of a society's collapse into totalitarianism. Democracies are not immune from self-delusion, although they tend to forms of oppression that are not overtly violent. Democracies in decline, however, will revert to covert oppression and the overt gradual erosion of human rights.

That's the way it was for me in the seventies and early eighties. I was a moderate drifting to right of center, although I was cautious about conservatism. But the center itself was shifting radically, drawn by the vertigo of social engineering. As I began to understand the mythological elements in the liberalism of the West, I wrote about what I saw with greater frequency and growing boldness. No one was much interested in my arguments, least of all the liberals. It is, after all, the nature of mythologies to be resistant to reason. When educated people are subjective, they can be so in a highly articulate fashion; they can sound eminently *reasonable*, and thus they become unable to see what the underprivileged have seen so clearly. It is the nature of blind spots to create dead-zones in one's range of vision. "Dead-zones?" says the liberal, "What dead-zones? I see no dead-zones!"

The first accusations trickled into "Letters to the Editor". I was an alarmist, they said. I was a decent enough young fellow, but given to overreaction and self-dramatization. That may have been true, and it may still be true. But the objective situation remained.

For the Thus, those years in Vietnam were occupied with less academic arguments. They lived under a cloud of suspicion. They were capitalists: they still sold things, although their sources for processed foods gradually dried up as the economy disintegrated. They were reactionary religious fanatics, agents of imperialist Rome: their boys served Mass, and Matthew and Jeanne taught a clandestine catechism class to the village children, a risky venture into "counterpropaganda". The church remained open, but all religious instruction was banned. For ignoring the ban, Father Tran was several times arrested, beaten, and returned to the parish with a warning. Certain lay catechists disappeared. Matthew was frequently ordered to appear before the local commandant and submitted to intense questioning. Jeanne, too, was questioned. Their store was vandalized by soldiers in broad daylight, and no reprimand was ever administered to the guilty. They became poor, but they usually had enough to eat. They grew a large crop of vegetables outside their back door, they raised chickens and pigs, though occasionally a few were confiscated. The family set aside a portion of the crop to give to widows, orphans, and underground priests. They waited. They hoped that eventually the situation would ease as the war years dwindled into distant memory. They delighted in their children; they worried; and they prayed.

One evening a woman came to visit them. In veiled language, she told Jeanne that Matthew and Father Tran would be arrested the following morning. This woman had a son who was thought to be a police informer. It was not known for certain if he had been responsible for the death or disappearance of anyone in the village, but somehow he had fallen under suspicion of the villagers. Jeanne was uncertain about the message. The woman was a notorious busybody and had a reputation for creating trouble between people. She was also a liar. It might only be harassment, perhaps even envy, for people considered the Thu family wealthy because of the modest success of their little store, their chicken shed, and membership in a large extended family of farmers and fishermen spread throughout the province.

The following morning Matthew attended Father Tran's pre-dawn Mass. His eldest son, Anthony, served. The boy was devout, and his father was proud of him. Matthew and Tran were close friends. They had grown up together on the same street and for a while in their youth had attended the seminary together. Then Matthew had met Jeanne during a summer vacation, and the paths of the two men diverged, to unite again farther along the river of time. Matthew thought much about the mystery of time and fate. He had three sons now. Tran had many hundreds of spiritual sons and daughters. They lived different kinds of fatherhood, but it was really the same mystery.

Father Tran must have had a sense, some spiritual intuition, that this might be his last Mass. At the homily he said: "My brothers and sisters, we do not know what will happen. Always remember this: Even if they destroy our churches, even if they destroy our tabernacles, they can never destroy the tabernacle of the heart, where Jesus and Mary dwell and await each one of you."

As the priest and the boy were leaving the altar after the completion of Mass, five Cong An swaggered in through the open door at the back of the church. They had their pistols in hand and were smirking. They pushed old men and women and children out into the street. Matthew went hastily to the sacristy.

"Tran, you must flee. I think it true what a neighbor told us last night. You and I are to be arrested."

Tran looked out the sacristy door and observed the police breaking into the poor box.

"You must go", Matthew whispered. "I will keep them busy."

"No. You must go. I will detain them. You have the children and Jeanne to care for. I insist."

While he was saying this, he closed the door to the sacristy, locked it, and pushed Matthew to a window.

"You go, run, hide. I am your parish priest; you must listen to me."

Matthew obeyed. He hoisted himself up and out. The priest lifted Anthony out after him. Then father and son ran for home. As they were running, they heard a gunshot. Matthew looked back, but there was no one in sight. He concluded that the soldiers must have been firing the lock on the sacristy door. A few minutes later there was another shot.

Jeanne and her parents were on the steps of the store staring in the direction of the church when Matthew and Anthony arrived. The boy ran to his mother and clung to her. When Matthew caught his breath, he explained what had happened.

Just then a teenage girl ran down the street wailing.

"They have killed Father Tran", she cried.

Jeanne turned to Matthew and said, "Go. Take the bicycle. Quickly."

Matthew did as he was told and was five miles down a back country trail before the Cong An arrived at the store.

The family knew nothing of his whereabouts. Repeated interrogations produced no information. Matthew Hoàng Van Thu had gone on a lengthy journey to purchase supplies for the store. He would not return for a very long time.

He lived for six months on the bicycle, moving from town to town, harbored by relatives and priests. His photograph eventually appeared in the provincial newspaper under the title, "Wanted for Questioning in Situation of Crime." The paper said that a priest had been murdered and the store owner had disappeared on the same morning. The villagers knew the truth, but it did not matter what they thought; theirs was a small village in an unimportant region, and the whole affair gradually faded against the background of many similar events.

Nevertheless, every few weeks the political police would burst into the two rooms behind the store that was the Thu home, hoping to catch Matthew. He did come from time to time, a few hours here and there, usually after midnight. He would always leave before dawn. The police would search the house, ask the questions they always asked, and then go, weighted with confiscated noodles or fish sauce.

One night Matthew was home and just beginning to eat a meal with his wife when the store's front door rattled and the hook ripped out of its socket. Matthew put the youngest boy on the floor—he had been dandling him on a knee—dived under a bed, and lay there motionless. The boy was close to two years old and thought this was a game. Police and soldiers burst into the room and eyed the two bowls on the table. Jeanne was perfectly composed.

"Why are you eating in the middle of the night?" they asked her.

"This little one is hungry", she said.

The woman would rather die than tell an untruth. In fact she was not lying, because the boy was indeed hungry. She set him before the bowl, and he ate from it. The police walked around the room, looking under beds, into a closet, behind a dressing curtain. Jeanne's parents, who slept in the same room with them, awoke, sat up in bed, clung to each other, and began to pray aloud. The little boy finished his meal and toddled across the room to the bed where Matthew was hiding. It was the one bed they had not yet inspected. Anthony and the middle boy were asleep on it. The child bent and looked under, singing happily, "Ba-ba! Ba-ba!" *Daddy, Daddy!* A policeman walked over. His boots were inches from Matthew's face.

Jeanne froze. The old people began to weep.

"Ba-ba! Ba-ba!"

Matthew held a rosary in his hands, and he prayed silently, "Mother of God. This is life and death. I ask you for help. Pray for me! Save me, and save my family, for the sake of your Son!"

Jeanne's old father got out of bed. He weighed less than eighty pounds and had lived more than seventy years. He walked with a cane. He came before the leader and scolded him mercilessly.

"Be quiet, old man", said the policeman, but he did not strike him. He looked bored.

"Ba-ba! Ba-ba!" the child continued.

The intruders turned to Jeanne and lectured her about her responsibility to raise her children as good citizens. They tore a religious calendar off the wall. They confiscated packages of tobacco and bottles of rice wine. And left.

Later that night, Jeanne and Matthew talked about what they should do.

"We must leave this country", said Matthew.

"But how?"

"On the coast for many months now, people have gone out to sea in boats. They have crossed over to Malaysia and Thailand and to other places. Some have arrived in America."

"There would be many dangers."

"What is more dangerous than remaining here?"

After much discussion, they agreed. Matthew disappeared for several more weeks, and when he returned he had gold.

"It is from my teeth", he said. His gold fillings had been replaced by dull gray metal, and in his hands lay a small ingot. Jeanne had petty cash from the store, and from a hole under the floor her father brought a knotted bag containing several ounces of valuable stones, mostly jade and opal.

"I have found a man who will take us across the South China Sea", Matthew told the family. "There will be thirty people in the boat. It is an open-top fishing boat. It is not certain we will escape."

"I have heard there are pirates who rob the people and sometimes sink the boats", Jeanne said.

"If we could have but one gun to defend ourselves!" Matthew replied. "But that is impossible."

"I have the butcher knives."

"Yes, and Grandfather has his bad temper!"

Everyone laughed.

"No pirate would dare to fight with us. We will be safe!" young Anthony proclaimed.

"I wish a little respect", said the old man, though even he could not hide his amusement.

In the end the grandparents decided to stay. They insisted that they didn't want to be a burden. They didn't want to slow the young people down. It wouldn't be difficult to manage the store. Moreover, they said, if the family business continued as usual, there would be little suspicion aroused. In time the situation would improve. Matthew and Jeanne would return some day from America to visit their graves and to pray for their souls.

That night Matthew left on the bicycle. He returned the following day after dark with a bamboo cart that could be pulled behind the bicycle. It had large balloon tires and could carry many things with little expenditure of energy. They left before dawn, Jeanne and Anthony walking, Matthew driving slowly, the two young ones asleep among the bedding and food on the cart. They zigzagged down the coast on back country lanes and secondary roads. No one stopped them. In four days they reached the rendezvous where the boat waited.

A crowd was jostling to get on board. The owner of the boat was angry and refused to take their excessive baggage aboard. Even so, it would be overladen. He demanded full payment in advance. Satisfied, he fired the ignition of the inboard engine, pointed the bow southwest, and they were off. The Thus cried with grief. The sound was hidden by the *bang-bang-bang* of the motor and the weeping of the other passengers. By morning the land was a pale green line behind them.

There are many horror stories about the boat people. It is said that more than a hundred thousand of them died on the South China Sea. Unstable craft were swamped and sunk. Government gunboats destroyed others after using them for target practice. The pirates were worst of all. Outfitted with powerful motors, they raced down upon the small craft of the Vietnamese, forced them to stop, pointed machine guns into the crowd, and demanded that all valuables be turned over. They had eyes like demons. They raped girls and women, then threw them into the water for the sharks. There were other atrocities, acts too unspeakably evil to repeat. These were evil men, who looked like evil men. The communist officials on shore seemed civilized by comparison. Some boats turned back, and the survivors told their stories. Many people in Vietnam heard these stories and never did depart.

The engine sputtered, tapped and pinged, all morning, until early in the hot afternoon it stopped altogether. Nothing the owner tried during the next few hours made it start again. He flew into a rage and began to smash the motor with a hammer. Then he sat in the stern, cursing the passengers and wringing his hands. Matthew borrowed the hammer and a rope. Someone else provided a large piece of silk. Others offered remnants of dresses, sacks, anything that could be used. Jeanne and the women sewed together a sail. Matthew nailed two long poles together and used oars as crossbars. When the sail was up, the boat began to move.

The owner of the boat was in a state of complete collapse. He wouldn't answer their questions. He had told them only that he would take them across the narrowest water between the southwest coast and the peninsula of Thailand. No one now knew in which direction that lay. Matthew took the tiller. He closed his eyes, and he prayed. He had no more knowledge of the sea than the rest of the passengers, but he remembered that someone had once told him the lands across the South China Sea lay in the direction of the morning star. Making a wild guess by the sun, he pointed the boat in the direction he thought that must be. With the coming of night and the next dawn, he was relieved to see it only a few degrees off to port. The three Thu boys, who were seated in the bow, burst spontaneously into a Vietnamese hymn to the Virgin Mary, titled "You Are the Morning Star".

They travelled in this way for twelve days, following the morning star. On the seventh day they ran out of water. Many people died of thirst. Their bodies were put into the sea, and before long the weight of the boat was considerably less. It began to move more quickly. On the morning of the tenth day, Jeanne abandoned her reticence and led a public recitation of the prayers of the rosary. The Buddhists and the atheists joined in. A cloud the size of a hand grew on the horizon and was overhead within an hour. It covered the whole sky and drenched the boat with sweet, sweet water. Then it went on, leaving them under a perfect stretch of blue from horizon to horizon. No one died after that, and two days later they sighted Indonesia rising out of the ocean. They had not seen a single pirate.

The Thus spent a year in refugee camps before they arrived in California. Matthew learned the art of cooking in a Szechuan restaurant in Los Angeles. But they hated the city. It was corrupt, like Saigon. A year later they were granted permission to settle in Canada. A few months after that they were hammering a home out of the big red scow and pulling whitefish from Canoe Lake.

* * *

"You see," says Matthew, "I not scared for you. Even you die, Natano, God see everything. Nothing lost. Nothing lost."

"I wish I could agree. Many good things are lost. Many people have suffered horribly and been lost. Think about those girls thrown into the sea. What about the people who died in your boat? We just lost Bill."

"Ah, Bill", he says thoughtfully. "Bill not lost."

Does he mean *saved*, like the TV evangelists mean saved?

"God see everything", he repeats. "He see. He wait. Nothing lost!"

How can you argue with that? Who would dare to contradict a man with his kind of firsthand experience? Not I!

My family history looks pretty tame from this vantage point. I thought my forebears were exiles. Old Stiofain and Annie. True, they were fleeing some real unpleasantness. Anne's was ideological. Stiofain's flight was rather more urgent: my murdered great-grandfather and all that. But they came from English-speaking lands and arrived in an English-speaking one. Despite the internecine warfare, their societies believed in the same universal truths. Things haven't changed all that much. We still live in a decent society, though crumbling fast and undermined by the hidden revolution that will soon tip everything in the direction of the collective mind. But soldiers are not yet permitted to rob the local Wal-Mart store with impunity. There are no pirates on the Great Lakes. On the other hand, we do seem to have a secret police now. And some of the fine points of the judicial system have been waived.

"What you do, Natano?"

"I don't know what I'm going to do. There's no place to go."

"No place to go?" He chuckles and looks all around him at the vast emptiness that is our land.

"I mean . . ." Well, just what do I mean? How do I say it, Matthew? How can I tell you that these aren't exactly the jungles of Indochina. This is a big land but a frozen one, and it will take an incredible amount of energy and ingenuity to survive out there, even if it's only at the level of savages. What do we do when our granola is all gone? When our socks wear out? Where do we buy fishhooks, and with what do we buy them? A little plastic card is replacing cash sometime in the next couple of years. So where does a homicidal maniac apply for one of those handy things? Hmmm?

And how do I convince you that the time of the end is the time of no place to go? Civilizations collapse slowly, just slowly enough so you think it might not really happen. And just fast enough so that there's little time to maneuver. Think, Matthew! Tell me why the Jews didn't run away from Europe in the thirties before it was too late. Tell me why the twenty thousand slaves sacrificed alive to the serpent-god Quetzalcóatl in Mexico City didn't run away before it was too late? Was it really too late? Or had they merely been convinced that it was too late? This is an important question. Life and death hang on it.

Get it through your head, Mister Editor, the paper is gone forever. You're trying to write an editorial in your mind, and mind is a transient substance. Even if you could get it down on paper, what would you say? What could they possibly understand?

Dear friends and fellow citizens, you who share with me the dubious honor of witnessing the end of the world as we have known it, dear "masses", for that is what you will soon become. I write only a simple question: Why is it so difficult to believe that the worst is happening? You who believe in progress? Look at the marvellous whisper-jets in our skies. But they are flown by a police force that isn't accountable to you or me. You believe in the elimination of poverty. Look at the efficient way the computers are planning a world economy, how they will number us, and we shall be made content, lacking nothing. Look at the ways they are eliminating the poor themselves by burning them to death with saline and cutting them to pieces in the womb. Talk about woks! A very strange age, is it not? But you experience it as normal.

Granted, every person in every era has felt his own times to be normal. Our times, too, are normal. As in every other era during that short passage from prehistory to the present, we cling desperately to normality. When events become more and more extreme, the temptation grows to bury ourselves in escapist dreams or in the distractions of comfort. The critical faculty is lulled to sleep. To stay awake and watch demands energy and the willingness to persist in a state of chronic tension. It's so much easier to be "positive", to trust in what our leaders tell us. Optimism eliminates many problems, though much that is human dies slowly within us, with hardly a protest.

What would Matthew think if I said all this in a stentorian voice? Heralds of the final war, unite! You have nothing to lose but your illusions! It's good private entertainment to be a prophet wailing in front of your bathroom mirror, practicing your style, but it doesn't raise the citizenry against a tyrant. And our tyrant doesn't even look like a tyrant. If we shout as loud as we want, it will make little difference, for this war is now almost wholly within. Few shots will be fired, and only upon those who dare to say that we are in a war zone, who dare to say that *we* are the enemy.

Another great twentieth-century cliché.

The time to discuss this was ten, twenty years ago. The social engineering class was just then gathering momentum. Counselors, therapists, social workers, psychologists, and *facilitators* of one sort or another sprouted everywhere. There was no denying that professional services were occasionally of help to families, but it should have been obvious that something was seriously wrong when the help became a growth industry. It soon became a way of life and eventually an entire culture. Now, ten, twenty years farther along, it has become nearly impossible to resist. There are few who aren't mesmerized by utopian dreams and alluring models of social reconstruction.

And who could have identified the point on the continuum beyond which there was no return? Even now, Matthew, would there be any response if a few noisy prophets appeared, shouting some final protests on streetcorners and in empty churches (thus losing all credibility, proving to a reconditioned humanity that the old world view did produce antisocial personalities)? Man has committed himself to the continuously shifting programs of self-improvement. Relationships are conducted with a psychological puritanism far more oppressive than the old moralism. "Dysfunction" has replaced sin. Society has become rather orderly and nonviolent (that is, if you discount clinical murder). Sociopathic elements are rehabilitated or bred out of the gene pool (oh, God, Tyler, Zöe, what will happen to you?). And no one seems to notice the absence of art, literature, prayer, and love.

I know what Matthew would reply. He would remember how he cast his life upon the waters and his life was given back to him. He would recall the operations of divine providence. He would point to miracles. He would force me to choose between real belief or a collapse back into skepticism. He would remind me that when every natural part of the equation indicates a certain end, that is the moment when the unexpected, the unknown element, will appear. His essential message: You must trust.

"What do you think I should do?" I ask him. It's a serious question.

"My heart want you stay. My soul say you go."

"But where do I go?"

I keep repeating the question like a runner with one leg chained to the floor.

He doesn't answer. His head is down, and I think I hear the whispering of prayers. These people are amazing.

Into my mind flashes the unsolicited image of my other grandfather, my mother's father, Thaddaeus Tobac. He lives in the North Thompson Valley, west of us, beyond the lake, on the other side of Canoe Mountain.

Why hadn't I considered him before? I suppose I had counted on Dad rescuing us and had disregarded everything else. Thaddaeus is perfect! They'll never think to bother an old Indian who lives in a shack by a creek on the flanks of the Cariboo Range.

Now I see. It's very clear. It will be hard. Much of the journey will be exposed to the sky. But if indeed all is seen, and if indeed all shall be well in the end, then what have we to fear? We may be spared the wok. The angels may blind the pirates. The hosts of Orcs may yet be driven back into the realm of the dark.

Six

January 20—early morning.
It's close to dawn. In a few hours from now we'll be crossing the lake. We intend to climb part way up the mountain, circle it to the southwest, then go down the other side into the North Thompson Valley. Hopefully we'll be at Grandpa Tobac's place by tomorrow sometime.

I had a good visit with Matthew last night. He told me about his war experiences and about the escape from Vietnam. It was heartening to have tangible evidence that people can survive the most impossible situations. I've been praying. It helps, but I'm still fighting stabs of stark terror and the suction of depression.

* * *

After last night's stars, a thick strato-cumulus has come in and blanketed the entire sky about three or four hundred feet above the valley floor. A few flakes of snow are falling out of it. In the dismal gray light you can just see where the layer decapitates the mountain across the lake. Not many aircraft will be flying today.

Matthew and I didn't sleep much. We took a few hours to rest after our marathon conversation, then awoke early to pack the toboggan. Sleeping bags, tent, snowshoes, and extra clothing. A hatchet and bow saw. Jeanne has been moving around the kitchen for two hours, making things at the stove, illumined only by the red candlelight. She's in charge of the cardboard boxes of food that will sustain us on the journey. I leave it to her. They're smart people, seasoned fugitives. Bushwhackers in the old style.

I wake Tyler and Zöe. Funny how I have dropped the years-old habit of using their pet names. Maybe they're growing up so fast I'm subconsciously abandoning their childhood. Or is it the enhanced sense of personhood among all these free humans that recalls me to their more fundamental identity, their dignity. I make a mental note to think more about this on the trip today. Now I explain the plan to the kids. They're groggy but interested as I tell them. They accept the news without question.

Jeanne serves up eggs and bacon on four plates. Four?

Four! Anthony comes down the stairs from the deck with goat's milk swinging in two pails. He was out in the barn doing chores while Matthew and I were busy with the baggage. I thought he was asleep.

"I go with you across lake, Natano", says the boy as he eats.

I'm not sure I like the idea. We look at each other across cups of scalding green tea. Noodles and raisins soaked in milk provide some additional distraction while I think.

"No. It's too dangerous. You're not in any trouble at the moment, but if you're caught with us, it might be bad news for your family."

"Bad news?" laughs Anthony. "Whole world is bad news, Natano."

He translates for his parents. They smile. But Jeanne's smile is less than full. Her eyes are troubled. She braids Zöe's long gold hair into a single rope down her spine. I can see what pleasure this gives my motherless daughter. She is memorizing each tug and twist, each untranslatable twitter and coo. My girl's chin is on her chest, her mouth is poised in a subtle, sweet smile, and her eyes are wet. I turn away.

Dawn is here when we gather on deck for a reconnaissance of the lake. Nothing is stirring in any direction. In the far distance we hear the sulphur trains pulling down into the North Thompson Valley on their way to the coast. Normal sounds. A raven flies overhead and makes its plaintive cry. The air is warmer and damp. Should we go or shouldn't we?

"Maybe we should wait another day, Matthew", I say. "Then we'll be rested and can start earlier."

"I not know, Natano. Radio say sun coming this afternoon. But tomorrow bad, bad storm coming this way."

"You stay here. Nice", says Jeanne.

A big conference begins in their language.

To be safe we should have left hours ago, but we needed those scraps of sleep. On the other hand, it's unlikely that anything will be stirring in the air this morning, and there are no roads where we hope to go. The only trouble spot will be the wide expanse of ice. The media is full of three missing people, and anyone spotting three figures racing across a lake into nothingness could easily guess who we are, even if we're only specks in the distance.

Wait a minute! Anthony's presence would make us four. Add to the equation the factor that no one but the Thu family lives by the lake. And there is no reason for traffic to be on the valley road at this time of year. We probably have a pretty good chance of making it across unseen.

"Okay, we go", I say firmly.

There are sighs and comments.

Anthony grins.

"We go!" he cries in a triumphant voice. The .22 is strapped to his back, and he's breathing heavily in excitement. His eyes are flashing, and his lips are red. Tyler and Zöe are looking mildly anxious. Their lips are pale and contracted into lines.

The good-byes aren't easy. There are hugs and handshakes and rehugs and rehandshakes. Even the baby has been kissed once or twice too often. Matthew kisses Anthony, which is a startling sight for our North American eyes. Then his mother kisses him and bursts into tears, pressing her head against his chest and clinging hard. She can't stop weeping. The boy pats her head tenderly and mutters reassuring words, but she's clearly afraid. Matthew inserts order into the scene by commanding a work brigade to get us down the gangplank onto the snow by the lakeside. More words, more blessings, prayers, cries, and that infuriating dog, barking hysterically.

The ice is dusted with fine snow, firm underfoot. It will be easy walking across the lake in our boots. The snowshoes are tucked under the ropes for later.

We look back repeatedly as the red boat shrinks behind us. The Christmas lights seem to increase their cheery glow as we penetrate the gloom. Anthony waves from time to time. He's enjoying the adventure. He and Tyler stride on ahead, talking enthusiastically, while Zöe and I take up the rear, pulling the toboggan. It doesn't weigh much on this surface, and I think she just wants to be with me. She takes my free hand in her mitten, the way she used to do when she was little and we went for Sunday walks.

"A real adventure lies ahead of us today", I say in my romantic quester voice. But it doesn't work.

"Yes", she replies in a whisper, looking back at the last homely house.

* * *

I estimate an hour's crossing. The lake is a couple of miles wide here. The mountain rises from its banks, soaring up six thousand feet above the valley floor. We won't have to climb to the peak because what we most need is cover. The mountain has been strip-logged from the base up to the thirty-five-hundred-foot level. Its flanks are bare white fields now, though in summer they're an impenetrable tangle of waste timber and deadfall snarled in devil's club and willow. Above that there's forest again. The increased costs of logging at that altitude, and the poorer quality of wood, have left a band of trees about a thousand feet wide that circles the mountain like the tonsure of a medieval monk. At around the forty-five-hundred mark the trees dwindle into stunted balsam and dwarf spruce. Above that is the moonscape of the high alpine. Our objective is to strike across the lake in a straight line, climb up the east face of the mountain as fast as possible to the forest, then go around the brow of the mountain to its western slopes. The trees should hide us well, unless the hell-cops have infrared sensors. Then down into the Thompson Valley, across the train tracks and the highway, and into the deep bush at the base of the Cariboo Range to Thaddaeus' cabin.

Simple enough. If you're built like a lumberjack. Me, I've been riding a desk for too many years, and I'm hurting from our recent physical exertions. But it's a good hurt. I know I'm alive. The fine clear air is a joy to inhale. The day is dark, but we're buoyed by hope. We have so far escaped the fowler's net.

About mid lake we catch up to Anthony and Tyler. They're leaning against a log that juts out of the ice at a 45-degree angle. At first I think it must be a deadhead, one of the countless waterlogged pieces of the drowned forest that surface from time to time and that make boating on the lake so treacherous. Then I see that it's a weathered cedar rail, with rusty barbed wire coiled around it. It could be from any of the hundreds of abandoned homesteads down the lake, drowned these past twenty years. But I like to think that maybe it's from Stiofain and Annie's farm, lying on the bottom eight fathoms below. I look north, east, south, and west. Yes, we're standing above their fields. An eerie feeling.

I sit down on the ice and lean my back against the fence rail.

We have made it halfway across in less than an hour. The kids are excited by our progress, chatting with Anthony about it, while my mind drifts into the past.

Just a few hundred yards toward the shore from which we've come is the spot where my father and I sat and fished that time, the last time we went out together. The time of our blunt conversation, the one I hope he's now remembering. I replay our painful dialogue, complete with my bombast. I feel a wave of depression. The surge of fear-and-flight adrenaline is suddenly used up.

"Poppa, Poppa!"

Zöe is shaking me. My hind end hurts. It's cold.

Suddenly I'm back on a frozen lake, sitting on a log that juts from the surface like a finger pointing to the sky with an objection.

"Dad! We better get goin'!" says Tyler.

"We go fast, Natano. Clouds thinner."

I shake my addled brains. I've done it again, for heaven's sake. "Okay, Anthony. Thanks, kids. I was just thinking."

They don't reply to that. But their faces say, *Dad, your thinking might get us in bad trouble!*

Poor children, how they suffer for the follies of their elders. Yes, it is indeed my thinking that has got us into bad trouble. Fathers should protect their children, should they not! Make a world safe for childhood, should they not! Ah, well, I'll try to master at least the external shape of my fatherhood. I'm sad and discouraged. Most of it's due to extreme fatigue. But I'll hide it; I'll fake it. I'm hearty now. All's well. Dad's back from Wonderland, kids.

They're relieved. Tyler and Anthony go stalking on ahead in swift strides. Zöe gazes back at the distant shore. Thu's place is a red dot beneath a black range. Ahead of us the mountain towers white and tyrannic. I can see the peak. That means the cloud ceiling has lifted. It's midmorning. Go, go!

Even as we trot, I'm able to think, though it's not word-think, it's image-think. My mind is a collage of memories. Like the cover Zöe made for the journal. Like my life. Shards of many conversations fall across the screen of consciousness and coalesce into an impressionistic work. But what is the work *about?* What does it *mean?* I know that one must stand back and be still before an impressionist painting, in order for its essential word to sharpen into focus.

Tonight when we camp, I promise myself, I'll have a few moments of stillness. For the time being I am running. As flight resumes, the depression recedes a little.

We're at the shore. The overcast is rising above the mountain.

Splinters of blue are visible here and there. Nothing is flying yet. We have a white canvas lying loose on the top of the toboggan. If a hell-cop zings over the horizon, we can throw it open and get under it in seconds.

The snow on the banks is less windswept, but it's fairly firm, and our boots crunch into it only an inch or so. We're making headway through a growth of willow bush. White rabbits rocket to the left and the right. Dear Alice, what can I say? Here in the twentieth century we're late, we're late, for a very important date! Find us a man-size hole that we can leap down. Gimme a looking glass! Gimme a key! Tell me the way to Wonderland, or show me a way to flee!

Another fifteen minutes, and the snow deepens and softens as the hill sweeps upward to the base of the mountain. We need snowshoes now. Anthony and I are pulling the toboggan, and Zöe is atop the sleeping bags, holding tight to the side-ropes. She's tuckered out and hot-cheeked and secretly enjoying her ride. Soon we're at the hard terrain. Flying buttresses leap out at us from the wall of stone. We have thousands of feet to go before we'll be hidden beneath the trees. Before us stretches a wasteland of rock, bush, snow, and a most primal element: height.

We're resting beside a tiny creek that issues from beneath a boulder. There must be hot springs below us, because the water is warm. We drink like animals, lying on the surface of the snow, sucking deep. I hear only the pip-pip of ptarmigans and the scutter of rabbits, even a chickadee or two scolding. Anthony whips his head up and around, leaps for the toboggan and unfurls the white canvas over us in two flips and yells at us not to move. We're opening our mouths to question, when the hum zings close by.

We freeze in terror. I hear Zöe whimper and Tyler swallow hard. My own heart is pounding. I don't like the funny skips and pauses that it has lately picked up. I look out from under the rim of the canvas, and sure enough a hell-cop is disappearing down the lake. It must have passed a few hundred yards to the east of us, and a hundred feet above the surface of the ice.

We climb. Pure, aching, slogging climb. Zöe hangs onto the belt of my parka, and though she's making a good effort, I'm hauling more than my own weight. Thankfully, Tyler and Anthony take over the toboggan without being asked. Good lads!

Gradually the sky clears off, and the sun begins to warm our backs. We eat snacks on the run. Cheese, a handful of chocolate chips, a frozen banana divided four ways. Dried fish strips are amazingly delicious. The salt is welcome. We pass another creek, but it's frozen over. At one point bubbles run beneath the surface, and after a little chipping with a hatchet, the water is liberated. It's sweet. So cold, my teeth ache.

Afternoon, the sun tracing a descending arc into the southwest. It will be dusk around four o'clock. We have maybe an hour left before we'll be climbing blindly. By chance we come upon a snowmobile track zigzagging up the mountain. Its surface is packed hard, and it feels as if we have been set loose on a highway. We remove our snowshoes and walk quickly. Legs ache, chests burn with the cold inhalations. But what a gift! Faster, faster. We're leaving no footprints. Great!

The sky is a deeper blue now, and the sun is behind the mountain. We have gone a little way to the northwest during our ascent. The treeline is no more than a short walk from us when the trail swings away due north and down the mountain.

We all stand around puffing. I debate with myself. If we follow that ski-doo trail, we'll be back at the bottom of the mountain but still not far enough west to take us out of range of the highway circling the base. Furthermore, where would we spend the night? We would be exposed to weather and to the vision of any trackers, and by morning we would still have a long way to go to get around into the North Thompson. By every measure we should climb a bit and go over the high places into the west. Then our descent into the valley will be nearly vertical and very fast. If we try bushwhacking through the valley floor, it will be too slow. How much exposure can these kids take?

Clearly, the best way lies up into the fringe of alpine trees and around that band toward relative safety. Then, down the mountain tomorrow, early.

Well, I'm still writing editorials in my head, and when I get a few moments I'll write them down in the journal. But the days when they could be read are probably long gone. I'm so tired. My brain is reeling from the extraordinary exertion and lack of sleep. But I'm strangely exhilarated. Perhaps it's all the gorgeous oxygen. The view from the heights is staggering. Below us lie the valleys that meet at Swiftcreek. The town's lights are twinkling on. Above us the sky is blue-black with pale green to the south, a pink curtain to the west.

Daedalus in Traumaland is now Icarus Ascending.

Here I am being literary, and we could all be shot!

No more cogitation, Mister Editor. Onward and upward!

Seven

We're at timberline now. The moon is rising, and it's almost night, a last salmon-colored streak indicates the departed sun. Above us are the first stars. We keep ourselves hidden under the canopy of trees at the lower fringes of the forest. We go uphill a stone's throw, where the growth is thicker by comparison, though still composed of dwarf conifers, none over a tall man in height. There is a clearing of sorts, maybe two body-lengths wide, more like a tuft of hair missing on the back of a dog. You'd never notice it unless you knew where to look. I have the dome tent out of its bag and sprung into shape, but the wind tosses it around the surface like a kite. The pegs will not hold it in the soft snow. There is no extra rope to tie it down to the stunted balsam.

As usual, Anthony the jungle boy is way ahead of me.

"Need warm, Natano."

He sets to work in the twilight, using a snowshoe as a shovel. He digs out a circle ten feet in diameter, tossing up a breastwork of white banks around the circumference. He excavates as far as the ground, and we're walking on a carpet of moss.

"Cut little trees", he says. Then he and Tyler, with hatchet and bow saw between them, set to bringing trees out of the surrounding growth. Anyone flying overhead could never tell that things are amiss down here, because he chooses his cuts carefully in order to avoid scars on the surface of the forest.

He erects the trees into a teepee, overlapping them so that there is a double thickness of wall around us. Tyler and Zöe, following his instructions, shovel the snow banks back onto the exterior of the teepee. Only a few feet of branches are visible at the peak. One side is left bare to provide an entrance. We crawl into the hole and find to our delight that it's warmer inside. Not much light or wind penetrates. Tyler snaps on his flashlight. I go out to make sure no light escapes. Not a flicker. We're safe!

Anthony asks me to cut soft balsam tips from the trees, and we spread them over the moss. Now it's perfectly dry as well as warm. I erect the dome tent inside the larger evergreen tent, but the cold synthetic seems harsh, distasteful, so we agree to collapse it again. Sleeping bags, blankets, baggage, and food box are arranged inside, and we pull the toboggan in after us. The entrance hole is covered with branches. Our refuge is snug, beautiful, and perfumed with incense. It smells exactly like a child's Christmas in here. We're sleeping under the tree and awaiting the holy morn with a thrill in our hearts that I had long forgotten, that, indeed, I had lost for a while. Grace has come down to earth once again. Peace on earth to men of goodwill!

Anthony opens a surprise parcel and tells us that there are gifts for everyone. Matthew has sent me a brass folding pocketknife and a bottle of half-frozen ginger beer. The Thu children have contributed candies for Tyler and Zöe. Grandma has enclosed a thermos of horrible fish stew for Anthony. For each of us there is a cotton handkerchief embroidered with our names—Jeanne's needlework. Then we open the food box and find fruit cakes, dried smoked meat and fish, nuts, rice balls saturated in sweet plum sauce, and cool eggrolls swimming in salty soy juice. More candies here: chocolate coins wrapped in gold foil. Clear mint droplets wrapped in green foil. Lemon bells wrapped in silver. I don't care if it is the middle of January, this is the best Christmas I've ever had. I tell Anthony and the kids. They laugh. They agree. We eat our fill and drink wassail.

The old circuits of the subconscious start flickering with lights. Maybe it's the fruit cake that prompts it, or maybe all the ice we've crossed today. Time for another flashback.

I remember once watching Turid L'Oraison make Christmas cakes. She was eighty years old at the time. She had a bad case of diabetes, walked painfully, and suffered a great deal. She lived by the lake, in a small winterized cottage not far from our house. A widow, her only companion was a mongrel dog named Buffy. Much of her life was spent watching the traffic of birds, squirrels, and the occasional wolf out on the frozen lake. She read the big city newspapers with a giant magnifying glass and spent much of her time growling over the follies of public figures, whose activities she watched like a hawk. She nursed a special dislike for her stepson, Maurice, who had gone on to great things in politics and was considered the town's favorite son. She was crude and decent and honest.

As I was saying, she was making Christmas cakes. She limped back and forth across her little kitchen, between the steaming stove and counter, then over to the refrigerator and back to the pans. Each step cost something in terms of pain. A thousand details, a myriad decisions, any one of which might change the texture, the taste, the peculiar charm of this cake. She was the queen of cakes, possibly a tyrant of cakes. She had a reputation for cakes. It was, I suspect, her only vanity, but she well deserved to be vain in this department. These cakes were her annual Christmas gifts to family and neighbors.

Of course, we could all have gone out to the supermarket and bought packages of commercial Christmas cake for $5.95. It wouldn't have been as heavy, as deep, dark, and rich as hers, but it would have passed. It would have looked like Christmas cake. It would have smelled like it, and it would, no doubt, have been sweet on the tongue, in a tired, generic, mass-produced way. It would have been *efficient* cake. But it wouldn't have been Turid's cake. It wouldn't have had her pain and her brutal wisdom in it. Nor her love.

That day she moved slowly and spoke slowly, though her mind was as sharp as the game of crack-the-whip Bam and Zizzy were playing out on the ice. The wind had blown the lake clean, and the kids were skating deliriously in all that space and freedom. We watched them from the kitchen window. They were young and strong. They didn't really believe in pain. It was late afternoon. The sky was washed with blue-black ink, and the first star had appeared. Turid smiled as she followed the antics, but before long she went back to fuss and brood over the mysterious instruments of her art.

"That's an awful lot of work", I said sympathetically, foolishly, nodding at the stove. A bachelor father overcome with nostalgia, soaking in the feminine mystique.

She gave me a look.

"It has to be right", she growled. "It has to be all good, or it's no damn good at all."

I thought about that. And it struck me suddenly how different my generation was from hers. She told me once that people have changed a lot since she was a young woman. It's true. We are different. We rush through our lives trying to get it all in, trying to get too many things done too fast. And as a result we make hasty decisions. We don't appreciate things all that much. We're seldom grateful. We work and play and consume on the run. We "improve" our minds on the run. We advance our careers on the run. We talk and cook and eat on the run. We settle for junk food, mass-produced filler that looks and smells and even tastes like food. We rarely choose to make a thing with passionate love for its being. We have developed the habit of doing many things poorly rather than a few things well. Is it really possible to think clearly in such a state?

And what of the sociopolitical food that has become our daily fare? We have grown accustomed to mass-produced projects and platitudes, half-baked concoctions that are sweet on the tongue but not nourishing. And what about those clever journalistic commentaries that mix selections of the truth with some very odd ingredients? We're being programmed to eat many a cake into which this or that cook has mixed tacks, bolts, and nails. But I'm wondering if we should be quite so reassured when they tell us that they graduated from the best schools of cuisine. Should we be relieved when they tell us that the cake contains some excellent ingredients as well as the controversial ones? And if they should warn us that our diet has been lacking in minerals of late, should we trust their judgment just because it's true that bolts, nails, and tacks are composed of minerals? Yes, we're very hungry. The cake looks good, smells good, and even tastes good until the real chewing begins. But if we trust this kind of cook long enough, we'll have a household full of broken teeth and torn stomachs. And in the end we'll be very hungry indeed. Perhaps we would be wiser to find an old cook who knows what hunger is and what real food is. As for me and my house, I think we'll stick with the wisdom of Turid, who says that a cake must be all good, or it's no damn good at all.

Okay, rumination over and out!

I ferret my pipe and tabaccy from the bottom of my rucksack. I light it and puff merrily.

"Bad for the health", I tell the children somberly.

They grin and sniff the sweet smoke.

"A mobile hearth", I add sagely. "Very useful in emergency situations."

They know smoking's a dirty habit—substance abuse—they've heard all about it at school. But they can't help liking the smell, and they lean back on their sleeping bags just watching me, smiling. Strange children! What a terrible example to set for them. I feel a trickle of guilt go down my throat, along with the soothing effect of nicotine. I'm a mess. Why deny it?

We're very tired. Limbs are beginning to ache in earnest. Tomorrow will be harder when the muscles take up their serious complaints, but at least from now on our way will be mostly downhill through thick snow, with soft landings if we stumble. After that, a quick dash across the highway and up Tobac's trail into the Cariboo Mountains. Even taking it slowly, we should be at Thaddaeus' by midmorning.

Why am I so lucky? Not many people in this world have grandparents who leave cabins strewn around the wilderness in case of emergency.

Every year when I was a boy, my grandparents Stiofain and Annie would pitch a huge tent on the pasture beside their cabin and invite the clan for a feast. It was usually held in late September, after the potatoes were harvested and my other grandfather, Thaddeus Tobac, had dressed his first deer. I can still recall the intoxicating smells of burning birch logs, autumnal leaves, and venison roasting over the fire pit under the dome of the tent. We all smelled like smoke-cured Indians—which is not surprising, because some of us *are* Indians, and some of us, like me, are half-breeds.

My Irish grandfather would pull out his flute or tin whistle and set the crowd dancing in a jig or a reel. My Shushwap grandfather would pull out his wheezing accordion, and together these two old forebears would make merry while the younger folk pounded the turf. I remember my quiet, prayerful mother knitting in a corner of the tent, smiling, smiling. She always seemed to have hours to listen to an adolescent's heartache. My English grandmother discussed world politics with anyone who was willing to brave her intellect. There were aunts and uncles who bounced babies and told riddles. There were cat's cradles, whittling, and skits. There were seed cakes and hogsheads of home brew, and dizzy light splashing over everything, as the kerosene lanterns swung on the rafter poles.

At a feast like that you could see the rich resource waiting to be tapped. The hard-won wisdom of the old married ones, who were glad to dish it up for the asking. I looked at their ancient, beautiful hands gently holding each other and wondered. I watched the hot, electric hands of the young intertwining and wondered about them too, pondered long those red cheeks, the flame in their hearts, the fire that burned but did not consume. I who was a child, my tongue's use sleeping, I dared not probe the secret knowledge of youth and old age. I was not like any of them. But what was I? Where did I belong? I did not know it then, but I belonged to them all—to the babies cramming coins, grass, and other things into their mouths. To the incoherent and the abstract. To the berry-brown aunties, sweating and jolly over pies; to their taciturn husbands, the farmers and millhands who struggled over plows, anvils, and words. To the strange solitaries—the invited—over there on the benches by the back wall, close to the door, ready to bolt into the forest. To the musicians, the jokers, the courters, the bush-philosophers, and the insane. To the gregarious strong, who occupied the central place in any bloodline, they who always seemed to know who they were, or perhaps never asked themselves who they were. To those who debated the timeless questions of local politics and weather. And to the others who listened and learned. Among this disparate throng was to be found in abundance the perennial laughter, clean of sourness and sarcasm, the practical advice, the rebukes, the praise, the pat on the shoulder, the stolen kiss, and the commerce of happy gossip. Above all, the storytelling—the passing down of our heritage and the forging of lore that bound us together into a family, a clan, and a people.

Where has it all gone, I ask? Is it still there, just waiting to be found again? So many of us have been scattered. So many missing. Where is the birth and death we used to share? Why did we not understand what was happening when the family began to disintegrate? Why did we not resist it? Why did we not fight against the corruption of our culture? Why did we not pray as we ought? Did we defend the little ones from the ravages of wolves? And now, lo these many years later, do we any longer cherish the very old and the very sick? Do we tolerate the young in noisy, demanding numbers? Do we bear with dignity the pain of existence (and the beauty of it), or avoid it at any cost? Have we lost bit by bit our reverence for the mystery of a human life, losing in the process our ability to love the poor and the plain and the mad and the difficult-to-live-with, the enemies, the saints, and the sinners? Is it our own face we see reflected in the mirror of their eyes?

Once, at one of those big tent parties, my grandfather Stiofain observed me casting a judgmental eye at the antics of my Indian cousins, who were, if I recall correctly, drinking a bit too much that day. At the ripe old age of twelve, I was already a social critic. I suppose my face must have been disfigured by a nasty curl of the upper lip—and he spotted it. He didn't reprimand me. Just looked me in the eye and said, "Tanny, a shepherd who loves his flock doesn't cull the black lambs or the mixed breeds without first finding out what's good in them."

That's all he said. No more. No less. I can still feel the shame I felt that day. My cousins may have been weak, but they were nowhere near as weak and stupid as a lad who is convinced of his superiority, a lad who has no mercy—me.

I'm trying to love, Grandpa, really I am. I've finally got me a tent and a flock, haven't I?

It's getting colder. We crawl into our sleeping bags and lie gazing up into the darkness. Every so often a trickle of clear, cold air comes by and parts a branch to reveal a star. I'm unspeakably weary but strangely content. I'm very proud of my children. They haven't uttered a single grumble. They've had a hard day but an interesting one. They're going someplace. They're having an adventure. A real one at that. I'm also quite impressed by this boy from a far country. I'll tell Matthew and Jeanne about it some day. I'll tell them that I'm as proud of him as if he were my own son. I hope my children will eventually develop at least half of his foresight and maturity.

Tyler is on my left, snuggled up to my back. He's not saying anything. During the last six months he hasn't done much except eat and grow. He's worn out now and is asleep within a minute. But Zöe is as bright as a new penny. She's under the crook of my right arm. Only her nose shows above the rim of her sleeping bag. What would the sex-police say if they saw this? I try not to think about it. It's cold comfort to remember that evil is in the mind of the beholder and that their ugly suspicions tell me more about the contents of their imaginations than about myself.

"Night, Poppa."

"Night-night, girl."

"I really liked today. It was hard."

Interesting conjunction of thoughts. I muse on it.

"This is how Frodo and Sam and Merry and Pippin felt", she says.

"Is it? How did they feel?"

"Scared and happy."

"Is it a good feeling?"

"Yes. Very good."

Pause.

"Dad, d'you feel it, too?"

"Yes, I do. Even big folk feel it sometimes."

How much we lose with the ambitions of adulthood. In my boyhood I had camped all over these mountains with a dog and a gun. I had been scared and happy many times in my life, but never quite this way. I have often gazed into the infinity that surrounds our solid little planet. Early on I learned that the universe isn't a flat theater backdrop to the human drama. It's deep. You look *into* it, forever. In my childhood I had often yearned for a sign coming out of that unfathomable mystery. I wanted a telegram from the transcendent; anything would do, a falling star, an angel, a vision. I longed for burning letters to be inscribed across the screen of my imagination. One summer, after a plunge into Malory's *Morte d'Arthur* and the medieval legends of knight-saints, I strained my eyes upon the darkened mountains, yearning, yearning for the appearance of a white stag with a cross in his antlers who would tell me what I was for and what word I was to bear into the world. He never came. I'm still waiting.

On the other side of Tyler, Anthony is in his sleeping bag with his tuque pulled down tight over his incredible Mongolian eyes. He should be strolling barefoot under bamboo trees, not huddled up here with us. He has an extra blanket draped over his head. He looks like a mad shepherd watching flocks. He has inched his body to the wall and parted a spy hole through the branches. He's staring out.

"Sleep, Anthony. It's been a long, hard climb."

"Yes. Soon I sleep, Natano. Now I look at stars."

"Anything happening up there?"

"Nothing. I think maybe morning star come up."

"It won't show till closer to morning."

"Yes. Not till then. But I like to wait. I like to watch."

I understand. He was a child once upon a sea, watching with his father for a star that meant life or death. This anticipation has become part of his personal mythology. It needs no reason. It has its own intuitive reasons. It's the *art* of waiting. The very gifted know that art, and the humble old. And the pure of heart.

* * *

January 20—evening
I'm writing by flashlight. We have made it safely across the lake and are now camped on the mountainside. The children and I are exhausted but doing very well, all things considered. Irrepressible journalist that I am, I can't stop taking my mental and emotional pulse. Too much has happened to record it all in the crude medium of print. I make do with the mnemonic archive. I'm still experiencing alternating waves of exaltation and depression—which are probably biological in origin. Tomorrow should be easier as we approach the refuge of Thaddaeus' cabin. We can catch our breath when we arrive, and then I may be able to articulate on paper some of the things that I've been pondering. One of the big surprises this outing has given me is a realization of the multidimensionality of the mind. I've done more musing, analyzing, and remembering during these past two days than I have in years. And done it at a gallop. Signing off for now.

* * *

I'm asleep when Anthony shakes my arm roughly. He puts his mouth to my ear.

"Natano!" he whispers. "Something out there. You no move, no make noises, please!"

We're motionless, breathing only the minimum necessary to preserve consciousness—puffs of frosted air in short bursts.

Something is definitely out there. It's walking past our shelter. You can hear the huffing of its breath, the crunch, crunch, pause . . . crunch, crunch, pause . . . of its passage. It can't be more than a few feet away.

Then silence. We hold our breath. I can hear my heartbeat.

Anthony lowers his eyes to the hole and peers out.

A sharp intake of breath, and the boy exhales. There's a suppressed cry in it, like the wind, which courses through sighing from fields of snow under the moon. It's amazingly bright out there, irradiated with blue light. He sighs again, but it's not a fearful sound.

"What is it?"

He pulls me over to see.

There. There.

It's white. I feel a rush of exultation. It's white as the snow, so white it's almost blue.

"Elk, maybe. Caribou, maybe", whispers Anthony.

Probably a caribou. Their hide is whitish-cream. I can see through the moisture in my eyes that the animal has stopped in midstride and is turning toward us, listening. It rears a great rack of antlers against the sky. I can't tell if it has the caribou's distinguishing shovel-antler jutting forward over its brow. It could be anything. But it's definitely white and majestic.

I feel its immense dignity. I feel it with us.

Anthony, I say in my heart, *do you feel it, too?* Feel it round us and before us, tall and fierce upon the mountain, no longer an *it* but a *he*. His crystal eyes are sent to stand and wait, simply to be, yearning for our silence. Is he jubilant when we notice, at last, the stars?

Indeed, there are shooting stars tonight. I think I've only noticed them in August before. A long, slow, orange burst falls through the sky and becomes nothing just above the mountains opposite, the place from which we came this morning. Minutes later a blue star, incandescent as a welder's torch, falls to the north and fizzles out. All the while the white hart—for so I have begun to think of him—gazes at us without moving.

I breathe at last. The hart shifts his head and walks slowly over the crest and is gone.

"Beautiful! Beautiful!" whispers Anthony.

"Beautiful", I whisper.

Eventually he's asleep, and I'm alone with my thoughts.

Is this the word I have waited for all of my life? Did it take a lifetime of preparation? If it had come too early, would I have held it in my heart the way I do now? How many, many nights have I begged for a word from beyond the boundaries of our mortality and, hearing none, suspected that out there beyond the last homely house, out there in the unexplored territory, there was . . . was what? Nothingness? I have jumped to ridiculous conclusions all my life. The arrogance of the educated, of course. How often have I begged to know, and instead was given the way of unknowing? Little did I understand that it's the best way of all.

Zöe stirs and rolls over. There's ice on her parka hood. Her cute little nose sticks out. I remove my own blanket and cover her, tuck her in. She doesn't really need it, because she has the 40-below-zero eiderdown. Mine is thinner stuff, but warm enough. Still, I think I need this fatherly gesture even if she does not. It's an act that has been repeated billions of times in the history of mankind. Perhaps it's such needless gestures that compose the true history of the world.

Children teach you most of the real lessons. That is, if you try to love them well. I don't mean yuppie love, the squandering of fortunes on their quality environments and their quality toys and their quality relationships and their quality experiences. Maya wanted that for them. She was a quality child of quality parents and came from a city where the best people experienced poverty only by theoretically, politically, becoming indignant about it. They didn't ever wish to experience it themselves. And who can blame them. Then she found me—an angry, shoddy, mongrel romantic who had sprung from two oppressed races. We were exiles within our own skins and didn't know it. She married me, not realizing that she was really infatuated with my mountain mystique. She was enraptured by the incense of birch smoke, the ecstasy of the peaks around us, of deer coming out of the morning fog onto an October field, of the purity of our glacier-fed creeks and rivers. She believed our way of life to be more genuine than her own, which it was, of course, but she didn't anticipate how it would feel actually to live this life. She didn't suspect that original sin is everywhere. No one had ever thought to teach her the term. She was a romantic, and I was a romantic, though we were two very different kinds of romantic. I fell in love with her, and she with me. But I never really knew her, at least not the soul of her, and she never knew me, either. We didn't have much of a chance to learn real love. The kind that surfaces when Pure Romance dies.

Shut up, shut up, Nathaniel! It's too beautiful a night for your old anguish.

Remember, remember when this little girl breathing under your arm taught you the thing you most needed to learn? It was winter then, too. She was a baby then. Remember.

* * *

Every father knows that there are seasons in the life of a family when troubles seem to mount up and spirits burn low. It had been one of those months around our house. In early December of that year we had had record snowfalls. Snow fell for weeks on end without a glimmer of sun. The accumulation of snow threatened to crack the roof beams, and the underlayer of ice forced meltwater under the shingles, setting off countless leaks that trickled throughout the house. Three times already that winter I had stood waist deep in snow on the roof, shovelling madly but enjoying the novelty of it all. Bam had great fun hurling himself off the peak to land harmlessly in the drifts below. Three times I had cleared the shingles, and the pile of white debris now reached the eaves. I had to dig a hole down to the living-room window to let some light in. But by the time a fourth shovelling was needed, I had developed a growth on my spine that was abscessed and infecting my system. Surgery was needed, but due to a long waiting list at the hospital there would be some months' delay. I was in a great deal of pain, unable to sit, stand, or lie without discomfort. By New Year's I was unable to do much of anything, which is perhaps the most frustrating thing of all for the head of a household. To watch and wait helplessly as one is buried alive is a terrible feeling. Family and close friends were too far away to come to our rescue and couldn't have got through on the blocked roads. Everyone else in the region was as desperate as we were.

On the day the snowplow finally broke through, I followed it into town to get the mail. I thought our troubles were almost over, but a distracted driver pulled out from a side street without seeing our oncoming car and demolished both vehicles. Thankfully, no one was seriously injured, but until the insurance was settled we were without transportation. Small disasters kept piling up, one of the more notable being a plugged toilet caused by a certain small member of the family throwing a toy truck down the hole and flushing, "to see what would happen", he said innocently. "I thought it would make Daddy laugh", he added. Then, grinning, he slammed down the two lids, *bam–bam!*

Enough to rattle the nerves of the dead. "Bam! Bam!" he said by way of a final statement. It was around that age that he was first called Bam.

The town plumber was holidaying in Florida, earning the envy and malice of his neighbors. I dismantled the toilet and did everything humanly possible to unplug it, but it was permanently jammed. Until we could afford a new one, we resorted to an antique chamber pot for a few weeks, a state of affairs that little Bam found rustic and exciting. This and other items had left us still able to chuckle over the uncanny way life is feast and famine. But at some point, shortly after, we lost our sense of humor. Daddy stopped laughing. For, with extraordinary timing, we were flattened by a virulent case of the flu. We couldn't telephone the doctor because the lines were down in yet another heavy snowstorm. The doctor's office was fifty miles away, and he couldn't have got through the blocked roads anyway.

There are ways of dealing with trouble in an affluent age. If you have enough money or influence, health and power, you can stave off trouble for a long time. You can pad and buffer and distract yourself until the illusion of mastery is complete. The only weakness in this seemingly perfect method is that your life must then be preoccupied with padding, buffering, and distracting. Most of us do it to some degree. We can't help it really. Pain just isn't fun; helplessness is scary. But suffering finds us all sooner or later. There is no hiding place, and, when raising a family, you are especially exposed to the dangers of human existence.

I didn't know it then, but the cost of a happy family is the death of selfishness. The father must die if he is to give life to his spouse and children. Not a pleasant thought but a true one. An entire lifetime can be spent avoiding it. It's simply not enough to provide and protect. In themselves, of course, providing and protecting are good and necessary things. That is our responsibility. But a father can provide a mountain of material goods for his family and defend it against all kinds of inconveniences, thinking he can rest easy, having done his part, and still have missed the essential point: he is called to be an image of love and truth. The house he provides, be it a cabin, a mansion, or a barge painted Christmas colors, must have at its core a heart that is willing to look at its poverty. As long as we're convinced of our own strengths, our cleverness, and our cagey ability to endure, we still think we're in charge. We construct a life-style of eliminating difficulties at any cost. It takes a lot of padding if you're to avoid the unexplainable, unjust blows of suffering. There will come a time, however, when this elaborate defense system crumbles.

I remember clearly the winter's night when my barricades began to fall. That night I had been unable to sleep from back pain and the steady tending of sick children. Moreover, our marriage was not going well. Maya hated living in a little backwoods town, far from the theater in which she had grown up and in which she had found her exotic identity. She wasn't only physically ill, she was deeply unhappy, and as a result, worry had begun to corrode me like acid. There were little skirmishes with discouragement from which I was still emerging the victor, but they were becoming harder to win, and they were becoming more frequent. Not only had I stopped laughing, I had stopped hoping. Spring, ha, spring was a primitive myth I no longer believed in!

In the notorious wee-small-hours of the morning, around three, the baby resumed a desperate cry from her bedroom. Her mother's body had resigned after four nursings since midnight. Utterly exhausted, Maya simply could no longer answer the baby's cry. There was only enough energy left to plead, "Will you get her?"

I groaned and maneuvered my back out of bed and made it across the hall to the hurricane of noise. Outside, the snow was falling in heavy, wet flakes, as it had for weeks. I was beginning to resent it. My head, my back, and all the cells of my flesh were in torment. I was feeling very sorry for myself.

Zöe was all of one and a half years old then, the apple of our eye, shining, crisp, and sweet. A baby who had emerged from the womb actually cooing and who early on displayed a wonderful wit and a gift for laughter. But, on the night in question, she stood there loudly protesting her predicament, a very tiny being, gripping the rungs of her crib and yelling with all the outrage of a prisoner unjustly condemned. There was a note of terror in her voice, too, because she was having trouble breathing. The soft glow of the night-light revealed eyes and nose completely clogged.

I gathered her up, murmuring our little code words of consolation, silly sounds I wouldn't care for anyone other than her mother to hear. But these old favorites were just not working that night. She refused to be consoled. I slumped into the broken rocking chair, the one with the cracked leg that squealed (when was the last time I had put off fixing it?). I began to wipe her nose and crusted eyes. Her limbs were tense, hands clutching my robe, her body shuddering and wailing in my arms. I reached down to see if safety pins had come unsprung or if her diaper was loaded, and, sure enough, she was badly in need of a change. She didn't want to be put down, and her anguish turned to hysteria as I lifted her onto the change table. First things first, for her pants were leaking as badly as the roof. But she disagreed. One frantic leg lashed out and pushed a pin into my thumb. Another bit of gymnastics, and she had tangled the diaper and its contents all over my hands, herself, and the table. Then, for one shattering moment, her mouth found my ear and bellowed into it with full intensity. I gritted my teeth. A flash of anger ran through me and was quickly gone. I had never seen her like this, though her mother had told me that it does happen. In the semi-darkness I couldn't quite see what I was doing. I flicked the overhead switch, and suddenly we were flooded with blinding, painful light.

Truth is sometimes like this, I thought. It's a searching light that reveals the fearful areas of our beings, the darkened rooms where we hide and refuse to trust. I examined my little flash of anger and was ashamed. Anger, I knew, has its roots in fear. A father at night may be afraid of any number of things: sickness, poverty, chaos, isolation, the collapse of the roof, the car breaking down again, his own mortality . . . or, even more to the point, his powerlessness in the face of reality. He may discover a secret in the fearful dark: he may actually learn to the depths of his being that he is not God.

Maya mumbled from the other room, asking if I needed to be rescued. But in a voice of supreme calm (despite the fact that I would indeed have liked to be rescued), I called out that all was well, all under control, and she should sleep. It was true, for a measure of physical order had been restored. Off went the light. I carried the baby back to the rocking chair. I rocked and rocked, holding her against myself. Between squeal and wail it was quite a symphony. She wouldn't stop crying, though the hysterical note was subsiding.

In the night, a father's raw nerve ends may begin to show, his fears and hidden neuroses begin to push up through the darkness like mushrooms. The innumerable little trials and strains of raising a family can add up to a considerable weight, especially if in coping with the storm of a thousand daily demands a father begins to forget bit by bit where his strength comes from. But in those years I knew only half of the equation. I knew that a father had to be strong.

Yes. But a father must also know how to be weak. For weakness comes to us all and is a blessing or a curse according to how we respond to it. In the night it may be hard to grasp this, for the dangers of life can thrust themselves like Orcs before our eyes: the corruption of values in society, the speed with which nations can rush to the brink of total war, the economy teetering on the edge of disaster . . . I could have gone on and on if I had allowed myself. Without realizing it, I might have reached for the weapons that many people use to protect themselves. In the night, overcome with darkness, alone and afraid, the temptation can be intense.

"Where is light?" my heart cried. "Have we been abandoned here in the darkness?"

As if in answer, a memory afflicted me: the day after this baby was born, her mother was attacked verbally by a stranger in the halls of the hospital. Maya had at first found him to be an intelligent and "grandfatherly" man, successful, vigorous in his seventies, concerned about many social issues. In the course of their conversation, he had asked if the baby was her first. When she said proudly that this was our second, his face looked solemn.

"Just how many children do you plan to have?" he asked.

"Three or four, maybe more", she said.

He looked at her with disgust and began bitterly and sarcastically to criticize her for "polluting" his world with too many children. She handled him patiently, but he stormed away after hurling some final insults. Certainly not a common incident, but a sign of the times, nonetheless. It had been the first major sting that Maya experienced at the hands of the brave new man. She didn't like it. She didn't like that man, and she clung fiercely to her beautiful new daughter, but from then on the stones began to crumble under the foundation. Her confidence was shaken. She had always been beautiful, talented, admired. Having a large number of people stand to applaud her as Titania, Queen of the Fairies or, better still, as Ophelia, was infinitely more delicious than being sneered at for her actual self.

The sneer was especially galling because it came from the enlightened, from people she secretly admired. Vibrant, intelligent, cultured people, who jogged and took holidays in Communist China or snorkeled in the Caribbean and who read the latest books and had token families. They were robust into their seventies, and they leaned far to the left on their ski poles. They believed it was better to kill a child than to kill a whale. I believed that both were forms of violation, but the former was surely the greater evil. Maya agreed with me in theory until she gradually discovered that all the *best* people thought differently. She wanted to be countercultural *and* a social success. She didn't mind despising that poor old yuppie and his kind for their blindness, but she never did learn to take it when they despised her in turn for failing to hold the correct opinions. There was a new orthodoxy abroad in the land, and she had somehow missed the cue during her few years tucked away in a remote valley with good old reactionary me. When she finally figured out what our way of life would cost, she began to suffer. She had been taught from birth to avoid unpleasantness. As a result, her inability to deal with the peculiar existential pain of the anathematized, the social pariah, later undid our marriage.

I think our baby Zöe taught me to respect suffering. On the night in question I didn't like the education. "So this is suffering", I thought sarcastically, hating it. Why did the experience not seem meaningful? Why was it just raw, ugly misery, with no artistic or mystical overtones and no inner consolations? I tried to pray my half-remembered, lukewarm prayers, but God seemed absent, and the words were as dry as Adam's dust. I was empty. A sterile heart with nothing left to give. No gush of affection for this poor, squalling creature whom I had helped to make, no profound insights about rising to challenges, about courage under fire. No recitation of Kipling's "If". No, nothing! But at least, I reminded myself, at least I have my will. I can choose to give the last dregs of whatever is down there in the bottom of this empty barrel of myself. And then I'll scrape the barrel's bottom and keep scraping, if necessary. For the rest of my life if I have to! I began by croaking out the broken words of a poem I had learned once. My grandmother had taught it to me. I tried to sing it, and the sheer oddity of this caught the baby's attention.

Out of the cradle endlessly rocking,
Out of the mocking-bird's throat, the musical shuttle,

Out of the Ninth-month midnight,
Over the sterile sands and the fields beyond, where the child
leaving his bed wander'd alone. . . .

I looked at my daughter, and she looked at me. This melancholy verse suited us both. Our moods were identical. Whitman's old hymn to mortality melted into the cycle of the broken rocker, as the man and his daughter were swept gently into the sea, the waters of presence, the great ocean of mysterious being that flows through everything, and beneath it and above it as well. Her cries sputtered and failed. She was quiet under the warmth of my hand.

"Well," I thought, "when everything's taken away from you, maybe they leave you a few little things like this: the only kind of power that means something. A warm hand and a song." Her bird hands fluttered, and she gave me little pats on the shoulder, a small mother consoling the consoler. We were both feeling somewhat better. Other words surfaced. My grandmother had taught me well, and memory was standing me in good stead:

For I, that was a child, my tongue's use sleeping, now I have
heard you,
Now in a moment I know what I am for, I awake,
And already a thousand singers, a thousand songs. . . .

Was she asleep? Did I dare risk it? Cleverly, I slowed the rocker and attempted to rise, to drop her gently into sleep. But her grip became suddenly fierce, and she cried. Down I went, rocking.

Then the final verse:

That strong and delicious word which, creeping to my feet,
(Or like some old crone rocking the cradle, swathed in
sweet garments, bending aside,)
The sea whispered me.

It took a while, but she was quiet again. I now found myself with a great deal of time to think. If I have to, I thought, I'll rock this baby till morning. I was strangely content to do so. If she needed me, I could carry this little beloved throughout the night.

"Yes," I thought, "I've nothing left to give you, Zöe. That's what I give you. Yes."

Crazy man in the dark. Listening and waiting. Rocking and stroking. Later, over the following months and years, I would often forget what I heard that night. I would sometimes disbelieve it in the flurry of distractions and burdens, sufferings, celebrations, and joys. But the sounds would return. I would recall the peace that filled the whole world, even though the world appeared to be falling apart. I heard again the music I hadn't suspected was there: the song of poverty, a child breathing easily at last, the cry of a night bird, the poetry of wind, and the whispering of snow. And in the depths of night a train's horn echoing across the wall of darkness. It seemed to me a reflection of the final trumpet, of a great and awesome beginning lying somewhere distant. Then the life of my wife and my children came before me with greater clarity than I had ever known. I had seen no star. I had heard no angels. Yet within my own arms lay a child as pure as an angel, and something more than an angel, for she was a living icon, "a strong and delicious word" never before seen, never to be repeated.

She was very fragile and very strong. She would awake to know what she is for, to find her tongue, to sing her thousand songs. And though the cities of our time are running more than ever with the blood of children, still her word shall be uttered, and the darkness cannot extinguish this word.

I lifted her and carried her to the crib. She sighed and turned, arranged her own body. I tucked the quilt around her, then paused to speak words that are soundless. I saw that outside the window snow continued to fill up the universe like mercy poured out over the world. As I closed the door, her bird-voice sang softly, "Night-night, Poppa."

I laid my body down in bed. Then, from the material of my little sufferings, I wove a word of thanks.

* * *

Now, nine or ten years later, the memory of that peace and that certainty has faded, and I'm in flight from Herod. Here I am, camped under a cold moon on a mountainside, huddling in a tent of spruce and snow with two of my children, a Vietnamese refugee teenager, and a white hart running around out there who could be a dumb deer or a projection from my now psychotic brain. All my bearings have been thrown into total disorientation. I struggle to keep a topographical map in my mind. We are going from here to there on it. We have departed. We will arrive. We will have a life that moves more or less in a linear progression, and we shall not, despite our feelings, dissolve into the universal blurring of distinctions. Nevertheless, the realist in me admits that there is no longer any sanctuary. My wife and my youngest son and my home and my career and my future have been whisked offstage without warning.

Herod, how did you do this to us, you old egomaniac? If I had you in the sights of my blunderbuss, I just might . . . I just might commit regicide! In the old days you were a tyrant who looked like a tyrant, and history remembers you as such. But for us there will be no accurate history. Our tyrants will be remembered as the saviors of mankind. Here you are again, two thousand years later. This time you have a public relations consultant; you have a pleasant bureaucratic manner and a business suit and a new, improved image. But you are just as furious with life now as you were then. Herod, Herod, Herod, you are still spilling a libation to your god. *Slay, slay,* you cry, *slay* these breathing words that contradict your chant of death: *Life is death!* your servants say. *Death is life! Darkness is light!* they say. *Light is darkness!*

My mind is rolling, wounded and weeping under the blue light sprinkled over these fugitive children who lie beneath a spruce sanctuary in a time of no sanctuary. I'm running, Herod, I'm running. I don't care if all the world is sated on your fat games and drunk on knowledge, their permissible children stuffed with good things. They have grown wise on electric candy. They are full of purple neon and the siren song of the arcade. They have seen acid visions. They know that their absent brothers and sisters fell under a knife, not at the command of a malicious king, but at the word of their mothers and their fathers. They have grown old too young.

You fooled them, you did. You seduced an entire age. Oh, I know that you are very clever and you gave them signs and wonders. But you have made a voice heard in the shopping malls, sobbing and loudly lamenting: it is our own cry, cracked, wired, and weeping for our children, because they are no more. But there are some who will have a childhood. There are a few who will slip through your fingers. You can't have *my* children. I won't let you.

I hope. Oh, God, I hope. Please, don't let everything good be devoured!

I'm afraid again.

It's winter, it's night. Is my life almost over? Am I going insane? Have I ever been sane?

It don't matter nohow, sang the cowboy on the radio the day before yesterday. It was the last piece of synthetic music I heard before the unexpected demise of my life. *It don't matter nohow.* Maybe nothin' matters nohow no more. Yet, I can choose to wait here on this final night and taste the bitterness of our times. I'll sit by the void where no voice is heard, no word, where only an absurd wind contradicts the bad news that men now call good.

I think again of the white hart. A coincidence? Merely a random movement of the interconnecting cycles of biological life? Or a word inscribed on the clean slate of nature? Who, then, invented the word? Who decides when it shall be uttered?

Powerful signs have been given to exiles in the past, fleeing their own land, going back into the country of their people's bondage. Angels in dreams, surprise stars, wise men from the east—yet we cannot live on signs, for we would soon become dependent on them. We live by faith, and if from time to time the veil is parted briefly, it is to encourage us for a specific task or to sustain us through a period we couldn't otherwise endure. But it is faith that we stand most in need of. Why did I let faith die? Why have I let so many years pass without giving it a thought? What have I missed? Faith is the great teacher and molder of hearts, the temperer of souls, as gold is tested in fire. Matthew could have told me that. In fact, he had told me without words. When our other strengths fail, there at the base of our empty souls is a mysterious silent wealth. There at the bottom of the barrel is the real strength, not power or resources, not worldly wisdom or a solid defense system, but rather the will to continue to love and to live by the truth. The human will! That curious faculty which can do so much good but which so often reaches instead for bombs and blunderbusses and even, at its worst, grasps for the ultimate illusion of being lord over all it surveys. Why do we grieve so when that grasping fails? Why is it that we resist the stripping down and flee from the knowledge of our fundamental human weakness? Is it really so bad when the true learning begins?

It's blowing hard out there. Only a little of the wind winnows through the lace filigree of the evergreens, our temporary encampment on the edge of the abyss. I lie here because of the internal authority of an abstract code within my mind. It seeks incarnate forms. I hug Zöe in her sleep. I turn over and hug Tyler. I love them. I reach beyond my son and tuck a blanket tighter around Anthony. He stirs in his sleep, mutters in Vietnamese, and hugs his .22 tightly.

Man, holding the frail scepter of his realm. Could Anthony kill or wound another human being with that thing? Yes. He could.

I, too, am grateful for my blunderbuss, though I don't sleep with it. It's over there, propped against the far wall of our shelter. Could I kill or maim with it? I think not. After tonight I know I could not. Though I just might knock a crown off a tyrant's head.

Eight

The luminous dial of my watch is blurred by frost. After some scraping, I find that it's the hour before dawn. I roust everyone out, and we eat scraps of leftovers from last night. We're on the move before the east turns pale gray. The long trek around the breast of the mountain is still to come. We'll travel horizontally until I can see the Cariboos stretching north and south into infinity. There's a certain creek across the valley, and my grandfather lives beside it, close to the massif. When I see that thread I'll know it's time to go straight down.

We're stiff and still trying to wake up. Anthony and Tyler are scouting ahead, going a bit too fast for me. They have hit their usual stride but carry their snowshoes in case the snow gets soft underfoot. Zöe is alongside of me, trotting in her boots. She goes too slow on snowshoes, and the surface is fairly firm here. The toboggan is singing on the crust. Even so, every now and then my leg plunges beneath the surface. I keep my eyes open for another snowmobile trail. It would make our journey so much easier. The sun rolls over the edge of the world, and the western ridges are bathed in a rosy light. A mile farther along we enter the shadow of Canoe Mountain.

The sleep helped. I'm not so depressed. The memory of that beautiful creature and the shooting stars also buoys me up. Fear is no longer the scourge it has been for the past two days. It's now only a sullen ache at the back of my throat.

We're travelling near the lower border of the ring of forest, yet keeping under the trees. I wish the boys would slow down a little. I call but they don't hear me. I see their parkas between the trunks of the pines. Tyler's is teal blue and Anthony's is bright red, an unfortunate color if you wish to avoid detection. They're getting careless and wandering onto the snowfields below us. It's softer underfoot there, and they put their snowshoes on, which slows them down and could make an emergency run more difficult. Now they're back close to the fringe of trees. No, they're drifting down into the logged area again. They prefer it because there are no branches to shunt aside or to crawl around, no pokes and rips in the parkas. Speed and the pushing back of limits is the proper exercise of youth.

I can see that they're talking animatedly, gesturing with their arms and joking together. Tyler pleads for permission to carry Anthony's .22. The older boy hands it over for a few minutes, then takes it back again. They're distracted from the seriousness of our situation; they're enjoying the excursion, two youths on a trek in a land that's big enough to match their appetite for struggle and spiced with just enough marginal danger to make it a thrill. Is there a dull ache in their throats? Are they carrying a load of ancient bitterness? Not likely. I'm glad for them. But they're getting reckless.

I call them back. I worry about the loud yell, because these rock faces slam the echoes back and forth nearly full force, saying to anyone within a five-mile radius that somebody's on this mountain. We stop for a break, and I warn the boys gravely. They nod. Anthony understands, but Tyler is in a giddy mood, and he has succeeded in infecting Anthony to a degree. And what is Anthony if not a boy at heart, albeit one who has been pushed rudely into manhood by the circumstances of life. Tyler doesn't believe in death. He has never seen it.

Anthony scolds and joshes my son into submission. He looks sideways at me for approval, and I smile at him, *thanks*. He is poised exactly between the childhood of Tyler and the weight of my kind of manhood. He is a bearer of burdens, but he hasn't yet begun to show any of the customary burn around the edges of the nervous system that I display in abundance. He checks the clip of his gun, a purely symbolic gesture. Tyler watches, admiring. He enjoys having an older brother, even one who has just smacked him into line. He knows it's all in good fun. Zöe is daydreaming, singing in a low voice, propped on top of the toboggan.

"How much far we go, Natano?"

"Not too much longer. Another hour like this, and we'll be opposite the mountain where my mother's father lives."

I point across the valley, farther south, farther west.

"Over there on that other range, there's a creek that comes off the high places. Down at the bottom is where he lives."

Anthony looks into the distance. He analyzes every contour that lies before him. Then he nods. "We go?"

"We go", I say.

The boys gradually pull ahead, and all's well for a time. Then, despite my lecture, they drift out from under the trees.

That's when it happens. So fast there's no warning. A hell-cop goes zinging down the valley at an altitude just above our right shoulders. It has come from the north and is flying out over the middle of the valley floor. Oh, no, don't look toward this side of the valley! The boys flatten on the snow.

Don't see us! Don't see us!

The pilot is so close I see his face turning our way. The whine of his jets alters. He banks sharply and does an impossible U-turn in the sky. I huddle with Zöe in the snow and drag the white canvas over us. She's whimpering. Tyler and Anthony are running on their snowshoes toward the edge of the forest. But they're going too slow. The hell-cop zips in a few feet over their heads, and I hear the *budda-budda* of his machine gun as he stitches a line between them and safety. Spurts of snow fly up, and the boys stop. They don't know what to do. The hell-cop hovers twenty feet above them, his nose tilted down for aim. He's speaking into his radio. Finished, he takes up another microphone, and we hear an electronic beep from a loudspeaker:

"Stay where you are, and surrender your weapons."

The metallic voice booms and echoes across the valley and back again.

Anthony twists sideways and unstraps the .22 from his back. Then with one swift movement he swings it up, and there's a crack. The plexi on the cockpit is punctured. Even from here I can see that the pilot's face is mad as a stung hornet. There's a pitched whine, and the helicopter shifts sideways. Anthony leaps sideways, too, and he's suddenly a fierce little Annamite warrior. With perfect control, he fires at the craft again, and this time there's a metallic twang. Gas dribbles out of a tank, and the stunned pilot lifts off high. As he goes up, I see him yelling into his radio. A hundred feet up, he tips the nose and fires a tracer burst at the boys. They're running to me. The tracer bullets creep toward the red parka, and I'm yelling, *run, run, run!*

Anthony twirls in a spinning wheel of snow, and falls. Tyler is in the trees now, sobbing, screaming, hurling himself upon us with white terror in his eyes. He scrabbles under the canvas. The hell-cop is lowering down, searching for us. I drag out the old blunderbuss, take aim in my shaking hands and squeeze the trigger, not expecting anything to happen. There's a thunderous *Blam!* that flings me backward with its kick. Smoke dribbles from the helicopter. It banks away and disappears over the crest of trees, trailing a smudge and a stream of fuel.

I yell at Anthony. He's crying out. I run to him.

Oh, God, it's a disaster! He's shrieking, twisting, and turning. The left side of his chest looks torn open in a stew of blood and snow. Red spatters on everything. Some bits of flesh, too. Where has he been hit? There's a mass of purple with small broken bones jutting out. Blood is gushing from some source I can't locate. But there are no spurts, so maybe the arteries haven't been cut. I smell burned cloth and burned tissue. I can't believe this.

I find the main source of hemorrhage just above and to the right of his belt. I pack snow in there and press hard. His screaming is the most terrible sound I have ever heard. His face is in agony until he shudders and falls into unconsciousness.

Steady pressure, steady pressure! Gradually the gushing slows to seepage, then stops. Sporadic puffs of frosty breath are coming from his mouth. He's still alive.

My children are standing behind me. Tyler is crying. Zöe is turned away, with her face hidden in her mittens.

"Tyler, get the toboggan! Quick!"

He's back down in a minute. We strip everything off of it except for two sleeping bag rolls, which I open up and spread out as a mattress. I drag Anthony's body onto it, then wrap him with the other two sleeping bags. I tie up the whole mess with rope. Thank God he's unconscious.

I take off into the clear-cut. We're heading straight down. The kids run and stumble as fast as they can behind me. We're all gasping and crying. Down, down, faster and faster, the toboggan racing us, sometimes pulling ahead.

I trip on a hidden log and smash face-down into a drift. The toboggan sails over me and crashes upside down. We turn him upright, but the blood is pouring again. I pull open the sleeping bag, stuff in snow, pressure, pressure, pressure.

It's stopped.

This can't be happening!

Once more we're plunging downhill, straight through a swath of exposure three thousand feet in height. If the hell-cop returns, we're dead.

Down.

Down.

The mind in flight is capable of its own aerobatics. What strange composite creatures we are, strange and beautiful, full of mysteries. While part of my self, the physical element, is hurtling its legs, arms, heartbeat, lungs, and skull down a mountainside, another part of me is wailing in grief and rage, while yet another part is coolly assessing the situation.

First objective: escape from immediate danger, which is the likely return of the hell-cop with reinforcements. Temporary refuge. We must get to the thick forest on the opposite side of the highway. Then, possibly, to Thaddaeus' place.

Second objective: find medical help for Anthony. I know little or nothing that would save a life in his condition.

Down.

Down.

Third objective: seek long-term refuge with Thaddaeus. (Think about this later!)

Down. Trip. Stumble. Get up, get up!

Down. Trees approaching. The highway is below us, only a few hundred yards away. I'm aching in every torn muscle.

Consider this as a possibility: flag down a passing car and send Anthony off to emergency at McBride Hospital. No good! Medics have to report these kinds of wounds to the police. They'll be watching for him, anyway. Anthony would end up in prison or worse. They just shot him. They killed Bill—and what does that say about the present state of justice? No, he'd be finished for sure.

Consider this possibility: get to Thaddaeus' and send for Woolley. He'll come. He can do bush surgery any day of the week, and he won't tell the medical commission about it, either. That's it, we'll do it that way!

We're now in the trees that flank the highway. Above us I see hell-cops hovering at the top of the mountain like wasps over a ruptured nest. How long will it take them to find our trail?

We plunge over the banks and tumble down onto the edge of the pavement. A big semi transport truck goes by, the driver honking his horn, waving. He thinks we're merry recreationists! I wave back. What a crazy world.

We're standing on the roadside, huffing and puffing, dazed, when I see him: a small figure in a black felt coat. An old man. He limps across the road to us and says in a heavy accent, "Come this way."

Zöe, Tyler, and I stare at him.

"This way", he says gently, and beckons. Who is he, and why is he standing right here of all places? I've never seen him before in my life.

"Don't be afraid. I will take you to Thaddaeus."

Now I stare hard. This is weird.

He limps off down the road, heading south. He doesn't look back.

We trot along the plowed shoulders, following him. There's enough snow for the toboggan to slide.

Who on earth is this stranger? And what's that accent? European?

He crosses to the other side. There's an awful scraping when I drag the toboggan over the wet, black pavement. Anthony groans, and his eyelids flutter. Another five minutes and we come to the Ministry of Highways' bridge at Cariboo Creek. We're close to Thaddaeus'. The stranger disappears over the banks beside the bridge. We go up and over too, leaving no footprints in the rock-hard pile of frozen slush and debris cast up by the plow.

Where is he? There he is, down in the thickets of willow beside the creek, hobbling his way upstream, west, into the foothills of the Cariboo Range. Tyler and I half-carry, half-slide the toboggan down the slope and follow him behind the screen of bush.

* * *

There is my ol' Thaddaeus, shuffling down the trail toward us. The foreigner meets him first and is talking to him. Snow flurries are falling. The day is graying. Beyond Thaddaeus I can see the shack where he has lived since the nineteen twenties. His wife is dead, his children all grown and gone. I'm the only grandchild who remains a local.

He stares down at the toboggan.

"Tanny, it don't look too good", he says in his slurred Shushwap argot. "Bring that boy inside."

For my grandfather, this is an extra long sentence. Ask him for a story, and he'll tell you one that could take hours to complete. But actual dialogue, never!

He goes to Tyler and Zöe and squeezes their arms. Then he herds us all into the cabin. Tyler and I, being the strongest, lift the toboggan through the doorway and place it on the pine plank table in the kitchen part of the main room. It's dim inside. There are a few kerosene lanterns sputtering. The cookstove is roaring. It smells a lot like Thu's place. Woodsmoke and fish, with the added spice of animal hides hanging from the rafter poles. Thaddaeus is a trapper, a little, old, bent Indian man who bathes a few times a year, changes clothing about as often, and is never, simply never, seen without a floppy cloth hat on his head and a Sacred Heart badge pinned to his breast pocket. The heart is crimson, surrounded by a crown of thorns, and topped by a flaming cross.

"This boy's in a bad way", he says to the old European. The foreigner takes off his black felt coat and reveals a neck dressed in a frayed Roman collar. I haven't seen one of those in years.

Tyler enters the lean-to bedroom. He lies down and turns his head to the wall. Zöe sits curled up on the couch with her face in her hands, suppressing sobs.

I peel the sleeping bags off Anthony. They're wet with blood, but not sopping. The priest and my grandfather uncover his body. I almost retch when I see what the tracer bullets did to him. Part of his lower rib-cage is blasted away, and there's a pool of black blood in the body cavity. I can see some upper intestines. But maybe we're lucky, because nothing vital appears to be torn. There's no smell of excrement, and no arteries are pumping out the boy's life. There's some seepage. We can stop that with ice and pressure. A lot of congealing, thank heavens. He's a healthy kid.

He's still unconscious. We can turn him, gently, gently. Oh, no, it looks as if the blast is higher up on his back, because I think I see some lung material that's torn or punctured. It's not inflating, and it's oozing a little. His breathing is shallow. He's gray and sweating. He's in shock.

If he has one functioning lung, we can save him, as long as there's no big hemorrhage inside that we can't reach. Even with that, it's still too big a job for us. Thaddaeus has some experience stitching together parts of children and grandchildren who got careless with axes or stepped on broken bottles. But nothing like this.

We turn Anthony onto his back again. The blast hole is the worst-looking aspect. But the numerous secret bloodlettings are the real danger. They've stopped now. The snow and pressure took care of that for a while. But they could open up again at any moment. A surgeon will be needed to stitch the mess together. If we don't find one soon, he'll either bleed to death, or he'll develop gangrene and die slowly.

"Father Andrei, what we gonna do?" asks Thaddaeus.

The two old men put their heads together and look for all the world like rabbis discussing a fine point in the Talmud.

"He must get to a doctor", says the priest. "But the journey would be dangerous for these wounds. Is there a doctor who would come here?"

"A friend of mine", I reply. "Woolley. I think he'll come. I'll go get him now."

"No. It would not be wise for you to go."

Once again I'm puzzled by him. Does he know who we are?

Thaddaeus nods toward the battery-powered radio.

"We been listenin', Tan. Better you don't go. I'll go."

An old man? Yes, but what an old man! He still walks miles of trapline every week and hikes into town for groceries once a month, pushing his dogless dogsled in winter or backpacking between break-up and freeze-up.

It's the only thing to do. This old priest limps, the kids might get lost or confiscated and reeducated, and I might get arrested. Okay, I nod, Thaddaeus goes.

I scribble a note to Woolley:

> Dear W.
>
> Recall well, *Herr Doktor*, our discussions regarding that mythical beast, the masses. Recall also that the political arm of the beast controls the media, and that the media control the politics. It is a closed circle, a serpent devouring its own tail. Do not believe all that you read or hear about me.
>
> I hope you explained to the cops about that asinine message I left on your answering machine. It was a dumb joke, my dumbest yet. The gunshot was a blank from T's starting pistol.
>
> I am alive and well and completely innocent of everything except crimes of the mind. One of my lambs is suffering in extremis. Please make haste with your little black bag. Collapsed lung, shattered ribs, burns, much bleeding. Can you muster a mobile surgical unit? I beg you to trust me. Follow the old man who bears this message. For friendship's sake,
>
> Yours, fugitively,
>
> Ed.

* * *

I approached Woolley a few months after Maya left. I hadn't yet met him, but I had heard plenty. He had just bought a small sheep farm at the base of the Cariboos, a few miles northwest of town. The village gossips said he was Not A Nice Man. He was a doctor, a recluse, British. He had set up an office on MacPhale Street and was open for business two days a week, but he didn't yet have many patients. He had privileges at the closest hospital, McBride and District Memorial, fifty miles away. It was rumored that he wouldn't do abortions or euthanasias. Swiftcreek's other two doctors were strident feminists who practiced abortions and geriatric terminations as if they were removing warts. They were very nice, intelligent ladies who conducted their medical arts with great sensitivity to the feelings of the families. They were well liked in the community. I tried never to get ill. I didn't enjoy being pawed by blood-drenched hands, let alone by impersonal female hands. It was a relief to know that the newcomer was antisocial and male.

We sat in his office for the first time, assessing each other. He sat on a swivel chair and stared at me sideways. He was tweedy and late fortyish, a bachelor, and had the usual uncared-for look of a man without a mate, though it appeared to be high-class absent-mindedness. There were a jumble of medical journals and heaped ashtrays lying about. A rack of pipes. His office didn't look any too hygienic. But the wall was covered with framed diplomas and prestigious papers.

They said *Bertram Woolley*, followed by a long list of initials.

I was ashamed of the peculiar medical problem that I needed badly to discuss with him—emotional instability is so humiliating. So I attempted some peripheral distraction.

"I see you were a professor of medicine at Edinburgh University", I said by way of opening. "You taught at McGill, too, and then the Mind/Brain Institute."

He grunted.

"And you were once an editor of *The Lancet*. That's very impressive!"

"What's the problem?" he asked in a cold voice.

"I think I'm having a nervous breakdown."

"What are the symptoms?"

"My hands shake all the time. I can't sleep. I've got a pain in my chest that feels like a running sore. It goes away when I drink Scotch. I continually want to cry for no reason, and periodically I want to scream. I tell people off in my mind all day long. I'm going crazy. Half my family is insane. I barely get my work done, and usually late. I've been making some stupid mistakes at the paper lately."

"Oh, yes, you're the editor of *The Ego*."

Was he kidding? His mouth twitched a little.

"*The Echo*!" I corrected.

"Ah, yes, *The Echo*."

We stared at each other. I didn't like him much.

"So what do you want me to do for you? Cram you full of pills?"

I could feel a slow sizzle start up inside of me.

"I don't know. You're the doctor", I snapped back.

His mouth definitely twitched.

"Do you want my opinion? With a little more effort, you could work yourself into a full-scale nervous collapse, if that's what you think you need."

"It's what I definitely don't need!"

"Then why are you making yourself have one?"

Of all the insensitive . . . ! I stared at him hard and boiled inside.

"Great bedside manner you have there, *Herr Doktor*! Does all your genius give you the right to insult people, you arrogant . . . !"

Without waiting for his response, I snorted at his diplomas, got up, and began rummaging around for my coat.

"Sit down, sit down!" he said, and to my astonishment I found him grinning.

"I've got just the medicine for you. It kills pain."

He was up and out of the office and back again before I had a chance to get an arm down a sleeve. He was carrying a brown bottle and two glasses.

He poured us each a drink of whatever it was.

He sipped his and watched me.

I sat down on my dignity. But I kept my coat on.

"C'mon, relax!" he said.

"I'm relaxed. I'm relaxed!" I snarled.

I took a sip. It was chocolatey and creamy and very alcoholic.

"You like it?"

"I like it."

"Good, good. Such a willing patient."

"Your social graces are really terrible, you know, Doctor. What gives with you? The whole town says you're a cold fish. And you're an awful long way from the British Isles for such a famous guy. What *are* you doing here?"

"To quote a mentor of mine, Jonathan Swift, *Principally I hate and detest that animal called Man.*"

"Aren't you in the wrong business for that sort of attitude?"

"I don't think so. I actually like individual human beings, when I can find one. It's the herd that revolts me. I also detest countries that turn human beings into herds."

"So why are you here?"

"Good question. Mostly because this land is empty. By the way, do you mind if I smoke? It's bad for the health. I don't recommend it."

He puffed up a Sherlock Holmes pipe, rosy briarwood and silver, and sent clouds through the room. He put his feet on his desk and leaned way back on the squeaking chair.

"Smells like camel-shit and bus-tickets, doesn't it. Why is it so comforting?"

"I smoked a pipe once, too", I said. "I gave it up when my ex-wife told me I cling to it because I never got enough nursing as a baby. And also the primitive fire-instincts—"

"You poor ninnyhammer! What made your wife such an expert?"

"She has a degree in psychology."

He choked on his drink and laughed for the first time.

"Addlepated. Totally addlepated."

"Thank you for this astute consultation. I'm getting better by the minute!"

"Speaking as your doctor, *Herr Redakteur*—dear, dear vehement editor—I assure you that smoking and drinking are definitely going to shorten your life. But they're definitely better than the obsessive pursuit of health."

"Spoken like a true addict."

"Listen, you'll drive yourself genuinely insane if you try to escape our lot!"

"Our lot?"

"Mortality. Everybody dies one way or another, not that it matters. Why should you die from the head downward thirty or forty years before your biological death?"

"Are you saying that these little addictions are Life?"

"Of course not. I'm saying only that, in moderation, mind you, they're humble pleasures. They're here for a reason."

"What reason? Why? From where cometh the thought that created the form?"

He puffed on that for a while and squinted.

"I'm not a theist, *Herr Editor*. But I think there's some intelligence at work in the cosmos. Other than you and me, that is. Does it matter, ultimately, if we ever give it its proper name?"

"Yes, it matters", I growled.

Woolley flung his feet to the floor and leaned over his desk with a mad, humorous, and intense look in his eyes.

"Do you play chess?" he asked.

"Yes."

"Do you wish to continue therapy?"

"I'll think about it. If your manner improves."

"I'll work on it."

He reached across and offered me his hand. I shook it reluctantly.

"As your physician, I order you to appear at my house every two weeks. Bring your brain in a detoxified state, bring your refreshing though limited honesty, and I'll supply the booze. Agreed?"

"Uh, not so fast. Are you gay?"

"Not in the least. You're quite safe in that regard. I shan't cough in your drink or poke you with an AIDS-contaminated needle. But your mind will be in great peril. I shall try to bend it into my own image."

"You have your work cut out for you."

"By the way, old chap, are you yourself gay?"

"No."

"That makes things simpler. Do you believe in friendship?"

"Not much."

"I see. Then I do have my work cut out for me."

I was just getting to know the Thu family around that time. I was hungry for any human face to reassure me, but at root I mistrusted everything. In those early years I suspected that the Thus might just want me because they were poor and I was useful. It took a long time to find out that this was untrue. They were pure gold. As time went on, I came to believe in their friendship, but even then it was always a community of the heart, not of the intellect. Poor ninnyhammer that I was, I believed smart people were infinitely more reliable.

I was grateful for Woolley. As ordered, I appeared regularly at his home. He didn't bend my mind. Nor did I alter his rather stark convictions. We drank, in moderation. He gave me a lovely old meerschaum pipe the following Christmas, and smoking became one of my few remaining vices. We took long philosophical walks in the woods. He taught me a lot about sheep and people, in that order of preference. My nervous breakdown failed to come off as planned. Woolley had sabotaged it completely. We became friends.

* * *

It's snowing heavily. Fat, wet, white flakes are falling slowly past the window. I hope Grandpa doesn't have trouble. Woolley loves cross-country skiing. Maybe he'll return by that method. If he drives his bright red Cherokee Jeep, with its MD license plate, and parks it out on the highway, it could look suspicious. The hell-cops aren't geniuses, but they aren't stupid, either. I hope he thinks of that. Why didn't I suggest it in the note? I worry about it but reassure myself that he's a smart fellow.

Good old Woolley. Not long after our friendship began, I tried to soften him up by calling him Bertram. He fixed me with his clinical gaze, the kind that performs autopsies without batting an eye. He asked me never to call him that.

"Don't call me Bert, either", he added.

"How shall we address each other, *Herr Doktor!*"

"*Hey you*, will do just fine. How about Doc and Ed? Or Woolley and Du . . . Duh . . . Dud . . . or whatever your convoluted Celtic name is?"

"You could try Tan."

"All right. Let's use that one. I'll consider it my little exercise in affection."

"Don't strain yourself."

He grunted. Then checkmated me.

"You're a bit of a bully, aren't you, Doc?"

"If you don't like it, pack your bags—*Tan*."

"I don't like it, and I'm not packing my bags."

He smirked. "You some kind of masochist?"

"Hey, I thought you despised psychologizing."

"Sometimes it's a handy little weapon. Drink up."

I drank up.

"I enjoy the honesty, Doc. I enjoy being my kind of honest, and I can even enjoy your kind too—for a while. But at some point you're going to have to progress beyond simple, basic nastiness. And I think you'd better call me *Ed*."

He looked at me, genuinely troubled.

"Bloody hell, you think I'm just mean-hearted?"

"No offense."

"For a clever fellow, you don't see much, do you, Ed?"

"There you go again. The petty tyrant act. How did you learn to talk like that?"

"By working with bureaucrats—nice, deadly bureaucrats."

"I know what you mean. They're taking over the world! They're breeding like rats!"

"Now who's being nasty? By the way, Ed, aren't you a sort of tyrant with that newspaper of yours? You're a pretty lucky fellow to be able to tell the world off once a week. One might even say you're a bit of a bully."

"Check, mate."

We laughed and drank up some more.

Nine

January 21
It's night. We're at Grandpa Tobac's cabin. This has been the worst day of my life. Young Anthony Thu has been shot by the police and is in very serious condition. I've sent a message off to Woolley, asking him to come here to try to save the boy. A priest is also with us, a Father Andrei, an old friend of Thaddaeus'. I suppose my faith is improving to the extent that I am wondering if we can call these coincidences providential. But I feel a certain bitterness as well. Where is God?

Tyler and Zöe are sleeping soundly. They're shocked and worn out.

* * *

I pull Zöe's thumb out of her mouth. *The Lord of the Rings* lies open and crushed under her elbow. Its pages are wrinkled with wet drops. I thought we had lost the book along with everything else this morning, but I guess she had it in her backpack when we plummeted down.

Father Andrei is kneeling beside Anthony. The boy is groaning again. He's conscious, talking to the priest in whispers. Occasionally he cries and shivers, and the old man puts a hand to the forehead of his penitent.

Is the snow falling like mercy throughout the universe?

Hurry, Woolley. Come quickly.

Dark. Only a dim oil light is burning on a hanger suspended above the kitchen table. Father Andrei is seated on the kitchen chair beside Anthony. He's reading Scriptures through wire-rim spectacles. Every so often he checks the boy. I lie down on the couch and try to rest. It's snowing hard outside, and the wind is blowing.

When will Thaddaeus return with Woolley?

Time. Time to think. In recent years there has been so little time. By force of habit I think of time constantly. I'm haunted by it. I measure everything by it. I'm a large white rabbit, late, late, late for a very important date, a date that I never keep. I have been frantically busy getting my life accomplished, and in the process I have failed to live. I have rushed past the abundant beauty that surrounds me. I have been so anxious about my children that I've not really looked at them.

Do we ever see another until he's gone? When Stiofain died, I knew that something had gone out of the world that was never before seen and would never be repeated. When Annie died, I was only a self-centered teenager, but even then I knew that the balance of the universe had been shifted. When Thaddaeus is gone, this place will crumble into ruins, and the memory of him will be lost in a generation or two. Many people have flowed from this shelter. I don't even know all of them now. They're scattered across the country, a splintered, demolished remnant of our extended family. When Thaddaeus dies, there will be nothing left to hold it together. His stories, his slow wit and powerful discernments, will be unlamented and unremembered.

And what about that old European over there, reading so peacefully, tending the ruptured boy as if this situation were normal: What memories does he contain? One scarcely knows where to ask. By contrast, the present generation, the brave new man, is a strangely homogenized creature, rushing, rushing, rushing toward an undefined end. Odd how the old ways produced a much broader (and need I say deeper) variety of human being.

These people are the last scraps of my own history. How often have I meditated upon their lives? Seldom, and then only with the crude instruments that came to hand. Now, my life is rushing before my eyes, but rushing *slowly*, if you will! I see the wife of Thaddaeus, my other grandmother. Poor Wanda was an alcoholic who went slowly insane. She's the source of my fears about mental illness, of course. I remember her as a thin, fierce person, whose answers didn't match our questions. She was a lot like my gentle mother in looks, but filled with a peculiar rage. Is this my inheritance from her corner of the gene pool? Dear Grandma—sometimes she was with us and sometimes not, and all that time, through more than forty difficult years, Thaddaeus looked after her with utter and indefatigable patience. He is the quintessential kind man. He had a lot to put up with. Wanda spent most of her life fighting battles in a wounded past. Although, when you think of it, we all do that, don't we? During yesterday's jolly outing hiking up the mountain, I talked with Maya and Dad and my other failed relationships. There are so many of them. I'm riddled with guilt over those failures. I *am* guilty. I didn't love one-tenth of the amount that Thaddaeus loved. I was too busy. If they catch me, they'll attempt to relieve me of my guilt. I hope they don't catch me. I don't enjoy guilt feelings, but at least they're honest.

Wanda's sickness was aggravated by alcohol, without a doubt, but it originated largely in a hard childhood and was more a case of emotional disorder than illness of the physical brain. However, she may have had a biological weakness in that department, and, if so, I've probably inherited it. That's why I worry so much about going crazy.

I hate the people who hurt her. I hate the man who murdered my great-grandfather Finbar back in Ireland almost a century ago. I hate MacPhale, who bought up this town and turned it into a factory. I hate the hell-cops. And I hate the gutless men who could have prevented the degeneration of our flawed but sane society into a landscape where all appears well but is not well. Indeed, it is perhaps sick unto death. And I hate the lies that blind my sincere father, and I hate the people who made the Thu family suffer, and the people who made the Jews suffer, and the ones who make Blacks and Catholics suffer, and the moderates who make us all suffer by their calm, measured assurances that all is well, all is well, all shall be exceedingly well. I can't forgive what's being done to us, the strangling of everything that's beautiful and true and good. The strangest of their lies is that, as the world dies, they say they are giving us an enhanced life. I find this an especially cruel form of deception. I hate them most of all for drugging everyone. Most people have been lulled into total apathy by the narcotic. I just barely saved Tyler and Zöe from becoming zombie consumers. I hate . . . yes, to put it simply, I *hate* this thing that has poisoned an entire world. Me, I think I'll just choose to remain awake until the last moment, guilty, full of aches and pains, neurotic as all get-out, dysfunctional to the end. At least I'm alive.

Woolley used to cut through the crap.

"You're a very angry chap, you are", he said.

"Yeah. I'm very angry."

"You care too much."

"Can one care too much?"

"Yes, one can."

"Did you ever love anybody, Woolley?"

"Yes", he said, in his quietest voice ever.

I glanced at the mantelpiece in his living room. There were several framed photographs of Cambridge, a rugby team, Penfield, the brain surgeon, a few assorted group portraits, a terrier or two. And the face of a woman. It was a plain, good face, and the eyes were thoughtful, the lips generous. I took a good look when he was out in the kitchen preparing drinks.

"Is she the one you loved?" I asked when he returned.

"She's dead." A voice delivering a cold fact.

"Your wife?"

"Don't probe into my secret wounds, Ed", he said in a dangerous voice. "And I won't probe into yours."

"I bow to your superior wisdom, *Herr Doktor*."

I asked him once:

"How come you don't do abortions and euthanasias?"

"How do you know I don't?"

"People talk. A man's foibles get around."

"Well, the rumor's true. I don't do aborts or gerries anymore."

I felt my heart go cold. "Anymore? You did them?"

"Yeah, I did them."

"How come no more?"

"Look, don't impute any righteousness to me. It's not a matter of morality."

"Then what?"

"I lost my taste for death. Plain and simple."

"Plain and simple."

I barely refrained from asking how he ever *acquired* a taste for death.

He saw me staring at him.

"Just call me Dr. Mengele", he grinned and raised his glass.

I bent my head and drank deep but couldn't manage a grin.

"Tell me, earnest young editor, are you my friend?"

"Sure, Woolley, I'm your friend."

"How much honesty can you take?"

"Lots", I said squarely, knowing I was lying.

"Would you care to know how I lost my taste for death?"

Without waiting for my reply, Woolley swivelled his padded leather rocking chair sideways and gazed out the picture window of his living room. He reached over and yanked my rocker sideways, too, so that we were both facing out at the soft light of dusk on a perfectly lovely spring evening.

"Let us behold neutral ground while ol' Doc tells you this bedtime tale, shall we?"

The sweet-uncle tone flowed over a black undertow.

"In the shadows of my illustrious past, between my periodic efforts to save humanity at its crisis centers in the Third World, I returned to normal practice. My trade is brains, actually, though I can tinker in just about any other part of the body. But as the number of physicians willing to shred live babies wavered, the medical profession turned to fellows like me to fill in the breach. You know, scientist types. A rank above your ordinary G.P. Now most doctors have no problem killing gerries, because it's just another needle. And because they can tell themselves that grandma and grandpa have had a full life and are ready for a nice rest. But vivisecting a baby is a little harder on the nerves. Only two kinds of doctor can stand it very long. The hack butchers and the idealists. I was one of the idealists."

I nodded assent. "I knew that."

"A clever fellow you are. To get on with my tale—eventually I thought, whatever this odd little inhibition is, this *thing* that keeps us from actually enjoying the dismemberment of someone else and keeps us feeling rather unhappy about the necessity of the whole messy affair . . . well, it's really quite irrational, I thought. If we can do it to a baby, then why not to a senile person? Why not a Downs or an epileptic or people with unusual gene disorders? We'll open them up in the interests of humanity. It's all very humanitarian, you know."

"That's enough", I muttered. "You don't have to tell me. I don't want to know."

"That's right, you don't want to know. A real journalist."

I stood up nervously. "Look, just forget it. I don't want to hear about it."

"You don't want to hear about it?" he mimicked, looking at me with contempt.

"That's right. Just drop it."

"You bloody phony little coward", he said in his professional voice, the autopsy tone. He was staring right into my soul: "You're a fake hero, Ed. You're the reason why my side is winning."

"What's that supposed to mean? I'm not the butcher."

"No, you're worse than the butcher."

"You're crazy!"

"You're worse because you know better than they do."

"They? Didn't you just say you're one of them?"

"You always overreact, don't you? Let me spell it out: I was an idealist who tried the meat trade. Even as I carved up the living bodies, I thought I was still an idealist, but I was a butcher. And when I saw it, I went back to my original form. Get it?"

"No, I don't get it."

"What you really mean is that you don't want to hear about it because it might deprive you of a pipe-smoking English crony who can discuss dead languages and dying literature with you and reinforce your illusion that the world didn't end a few decades ago. But more than that, gore upsets your stomach. Horror makes you mad, and when you're mad, you do stupid things. You might embarrass yourself in public."

"That's not true. I say all kinds of unforgivable things in public."

"Maybe. But let's say for the sake of argument that you're a real journalist and have a professional interest in hearing me out?"

"I don't want to know about it, because you're my friend. And what you're telling me makes me think I don't even know you. If that's true, then everything's an illusion. What's true? What's not true?"

"You never stop spinning your tires long enough to find out. You never listen. I was about to tell you, but you couldn't take it."

"All right, Woolley, but this better be—"

"Be what? Good? It's not good, it's evil."

"A strange word in your mouth."

"Bear with me long enough to find out just what I mean."

"Proceed."

"Before I came here, I was a professor of neurosurgery at a brain research laboratory. We had millions of dollars at our disposal. We purchased bodies. Living bodies. I was especially concerned with pushing back the research frontiers that would permit us some advances against Parkinson's disease, Alzheimer's, and epilepsy. You see, most abortion techniques tear babies to shreds, and it was a gruesome business for the junior research assistants to pick though the parts in search of good brain tissue. So we paid women who were going to have abortions to carry their babies to term and deliver them at the lab. We paid many of them to become pregnant. We inseminated many of them artificially. It can take dozens of babies to provide tissue for a single patient."

"Okay, that's enough. I get the picture."

"Maybe you get the fright-show part of the picture, but you don't get all of it. Are you going all the way with me, or are you going to run and hide?"

I was silent.

"Killing is easy. You give the woman a local anaesthetic. You reach in and grasp one of the baby's legs with forceps and pull it into the birth canal. Then with your hands you deliver it, but taking great care to leave the head inside. You wouldn't want noises. The base of the skull is exposed. You force scissors into the base of the baby's skull, then open them to enlarge the hole. It struggles. Then you put a suction catheter into the hole and the brains are sucked out."

The room was dark, and I couldn't move. I felt sick. For an instant I wanted to kill Woolley, with scissors.

"I know precisely the emotion and the thoughts you are feeling right now", he said.

"Do you?"

"I assure you that in recent years I have felt all that you feel and more, a hundred times more."

"I don't get it. What are you saying?"

"One day there was a birth that didn't come off as planned. The baby slipped out too fast and slid round in my hands before I knew what was happening. Its eyes opened. It gasped and it cried. The mother heard it and jerked her head up and saw it. She began to struggle. You could tell she was having doubts. A nurse sedated her while I clasped my hand around the child's mouth. I pinched off its air with my thumb. It wriggled mightily. It looked at me as it died. It looked at me."

Woolley's voice broke, and he paused.

"I looked back. I shouldn't have looked back."

"You saw."

"Yes. I saw. It was a child. A person. That anonymous little girl was—in a way I can't explain—she was my daughter, or my son, or . . . my wife. I said to myself, that's it, no more working on the death gang for me! No more saving humanity! I'm going to go raise sheep."

"I'm going now, you bastard", I said in a low voice. "You stay away from me, and I'll stay away from you."

I left him there in the dark room.

I didn't return to Woolley's for several months. He didn't call me. But one night in late summer when my hatred of him had abated and my curiosity revived a little, I had the urge to find out if what had happened between us was irreparable. Friendship without *eros* is still a form of love, and one cannot root out love in one stroke. I drove over without calling ahead. On the way I rehearsed how I was going to tell him that I despised him. I was going to let him know that strangulation was too merciful for him and that he deserved to be shredded. But I couldn't shake the memory of how his voice had choked. And by the time I pulled off the highway into his lane, I kept seeing the look in his eyes when he told me that he felt everything I felt against him and more, a hundred times more. Then I understood that he hated himself more than I could ever hate him.

When he saw me coming up the driveway, he was out the front door in a flash, waving a newspaper.

"Eddie," he shouted, "did you see what that idiot L'Oraison and his gang are proposing in the Commons? It's a disaster, old boy! Come in and have a drink."

"I . . . I—" I stammered.

"Oh, nonsense, you blabbermouth. Why are you always monopolizing the conversation? Come right in. I have a truly nasty chess ploy I've been wanting to try out on you."

Woolley was his old self. But things were never quite the same again. Thereafter, I would always be uneasy about the exact nature of our relationship. Was I merely intellectually useful, a confessor to an unbeliever who couldn't forgive himself? Or was I a foil for his ironic thoughts, a looking glass into which this solitary man occasionally glanced? At some point, doesn't a true friend acquire the right to every key in the house? Otherwise, what is the household of the heart but a maze with passages that end in walls, windows that open onto empty space, and doorless rooms from which faint noises escape? But maybe his confession had been about precisely that.

And what of me? What key to myself had I given him? Perhaps I had been merely using him—the pleasures of intellectual stimulation, a relief from loneliness, or a goad for my hunger for laughter? Perhaps a mirror into which I myself occasionally glanced and found, to my own surprise, *my self.* Most of all he reassured me that I was sane, or at least had not yet become completely insane.

Maya once told me that I was the sanest man she had ever met. I was inordinately gratified by the observation. When I asked her why she thought so, she replied, "It's not just because you're a really bright guy, Tan. It's because you can laugh at yourself. And you can laugh at the world, even when it's going nuts."

That was in the beginning. She hadn't yet seen the unexplored depths of my anger. She was right, of course; I did have a certain gift for gallows humor. But there was also that rage and the thinly disguised despair. I was sane *and* crazy. My grandma Wanda went genuinely mad because the extremity of her environment brought intolerable pressures to bear on a genetic vulnerability. It bears repeating that I have probably inherited the weakness, and my environment is looking worse by the hour. What next? If I follow in her footsteps, I hope my life will be short. Insanity is so humiliating. Like a teenager, I believe that death is preferable.

Dysfunctional or what! Yep, that's me, and a good measure of my family, too. But I wouldn't trade 'em for the world!

I begin to laugh, and I laugh till the tears spill from my eyes. Father Andrei looks up from his Scriptures. A penetrating, compassionate look. He says nothing, just looks.

That's when Thaddaeus bursts in riding on a gust of snow. The door bangs closed against the wind. The old man's cheeks are whipped raw and red. His eyes are dark.

"That guy won't come, Tanny."

"Woolley?"

He hands me a piece of paper.

Herr Redakteur,

Greetings! You will be intrigued to know that the comedy took a serious turn when I tried to explain your suicide prank to the cops. They weren't in the least amused. They have a recording of it—I guess your phone line must be tapped. They weren't interested in my explanation, Ed. They're playing it over and over on the radio, and no one, I mean no one, is laughing.

I am sorry for your lamb. I do not wish it to die. But nowhere in our agreement did I promise that I would sacrifice my life to sustain yours. I resigned from our civilization a long time ago. History is a cycle of endless repetitions. If you wish to survive its quibbles, you must swerve to avoid disaster, not walk straight into it. You never learned that, did you? Have I taught you nothing? Must you be forever oozing fiery quixotic ideals and righteous ardor? Intemperate man! Can't you see that what transpires among your fugitives has occurred countless times before? The collapse of an age produces innumerable sacrificial lambs. It is unfortunate, but it is your lot. Think of it as a mega-drama, the long-awaited shattering of the mind's ghetto walls. Is that so terrible? Paranoia is no longer an issue, is it? But survival is. Be honest with yourself: though you are frightened or enraged (the latter more typical of you), you must admit that you feel more alive than you did three days ago. Isn't it so?

As you read this note, you will doubtless consider me a heartless coward. Try to grasp it, Eddie, I am a technician, not a doctor of the soul. You want me to heal your world, despite the fact that nothing now is going to heal it. It must self-destruct, old boy. I refuse to save the world. I tried to save thousands of your bleeding lambs in refugee camps in Ethiopia and Thailand, in Turkey and Croatia, in the Sudan, Rwanda, and Mexico. Some lived, but many more spilled through my fingers back into the dust from which they had come, leaving only a dead ache in me. It hurt too much then. And it will hurt too much to try again. Your lamb will die sooner or later. Why not now? It doesn't matter. Nothing matters, ultimately. You care too bloody much about everything. Damn it, Eddie, don't ruin my life, too, what remains of it.

Doc.

P.S.: When was the last time we played chess? How about a game tonight? If strategy permits it, knight could move to king's rook. I might be able to repair the broken pawn. But, for the time being, I am enclosed within my own parameters. I play by the rules. I aim to win. I survive.

An abyss opens up under my eyes. I stagger back from it. Woolley, Woolley, you are my friend. What happened to you?

"Thaddaeus, did you see any police?" the priest asks.

"There was a cop sittin' in a car down the block from the clinic with his lights off. The doctor wasn't there. So I walked out t'his farm and found him. No police there."

"Did he say anything?"

"Nope. He don't look like nothin' after he reads your letter. He just writes this one back t'you."

"There's something crazy about this", I say. "Maybe he's being watched. It could be he's trying to warn me in his cryptic way."

Of course that's it! Woolley is as clever as ever. He knows I can read him. He's the only physician from here to Prince George who refuses to do abortions and euthanasias, and a guy like him isn't going to let a lamb die. The note is a ruse, I'm sure of it, in case of interception by the police. He wants me to read between the lines—knight, bring pawn to the castle. He's saying loud and clear: Come to my place tonight, clandestinely.

"He's trying to tell me we should bring Anthony to his house."

The three of us turn and look out the window. It's a blizzard.

"Nobody's goin' anywhere till mornin' ", says Grandpa.

"Can Anthony make it till then?"

"Maybe, Tan. Maybe."

* * *

I awake with a start. The cabin is dark, save for Father Andrei's lamp. He's still reading beside Anthony. The boy is no longer groaning. The wind howls. The world sleeps.

I lie on my back in the eiderdown bag Thaddaeus lent me. I'm on the floor in a corner, hidden by shadows. I look at the priest for a long time.

That's an ascetic face. It has suffered. I think it's a purified face, though it's hard to know what that really means, because I haven't seen many like it in my lifetime, and there are no accurate scales on which it can be measured. He radiates interior stillness. He's physically fragile in appearance, and his voice is gentle. He uses words with economy. But when he speaks, everyone listens.

Without looking at me, he says, "You cannot sleep?"

"No."

"We have not had an opportunity to talk with each other. Would you like to visit with me?"

The Slavic notes are savory. His eyes, when he glances over to the corner, are like crystal—deep pools of it.

"Yes", I reply. I move onto a kitchen chair across from him. He pours two cups of tea from the kettle behind us. I put a spoonful of honey in mine. There's no milk.

"How's Anthony?" I ask him.

"He's conscious, then unconscious, then conscious again. Now, he sleeps. He is a good soul."

Right, padre, he's a good soul. But me, I'm not a good soul.

I deserve to be taking that lad's place. He's suffering because of my mistakes. I don't say this aloud, but the words shoot through my mind, and instantly I'm wrestling with grief all over again. The lava beds of rage begin to bubble. I want to fight. I want to kill. Most of all I want to kill Death.

The priest is watching this interior struggle. I don't want him observing my anguish. It only increases the guilt. The pain is too great.

I try to distract him.

"What are you reading, Father?"

"An old story."

"The Bible?"

"Yes, the story of Joseph, son of Jacob."

"Uh, sorry, Father. Jacob who?"

"Jacob who was renamed Israel."

"Oh, yes. I guess I forgot a lot of that. It's been a while since I went to Mass."

"Why did you stop going?"

I shrug. "Mostly because I couldn't hack it any more. Too much of a black sheep. Unworthy."

"We are all unworthy", he corrects.

I grimace. *Thanks for the homily, but no thanks!*

"I guess I just got sick of the way things were going up there on the altar. Fiddling around with the Scriptures. Showmanship. Balloons. Charm. I was in need of real help in those days, and all they dished up was smarmy theological pablum. It gave me the creeps—especially those canned sermons. The ideas were sweetened with pseudoreligious mystical talk, but it was politics sheep-dipped in religious jargon. I'm a journalist. I can spot jargon a mile away. In place of a collective utopia, they wanted us to become cells in some vast organism-utopia. Spiritual protoplasm!"

He looks at me sympathetically but makes no comment. He's the charitable type.

"By the way, how come you don't have a parish?" I ask him.

"I am retired from active ministry now. I live near a convent of cloistered nuns, and when I am not travelling, I assist as their chaplain. I was a missionary for years. During the last war I was sent to this valley for a time, and it was then that I met your family. Your grandmother was my friend. Thaddaeus, too. I come here now and again to see him."

"Where do you live?"

"Nowhere. And everywhere." He smiles.

"Ah, like the birds of the air and the lilies of the field, et cetera?"

"Something like that, yes."

"So. How do you live?"

"As you say, like the birds of the air. I visit with people. I pray with them. I offer the Holy Mass and hear confessions. We talk."

"So you're still a missionary! In darkest North America."

He doesn't smile. "Yes, it is very dark."

We're agreed on that point.

He looks down at his Bible. "It was dark for them, too", he says.

"For who?"

"Jacob who became Israel, and his son Joseph. This boy was especially beloved of his father. Joseph was a boy who had dreams. He dreamed many dreams, and the Spirit of God gave him the gift of understanding. His brothers were jealous of him and decided to kill him. Would you like me to read it to you?"

I really don't want an old man with a heavy accent to read aloud lengthy passages from the Bible in the middle of the night. I haven't eaten in almost twenty-four hours. I'm very tired.

I don't say any of this, of course. But after that last thought, he surprises me by reaching behind and cutting a thick slice of dark bread. He hands it to me without speaking.

"You eat. I read."

"Go ahead", I say with a full mouth.

And this is the story he tells:

One day, when Joseph's brothers had gone to pasture their father's flocks, Israel said to Joseph, "Your brothers, you know, are tending our flocks at Shechem. Get ready; I will send you to them."

"I am ready", Joseph answered.

"Go, then", he replied. "See if all is well with your brothers and the flocks, and bring back word."

Joseph went after his brothers and caught up to them at Dothan. They saw him approaching from a distance, and before he came up to them, they plotted to kill him. They said to one another, "Behold, here comes that man of dreams! Come on, let us kill him and throw him into one of the cisterns here; we could say that a wild beast devoured him. We shall then see what becomes of his dreams!"

When his brother Reuben heard this, he tried to save Joseph from their hands, saying, "We must not take his life. Instead of shedding blood, just throw him into that well there in the desert, but don't kill him outright." His desire was to rescue him from their hands and restore him to his father. So when Joseph came up to them, they stripped him of the long tunic he had on. It was a beautiful coat of many colors that his father had made for him, for he was the child of Israel's old age. The brothers took him and threw him into the cistern, which was empty and dry.

Then they sat down to their meal. Looking up, they saw a caravan of Ishmaelites coming up from Gilead, their camels laden with balm and resin to be taken down to Egypt. Judah said to his brothers: "What is to be gained by killing our brother and concealing his blood? Rather let us sell him to the Ishmaelites and reap a profit from it." They sold Joseph to the Ishmaelites for twenty pieces of silver. They took his coat, and, after slaughtering a goat, they soaked it in the blood. Then they sent it home to their father, with the message: "We found this. Is it your son's tunic or not?" The coat was of exceptional beauty. There was none like it. Israel recognized it and cried out: "My son's tunic! A wild beast has devoured him! Joseph has been torn to pieces!" Then he tore his own clothes, put on sackcloth, and mourned his son for many days. He was inconsolable, saying, "Now I will go down mourning to my son in the netherworld."

Father Andrei pauses and looks up.

"The story is very long. Do you wish me to continue?"

"Does it end well?"

"A good story must not be given away too soon."

"Keep going."

The priest reads for a considerable period of time. The story of Joseph in exile is one of the most moving in the history of mankind. It is an account of divine providence and a cautionary tale about abandoning hope prematurely. Joseph's life appears to be over. He is sold into slavery. Then, in Egypt, he rises in his master's house. He is slandered and cast into prison. There he rises again, because of the greatness of his personal qualities and the blessing of the Lord. He is released and becomes a servant in the palace of the Pharaoh. Here, too, he rises, on the strength of his ability to interpret dreams. He is given charge over Pharaoh's palace and eventually saves the country from famine, being forewarned in a dream to prepare ahead. He is now second only to Pharaoh in authority.

When Jacob learned that grain rations were available in Egypt, he sent ten of his sons to go there and buy some, that they might avoid starvation. Jacob kept Joseph's full brother Benjamin with him, for fear that he might lose yet another son. Since there was famine in the land of Canaan, the sons of Israel were among those who went to procure rations. It was Joseph, as governor of Egypt, who dispensed rations to all the people. When Joseph's brothers came and knelt down before him with their faces to the ground, he recognized them as soon as he saw them. But he concealed his own identity from them and spoke sternly to them, "Where do you come from?"

They answered, "From the land of Canaan."

"We your servants", they said, "were twelve brothers, sons of a certain man in Canaan; but the youngest one is at present with our father, and the other one is gone."

"You are spies", accused Joseph.

"We are not", they protested.

"This is how it shall be tested to see if you are telling the truth", said Joseph. "Unless your youngest brother comes here, I swear by the life of Pharaoh that you shall not leave here. So send one of your number to get your youngest brother, while the rest of you stay here under arrest." With that, he locked them up in the guardhouse for three days.

On the third day Joseph said, "I am a God-fearing man. If you have been honest, only one of your brothers need be confined in prison, while the rest of you may go and take provisions to your starving families. But you must return with your youngest brother."

To one another, however, the brothers said, "Alas, we are being punished because of our brother. We saw the anguish of his heart when he pleaded with us, yet we paid no heed; that is why this anguish has come upon us."

"Didn't I tell you", broke in Reuben, "not to do wrong to the boy? But you wouldn't listen! Now comes the reckoning for his blood." They did not know, of course, that Joseph understood them, since he spoke with them through an interpreter. Turning away from them, he wept. He privately gave orders to fill their containers with grain, to return the money to each one's purse, and to give them provisions for the journey. The brothers loaded their donkeys with rations and departed.

Father Andrei takes a sip of tea. His voice is frail. He rubs his eyes, then replaces the spectacles. He looks up at me. I nod at him to continue.

The story is rich in twists and turns. The brothers passed test after test, each time proving their honesty. And they returned with their youngest brother, Benjamin. Then Joseph put them to a final test. He secretly planted a silver goblet in their possessions as they departed and "discovered" it in Benjamin's baggage.

The brothers flung themselves on the ground, pleading for mercy. They offered themselves as slaves to expiate the crime. Joseph relented and told them he would keep only Benjamin as his slave. The others, he said, could return freely to Canaan. Judah stepped forward and argued.

"If the boy is not with us when I go back to my father, whose very life is bound up with his, he will die when he sees that the boy is missing . . . I could not bear to see the anguish that would overcome my father. His white head would go down to the netherworld in grief!"

Joseph could no longer control himself in the presence of all his attendants, so he cried out, "Have everyone withdraw from me!" Thus, no one else was there when he made himself known to his brothers. But his sobs were so loud that the Egyptians heard him, and so the news reached Pharaoh's palace.

"I am Joseph", he said to his brothers. "Is my father still in good health?" But his brothers could give him no answer, so dumbfounded were they at him.

"Come closer to me", he told them. "I am your brother Joseph, whom you once sold into Egypt. But now do not be distressed, and do not reproach yourselves for having sold me. It was really for the sake of saving lives that God sent me here ahead of you."

Thereupon he flung himself upon the neck of his brother Benjamin and wept, and Benjamin wept in his arms. Joseph then kissed all his brothers, crying over each of them, and only then were his brothers able to talk with him.

The story continues and covers a great deal of Joseph's life, including a reunion with his father and the entire family.

"You see", says the priest gently.

"See what?"

"He forgave them."

I ponder that.

"That's nice, Father, but what would have happened if they had killed him in the first place?"

"Perhaps his great heart would have forgiven them even then."

"Do you know that?"

"I know only one thing."

"Which is . . . ?"

"The human will is a great mystery. We *choose*. We choose to hate. We choose to forgive. We are free to do either."

I don't like what he's saying. I'm angry.

"Are you telling me we have no right to be upset about injustice?!"

"You have every right to be angry. What is happening is evil. But if the evil infects you with evil, then it has won a hundredfold."

I feel an anguish so terrible it threatens to tear my chest.

"Your anger is just," he continues in his kindly voice, "but your hatred is not."

Why are his words stinging me so bitterly! The pool of lava is waiting to erupt. The rage, the pain, the fear that neither forgiveness nor hatred makes any difference. *It don't matter nohow!* Is that the source of it? A fundamental terror of abandonment in a dark place from which there is no escape? Is it because I think I'm alone at the bottom of a deep, deep pit? And that pit is myself.

I crack.

My hands are shaking. A torrent of grief pours out in sobs. The priest comes over and puts his hand on my shoulder.

Later, maybe hours later, there is an actual sacrament in which

I employ the objective words of admission. I accept full responsibility for my acts, my anger, my hatred, my failures to love. He speaks the words of unlocking, of pardon and peace. He blesses me with the sign of the Cross.

And as the dawn breaks, I am at peace. There is no guilt, and there are no guilt feelings. No fear, no anger. Just clarity.

* * *

Clear sight demands that we cast a glance within. There, in the old garage sales of the heart are to be found a few embarrassing items.

Maya left me because she was pumped full of every distorted perception that our century has been able to produce. But she also left me because I was not listening and because I failed to love, and she needed to be loved very, very much in order to resist the distortions. But I was too busy.

Everyone in our era needed to be loved *first*. We poor men with our pathetic male egos—we needed women to love us so we could become strong enough to love them. And they needed us to love them in order to be able to love us. Somebody had to go first, and practically no one felt he should be the one. It was messy. It was ugly. It was riddled with resentment. Relations between men and women lost their mystery and simplicity. They became terribly complicated and infested with ideology.

I panicked whenever I heard Maya spouting nonsense in that determined voice. I was afraid, and I got angry, and I ranted. Not in a loud, frightful voice, of course, but in a didactic voice that went on and on, spewing out an encyclopaedic knowledge of, and loathing for, the mind of degenerate Western man. Ranting shuts down communication instantly, but few ranters know that until it's really far too late.

I don't think she was upset with me because I was no longer a liberal or because I had reverted to what she considered to be sexism. Or because my sociopolitical convictions had kept us poor or because we had a lot of enemies in an era that was just made for niceness. No, she was profoundly hurt by the fact that I had a mistress. Perhaps if the mistress had been a woman, she could have hated her rival and fought. But it was nothing so accessible. I was completely absorbed night and day in my newspaper. *The Echo* was my true bride. Maya knew it long before I did.

She tried to tell me.

"I know you don't love me, Tan."

"Of course I love you."

"You *think* you love me."

"I don't *think* I love you, I *know* I love you."

I went to hug her, but she turned to stone, and a tiny mean voice said, "You're in love with only one thing."

"What's that?"

"Your ego. And that paper which makes you so famous. You enjoy the whole thing. You enjoy being admired, and you enjoy being hated by people who don't even know you. You especially like being a hero."

"That's ridiculous. Do you think I like being sneered at by my neighbors?"

"You don't care about them, because you despise them. Because they're ignorant."

"I don't despise them! I'll grant you that I don't think much of their bottle-fed prejudices—"

At that point I began a lecture, and she walked away into the kitchen while I was in mid-sentence. She plugged in the kettle.

"You want some coffee?" she said sadly.

"Don't call it coffee, Maya."

"Okay, it's not coffee. It's a socially responsible, environmentally sensitive hot beverage."

For a moment I wondered if this was a hint of self-deprecating humor. She bought the stuff because real coffee, she said, was produced and marketed in North America at prices kept low by the unjust wages paid to the native peoples of Central and South America.

I switched to tea.

Then she informed me that the huge tea monopolies made their fortunes on the backs of Asia's poor. She purged the house of our guilt-ridden addictions and replaced them with potions that looked and tasted like twigs and dried berries put through a blender.

I switched to alcohol—socially irresponsible and dangerous as it was.

For years it was our standard joke, the safe peg of disagreement on which we could hang our larger disagreements and laugh from time to time. Gradually the laughter became more strained and then ceased altogether, leaving only a bitter herbal taste.

"So, do you want some socially responsible beverage or not?"

"No, thanks."

I suddenly had nothing to say.

"Tan, I'm finding it very hard to stay here."

"What! Why?"

"Take a look at my life."

"*Your* life? What about *our* life? What about Bam and Ziz and Arrow?"

"Don't bring them into this. It's us that's the problem. The fact is you have a family that isn't really a family. We're your *idea* of a family. You've parked us in this beautiful cage, and we sit here and wait for you to come home six and a half days a week. We wait and wait. Like Godot, you never come."

"What are you talking about? I'm here most of the time. Why do you think I moved my office out here from town? It was so I could be more available to you and the kids. It cost something, Maya. The paper isn't as fine-tuned as it used to be—"

"I keep waiting for you to come home even when you are home. You're glued to that computer all the time. You've got square eyeballs, for God's sake. You used to look at me."

"I look at you", I said lamely, but I knew she was right. How often had I fled the supper table in order to get back to the red-hot editorial I was composing? How often had I put off Bam and Zizzy's pleas for a bedtime story with a mumbled, "Not tonight kids, maybe tomorrow"?

But tomorrow never came.

"I think I could bear it if you weren't so intolerant of the things I believe in."

"The things you believe in?"

"Yes. I *believe* in them. *I* believe in them."

I said nothing and controlled an impulse to counter with a sardonic twist of the lips.

"Don't give me that poker face, Mister Editor. I know that look all too well. You think I'm not capable of ideas. You think you know more than a lot of people in this country who are a whole lot better educated than you are."

At that I let slip the curl of a lip.

"Granted, Maya, I do not have a single university degree, and you have three of them—"

"And so do most of my friends, who, by the way, are simply aghast that I continue to stay on here at great personal cost, the destruction of my career, my art, with a man I barely recognize any more, only because I signed a paper stating that I'd remain loyal to him, a stranger drifting into the worst kinds of revisionism and eventually probably *wife abuse*!"

The hysterical note in the last phrase, the whine, pushed a button in me.

"First of all, Lady Ophelia—"

"Don't try pushing me around any more. You called my friends murderers once too often."

"What are you talking about?"

"In the paper. When are you going to get it through your head that the abortion thing was settled a long time ago? It's not a crime. It's a medical procedure. Margo, Crysta, Tara, they've all had abortions. If you keep calling them killers, you're going to get slapped for hate literature."

"Read those articles again, Maya. Never once did I call those women murderers or killers."

"But you said—"

"I said the *act* was murder."

"Well, there you go!"

"I said, any nation that lies to itself about the nature of such acts will go on to do worse —"

"Whatever. The point is, you don't really understand women's issues."

"I understand a dead baby when I see it."

She rolled her eyes. "*You*", she said, pointing a finger, "are a sexist!"

"I am not a sexist."

"You're definitely a patriarchist of the worst kind, the kind that thinks he isn't. And you subscribe to a religion that enshrines patriarchy as something *sacred*. Something *holy* —"

"First of all, I was born and raised in a *matriarchal* clan. The person I admired most in this world was my grandmother. I do not think women are inferior to men. But they sure are different. Now if you look at last week's editorial in *New Womanspeak*—"

"Tan, it's the nineteen nineties. You're so dumb you're still fighting battles that were fought in the sixties!"

And so it went. It went like that for about eight more months. She read the pop literature steadily and got deeper into it. Eventually Tara sent her some titles that fairly dripped with the stench of dragon. And at last Maya found her own heroes—I mean, heroines.

We both became horribly silent, dutiful parents. And one fine day I woke up and didn't even notice the empty space in the bed beside me. I padded down the hall to switch on the computer. I wanted to get an early start that morning, because I was heavily into an article that *Atlantic Monthly* had commissioned. I was excited by the job because it was a daring foray on their part into the realm of the politically incorrect.

Scotch-taped to the screen was an envelope. A pair of scissors lay across the keyboard. The power line to the screen was cut. The mouse line was cut. And so was the umbilical that coiled between the keyboard and the big electronic subconscious.

The envelope contained a letter:

> Nathaniel,
>
> It would be a lie if I said I don't love you. I do, or at least I still love the guy I first met way back then. Is there always somebody else inside the people we marry? Why is it this way? Why couldn't you find in me what your real love—that echo—seems to give you?
>
> I need to go away for a while and be with people who understand me. Creative people. People who love life and don't spend every waking minute hating and criticizing everything under the sun. Why can't you just live? Why couldn't we just be happy?
>
> I know what you'll say. Your eyes will glaze over with the forced effort of listening to me, and then you'll say something very intelligent about us being in a war zone and life is a grave affair, etc. Well, to hell with that. My life was fun until I married into your kind of social consciousness. It was pure pleasure. It was great to be alive. What war? There is no war. The war's all inside you, and I'm not going to be your collateral damage. If I don't get some fresh air for a while, I'll end up cutting something more permanent than an electric cord. You wouldn't enjoy it.
>
> I've cut your power lines to make sure you read this. I also suggest you go down the hall and take a look into Arrow's crib. You'll find, after some reflection, that he's not there. He's with me. He's safe. He's fine. I'd have taken Bam and Ziz too, but they'd cry and want to say good-bye to you, and then you'd sit me down and talk, talk, talk for an hour, and I'd weaken and change my mind.
>
> You don't need to know where I am. I'm safe. I'm with friends. I'll phone you in a few weeks. Tell Bam and Ziz that I

love them. They won't believe it, but tell them anyway. Tell them I wanted to take them. No, tell them I wanted to stay and be a Mum. Tell them I took Arrow, not because I love him best, but because he's nursing and he's so little, and dammit, because he looks so much like a guy I once knew and loved for a while.

Maya

* * *

Father Andrei is sleeping on the couch. I haven't slept a wink. Ordinarily this level of exhaustion would have me plunging into despair, but I am peaceful. Never discount grace. Odorless, tasteless, soundless—but powerful stuff it is.

The window is trading black for soft purple. The wind has stopped howling; the storm is over. It must be about 7 or 7:30 A.M. Tyler (of all people) stirs. He lies quietly in the dark for some time, then gets up. He comes over to the corner where I'm curled in my sleeping bag and sits down on the cold, bare planks, hugging his knees. I keep my eyes closed, pretending I'm asleep. I'm not much good for father–son banter at the moment.

He stays beside me, perfectly still—very unusual behavior for him. Tyler is the sort of lad who is either asleep or in perpetual motion. Two gears. Stop and go.

Eventually he reaches over and shakes my shoulder.

"Dad?"

I produce a fake snore, hoping he will go back to bed. He shakes me again.

"Dad?"

"Yeah, Tyler? What time is it?"

"I dunno . . . Can we talk?"

"Sure," I say, getting up on one elbow. "Fire away."

"I don't know how to tell it, Pa. I was dreaming."

"About Captain Coco and the adventure of the lava pits?"

He shakes his head. "It was really strange."

"How 'strange'?"

“We were living in a place in the mountains. Me ’n’ Zizzy and some other people. But we were older.”

“Was I there?”

He shakes his head again. “No. You weren’t there.”

“Your mother?”

“No. But Grandpa Thaddaeus was.”

“Father Andrei?”

“No . . . That was the funny part. It was like everyone was there, but some of us weren’t.”

“Sorry. You just lost me, Son. Non sequitur.”

“Like some of us weren’t there but no one was missing. At least . . . well . . . we were together in our hearts.”

He fumbles the last word. This is pretty shaky ground for a lad who hates mush.

“Yeah,” he goes on, “and there were people living with us I never met before, but it was like I’d always known them.”

“Any idea who they might be?”

“Well,” he says slowly, pondering, “one of them was Arrow.”

“Arrow? Your brother?”

“It was him. But he was a man.”

“A man?”

“All grown up. He sure didn’t look like a baby, but somehow I knew him. Zizzy, too—she had white hair and lots of little kids around her. I knew they were her grandchildren. Weird, eh?”

My spine begins to tingle. I sit up straight and lean against the wall.

“There were lots of people with scars and burns. And a baby with a giant head. We were all living in small houses made of stones and logs. We were all poor. But we were happy. I never felt so happy. No one was ever scared there. Ever.”

“You say Arrow was there? What was he like?”

Tyler furrows his brow and looks at his wiggling toes, trying to remember.

“He was tall and brown, like you. But his hair was gray. He was a quiet guy . . . but kind of a leader. He had Grandpa Steve's cross in his hands—you know, the one that came from Ireland—and we were talking about it. We were talking about you."

"Hopefully you were saying only the nicest of things."

Tyler smiles pensively. "I can't remember exactly what we were saying, but it was good. I was telling him what you were like. He cried. Yeah, that's right, me and Ziz and Arrow were all crying, but we were really happy, too—hope you don't mind, Dad."

"That's okay. Carry on."

"See what I mean about weird? Feeling so sad and so happy all at once?"

He closes his mouth firmly on that.

I digest it. Is the dream just wishful thinking projected on the screen of consciousness? Or is it a case of *Behold this dreamer cometh*?

He looks up at me suddenly, a light in his eyes, and says, "Dad, I think it's going to be all right. We're gonna get through this."

"I think so too, Son."

"When it's over, do you think we could start going back to church?"

"A good parish is hard to find. But we could try to find one."

"You promise?"

"Yeah", I choke. "Yeah, that's the first thing we're gonna do. I promise you."

"Okay!" he says, pleased. Then he jumps up, stretching his lanky frame, the dreamer reverting to Track Team Bam. He goes over to the table and checks Anthony, who is sleeping, his breath whistling shallowly, his eyelids twitching, his skin gray. Satisfied that his friend is still alive, Bam proceeds to poke about in the kitchen.

Then the second surprise of the morning: Zöe is tiptoeing across the room, golden braid atangle. She plunks herself down on the floor and sits crosslegged beside me.

"Morning, Poppa."

"Morning, girl."

She smooths a piece of Day-Glo fluorescent orange paper on her knee and proceeds to write on it with a green crayon.

"What's that, Honey?"

"No peeking!" The pink tip of her tongue protrudes from the corner of her mouth as she concentrates. She folds the paper carefully and tucks it into my breast pocket.

"Can't I read it?" I protest.

"Yes, you can", she replies demurely. "But not now. Later. Save it for later."

"When?"

She pauses and tilts her head reflectively. "Sometime when you're sad. Only then. Promise?"

"I promise."

She kisses my cheek, then scampers off to check on Anthony. She stations herself by him and strokes the wet black strands of hair off his blood-spattered brow. Over and over, stroking, crooning, whispering. A small mother.

I can't watch it for long.

Then I hear Father Andrei stirring. He sits up on the couch and rubs his eyes distractedly. Thaddaeus is awake, too, firing the wood burner. Soon I smell oatmeal, tea, bread toasting on the stove top.

I get up and start to roll the sleeping bag.

"Dad," says Tyler tentatively, "Grandpa has a dogsled that y'push, y'know. I want to take Anthony to Doctor Woolley's. I'm strong. I'm almost thirteen. Even if they catch me, they won't put me in jail."

"Tyler", I whisper, hugging him. "Thank you, Son. But they might put you under lock and key in a juvenile detention center."

"I'd run away. I'd get back here fast."

"Maybe, maybe not. We can't risk it. But you make me proud just by offering."

"I will go", says the priest.

"No way, Father. To be blunt, you could hardly get yourself up the trail from the highway yesterday."

"I will find strength, somehow."

"No, you won't. I'm going. It's me that got him into this mess in the first place. It's a fairly simple matter. We just travel north along the base of the range, swerve by the town, and a few miles farther on we're in the doctor's fields. I'll make sure there are no police around before I go in. I'll be back in six hours."

Thaddaeus orders Tyler and Zöe to stand by the stove and keep the porridge from boiling over. Father Andrei is filling cups with tea. Thaddaeus asks me to step outside on the excuse that he needs me to help bring in an armload of firewood.

"Tanny, the town was swarmin' with cops yesterday. It's dangerous. I'm taking the boy!"

Those lips and eyes are so firm you couldn't budge them with a pry bar.

"Grandpa, I need you here. If they catch you, even if you don't say a word to them, they'll have somebody identify you. They'll just figure out instantly where we are. They'll whip back here and nab us all. On the other hand, if they catch me, I can keep them busy for days. If I'm not back here in six hours or so, you'd better clear out and go someplace safe."

"Okay", he grumps at me.

"Grandpa, if I don't come back at all, it means Tyler and Zöe are going to need somebody to look after them."

"I thought about that. I'll look after 'em, Tan. I got trap-cabins back in the bush, and one big livin'-size cabin over on the other side of the mountains in the Cariboo country. They'll never catch us. It'll be a good life. Then, when you get exonerated or out o' jail, you come and find us."

He tells me the clues I might need: a certain lake, a certain mountain, west on a logging road, then canoe along a river to a portage, another lake, then hike east eighteen miles, and so forth.

"Grandpa, if they catch me there's always the possibility they won't ever let me go. Things are getting crazy. Quiet, secret crazy. All kinds of laws are being changed. They can do just about anything they want now."

He has no reply. He hugs me sideways, and I hold on tight. I lay my head down on the hat atop his old skull. He smells of seventy years of woodsmoke and sweat, my strange, dear little forefather. He thumps me on the back.

"Need firewood", he mumbles, and we gather some for our excuse.

During the next fifteen minutes I pack the sled with sleeping bags, a thermos of coffee, some biscuits, Grandpa's .22, which he is lending to me for the trip (the blunderbuss is lost forever on Canoe Mountain), and some Tylenol tablets for Anthony. Thaddaeus gave him two pills a half hour ago. If I can make it to Woolley's farm within three hours, he shouldn't need another dose, but just in case I'll bring the pain-killers along.

Back inside the cabin I glance around, wondering what else I should take. I spy the top half of the plague journal jutting out of my knapsack. Should I take it with me? There doesn't seem much reason to do so, because it's not likely I'll be writing today. But on an impulse I decide to bring it along. You never know what will happen. I remove my parka and plaid shirt. Beneath that is my double-layered thermal undershirt. I take that off too. Brrrr! The top seam is ripped at the collar, and I widen the rip enough to slip the scribbler inside. There, it's snug in its pocket. I quickly dress myself again.

Father Andrei is standing at the door. He beckons me outside.

"Before this day is finished, Nathaniel, we may all be sold into slavery."

"It's possible. Let's hope not. There won't be much left of . . ."

"Of?"

"Of a world that's fit to live in. But maybe it's still possible for us. If people can start thinking again and believing there's something better."

"It is not too late. But there is always a cost. If this is the time for you to bear that cost, then do it in peace. Hold fast to the forgiveness you found this morning. Tyler and Zöe will be cared for. I do not think they will fall into the jaws of the beast."

"And what about you?"

"It is not my time yet, even though I am old. My time is for later, though it is not far off."

"How do you know these things?"

He looks at me without answering, a profound, sober, and tranquil glance from ancient blue eyes. Why is it that most of the truly human people in my world are either children or old people?

We stand there looking at each other for about a minute. Then he closes his eyes. He reaches up with his right hand and touches the center of my chest. Very gently he says, "Nathaniel, the only indestructible sanctuary is in the heart."

What does he mean?

"The heart, Father? I'm afraid I've lost all confidence in my heart. My emotions have been a mess for too long—"

"I do not mean the emotions. I mean the heart of the soul. The interior tabernacle."

"Oh, I see", I murmur, knowing that I do not see.

He opens his eyes and says, "Do not be afraid. You will not be alone."

"Yeah, you're right. I'll be back here in a few hours, and then we can all hightail it into the west."

"I am not going across the mountains."

"You're not? Where are you going?"

"I wish to try to find your wife and your little son."

This startles me.

"They, too, are in danger," he adds, "though not immediate danger. A spiritual danger, I believe."

Perplexed, wondering how he arrives at his mysterious decisions, I go back into the cabin, find my knapsack, and return in a few moments.

I place a stone into his hand.

The Celtic cross is my one inheritance. My great-grandfather bled upon it. It once saved my mind during a wrestling match with a fallen angel.

"Father, if you find Arrow, please give this to him. Tell him I'm sorry I wasn't a good father to him. Tell him I love him and I'll find him some day. Tell him . . . well, tell him that my white head will go down to the netherworld in grief if he never knows how much I wanted to love him."

"I will tell him. He will know."

"And if you find Maya . . . please tell her I'm so sorry about the way things were. Ask her to forgive me. Tell her that if by some miracle I ever get out of this mess, and if she ever *can* forgive me, I want to try to love her the way she deserves. Tell her that. Please."

"I will. You must pray for this. It will be more difficult than reaching the heart of a child."

"Yes."

He embraces me and blesses me.

Shortly after, we say our good-byes. It's a script in which we must all assume heartily that I'll be back by afternoon and, at the same time, take into consideration the fact that we might never see each other again. We assume the former in public and the latter in private. They come at the problem from different angles, but it amounts to this: I have two good-byes with each of them. Zöe's is the hardest.

"See you later", she says in a bouncy voice, then bursts into tears. She clings to me tightly with her arms around my waist. It hurts.

"Poppa, Poppa", she cries. Her face is pressed into my stomach. Jeanne's braiding job has come undone. Thaddaeus takes over, and she buries herself in his chest.

Tyler is looking stoical. "Six hours, Pa."

"Right. Six hours, Tyler." I can tell he's been crying someplace privately. We hug. I mess up his hair, an act he has always hated and now seems to appreciate.

We carry Anthony out on the toboggan and as carefully as possible transfer him onto the thick blankets of the dogsled. He cries once as we move him. Then he's quiet, his eyes open, following everything that's going on. We heap him with eiderdowns.

The others make their good-byes to him. He whispers to each. The two old men shake hands with me, mutter encouragements and promises of prayers.

The sled is an eight-foot-long wicker basket on ski-runners. Toward the stern the sides sweep up and bend into handles for the driver. It's better when pulled by dogs, but even without them I can push easily from the rear. We look like a snow scene from a nineteenth-century romantic painting, jolly woodsmen with our sledge packed and the sun just breaking through the clouds above a quaint cabin in the forest. This is the moment for the driver to crack his whip and eight huskies to lurch forward and disappear with a musical fanfare into the pines. Lights, camera, action!

I wish it were so easy. I kneel beside Anthony and tell him, "It's about three hours to the doctor. It's going to hurt. But you'll make it."

"Okay, Natano", he says, and gives me a weak smile.

Then we go. I push, and the runners creak, then slide, and the sled moves slowly into the trees. I look back once. The two men and the children are standing motionless, watching us. The meek shall inherit the earth, I think it says someplace.

Ten

It's gorgeous weather. The sky is clearing, and the blue is a great boost to the spirits. It's cold, though. Around five below zero. Our breath is frosting the rims of our hoods.

Anthony has held on very well. If all goes as planned, he'll be in surgery within a couple of hours. Woolley can return him to his parents when he's out of danger. I won't stay. Back to Thaddaeus' pretty quick. Sooner or later someone is going to remember that the fugitives have a relative living in the bush. They'll mention it to the authorities. I think we'll all just quietly go up over the mountains into the Cariboo country when I get back this afternoon.

This sled is an amazing invention. With only a light push it can skim over the snow carrying heavy weights. Thankfully, Anthony is just a little bitty Oriental who weighs not much more than Zöe. We're flying, making good time. The woods are composed of sparse poplars. For a while we thread in and out of them, following one of Thaddaeus' traplines. His old feet have made a thin Indian trail that's perfect for my boots. The sled runners straddle it. About four miles north we come to the Canoe River. At this point it isn't very wide, and it's travelling due east as it crosses the top of the valley toward the big lake that it feeds on the other side of Canoe Mountain.

The river is frozen over. I have to pull back when we go down the embankment and push hard going up the other side. Other than that it's really quite easy. It will probably take less than the estimated time. It's 8:30 A.M., and the sun just jumped up over the mountains above Swiftcreek. A soft yellow light bathes everything. Blue jays are scolding us. Woods ptarmigan scatter here and there. The white rabbits are out in force too, bolting toward Wonderland. Oh, Alice, Alice, Alice, if you only knew. Truth really is much stranger than fiction. If the Conditioners succeed in reshaping mankind, and if my journal survives, will there be anyone left in a hundred years from now who will believe there was a person such as me, or Anthony, or Thaddaeus, or, most of all, our Father Andrei? They will consider him a myth or a kind of Druid, no doubt.

No, Nathaniel. Swerve away from the old plunge into bitterness!

Curiously, I'm still free of it. I can reflect. And I can speculate on the nature of the future, but it no longer drags me into emotional chaos. That terror used to breed violence in me, I see now. And in an orderly society there is no outlet for such violence except the target range that lies within. So many madmen in our times, so many criminals, and so many youths shooting themselves. Don't the Conditioners grasp it? No. They rarely do. They simply increase the dosage of the medicine that's poisoning us. Perhaps the best we can hope for now is the collapse of everything. Then people will begin again to search within themselves, and among themselves, for what is authentic. They will find it. It is there. In the meantime I will try to save this boy, this seed of a better future.

We stop. I check his covers.

"You cold, Anthony?"

"I okay, Natano."

"You hurting?"

"Hurt bad."

His face is still gray, though pink spots have appeared on each cheek. His eyes are heavy but clear.

"No bleeding?"

"Nothing. No wet."

I check anyway, a swift play of hands around the bottom blanket closest to his skin. He flinches. It's dry.

Off we go. Oh, for a good dog team at this moment! Still, we're making progress. A light wind buffets us from behind. I'm tired, though not exhausted, despite the lack of sleep and little to eat. My heart is at peace. It hurts. Yes, it hurts a lot. But the razor bite of anguish is gone. If I cry, it's not the bitter waters of despair but the sweet waters of a cleansing grief. Woolley would probably quip that real men don't cry. Wrong, Woolley, only real men cry. They have hearts to accompany their prodigious minds and their bravado. Please don't lie to me any more, old chap. I know that somewhere, in some dark room, when all the medals and honors and diplomas are invisible, you, too, cry for your lost love and for a world that might have been and is no more.

I understand your pain. The most horrible pain is to think that your pain counts for nothing. You either wrestle that lie to the ground, or it wins and you run from it. Real men don't run, Woolley. Oh, I'll grant you, they should run from dumb kids fantasizing with machine guns and helicopters. And we should probably run from a virus or a bomb or a maniac. But we can't ever run from the wrestling match that is within. If we do, we end up hating ourselves and hating everyone else forever.

Woolley, why do you always play it so safe? You should try being a loser once in a while. It's good for the soul, and you learn so much in the process. One of the things you learn is that reality, on a human scale, is never final. Evil is not absolute. You must never lose hope. There is a more complete reality that exists beyond the clutching fingers of our senses and our proud intellects. Try to find it, my friend. Don't let the liars win. It matters that you do, Woolley, it matters. Everything we do and say is counted. The universe isn't on trial. We are.

Off to my right I can see the smokestacks of the mill. The town lies in that direction. Ravens are spiralling in the heat waves rising from the beehive slash burner. I can hear the whine of the saws. Business as usual.

The wind veers and is gusting at my left side. I feel the cold now. I hope the boy doesn't.

"You okay, Anthony?"

"I okay."

The skis are singing on the crust, and we're still making great time.

I cringe and swallow hard when a hell-cop goes down the valley. It's soundless, a mile to the east. I have the white canvas folded in the carrying box under the handles. It would take me two or three seconds to get it unfurled and over us. I pray for that much warning.

We come to a snowmobile trail. It crosses our path at an angle from the direction of town and heads northwest toward the Cariboos. I'm uneasy. There are a billion ski-doos in the woods these days, and one of them could be the police. I stop and kneel. I feel the surface with my bare hands. It's iced. The machine must have gone past days ago, leaving treadmarks that melted, froze again, then blew clear in last night's blizzard. Well, this is a bonus. We can fairly sail our way on this kind of surface.

The trail follows the heave and dip of the land, into snowy dells and around islands of pine-covered rock. The forest gradually thins and flattens, and we are now on a wide, open range that is swamp in summer. Suddenly we are clattering across pure ice. I'm a little uneasy about all this exposure, but at least we are going very fast. We pass a cluster of discarded beer bottles, cigarette butts, and a few bullet casings scattered around. Kids, probably. The sky is empty. I trot and push with little effort, skidding across the frozen surface.

I know this place. It's Cranberry Swamp.

And suddenly I am overwhelmed with the strangest feeling. Disoriented, like a drowning man, I grope for the surface of reality, for light and air. For a moment I cannot tell if I am submerged in the past, the present, or a *déjà vu*. In any event, literature is becoming remorselessly incarnate. O my brave and blind words, O my unknown name, O my dazed mind, waiting in darkness for words to shatter my unhearing! Plying my power, singing loud the great, sharp bark of my humanity, am I a child becoming a form of man? Is Daedalus at last ascending, bearing the weight of beloved Icarus? As we fly, I hear my children laughing, and we are rising, rising, rising fearless in our fear. For an instant, in the liberty of the mind's imagination, I gaze on trees burning with green fire and an expanse of water freed.

The skis bump over a band of pebbles that borders the swamp, jarring me, breaking the spell, catapulting me back to the present. Anthony and I are now entering a swath of willow thickets. Rabbit pellets are everywhere, and white chew marks on amber and purple bark. The snowmobile trail veered off in the wrong direction back out on the swamp ice. It's all bush-whacking now, but at least the surface is still relatively firm. I sink in a couple of inches with each step. The sled continues to skim.

We jar to a halt. The left runner has rammed under a snow-covered windfall. Anthony gives a sharp cry, then groans.

"You okay?"

"I okay."

I check his face. It's the same. He flashes me a look of reassurance.

A bit of maneuvering, backing up, and we're going forward again. The snow is definitely getting softer. I put my energy into second gear in order to make slow, steady headway. I'm tiring.

My watch says nine-forty. We must be getting close. The town is back there, hidden behind the woods over my right shoulder. We come to an open gate. Barbed-wire fencing runs east and west. A ski trail comes through the gate and swings off some-where. This has got to be Woolley's property!

"Hang on, Anthony, we're almost there."

He whispers something back at me.

In my excitement I push us through and am trotting with the sled runners straddling the ski trail. I know that Woolley's place is big, six hundred acres at least, and most of it in bush. This trail has got to take us to his house. And so it does. Another five minutes pass, and we come to the creek that bisects his land. On the other side the woods are interspersed with pockets of open pasture. There are still some hollows and hillocks to navigate. We're coming out of one now, and there across the field is the house!

I always loved Woolley's house and coveted it a little. It's a portrait of order on the outside, although inside it's heaped with books, dust-bunnies, dishes in the sink, the usual bachelor mess. By contrast, Grandpa's place is a wreck on the outside, and the interior is fastidiously neat. Yes, Woolley and Thaddaeus are converse images of each other. Still, if I had to choose a place to live, I'd probably fall for Woolley's myself. It's a new bungalow painted white with yellow trim, surrounded by mown lawns, clipped shrubs, and paved driveway. A mile of tarmac leads out to the highway.

I see there's a plow on his blue pickup. The red Cherokee is parked beside the garage. His sheep are out in the paddock discussing bales of hay. The barn is fire-engine red with a new galvanized roof. Smoke is coming from the chimney of the house. In the backyard a satellite dish points to the heavens. There are multicolored towels flapping frozen on the clothesline. There is not a cop-car to be seen or a zing in any quadrant. On this cold winter's morn with blue, blue skies and rescue before us, it's an incredibly cheery scene.

"Natano, Natano."

He's groaning in pain. The pink spots are gone from his cheeks.

I get down on my knees. What did he say?

"I die now, Natano", he whispers.

"No, no, you're not going to die, Anthony. We're here. The doctor's house is just over there. Hold on for a few more minutes. We're on our way."

"I wet."

I feel under the blankets. Oh, God, it's sopping in there. I strip off the heavy covers and find them badly stained on the undersides. The bottom blanket is dripping, totally soaked. He's lying in a pool of his own blood. Oh God! Oh no!

The blood is pouring fast. I press hard. It won't stop. I press. I press. It won't stop, it won't stop.

His eyes are clouding and his voice is thin. He forces a weak smile.

"I happy, Natano."

"What!" I cry.

"I happy", he says, and the breath goes out of him.

I don't believe this. I kneel in the snow and stare at his face. It's empty, a mask. His eyes are dull charcoal orbs. I draw the lids down over them. I stare at the white teeth and the blue lips. I close his mouth. I stroke the black hair away from his forehead.

No. It can't happen like this! You must be able to shovel blood back into those veins. My hands are covered with it. It's spilling through my fingers. It's cool, clotting, smelling of astringent minerals.

Oh, Anthony!

I can't bear it. The world around us grinds down into a total stop. The wind, the birds, the traffic out on the highway, it all just fades into silence as time slides into slow motion.

Oh, God, I sob. I hold him. His head flops sideways, and the mouth opens. Light glints from under the slits of the eyelids. I kiss his forehead. I trace a cross on it. I lay him down in the blood and wipe my hands on my clothing.

This is a pain that numbs. You can't feel this kind. It's just deadly.

I push the sled slowly across the field toward the house. I don't care if hell-cops swarm out of the bushes.

At the back end of the barn there is a lean-to shelter that Woolley uses during lambing season. It's empty now. Its floor is covered with clean straw. Snow skiffs in from both ends of the shelter, but in the middle it's dry. I steer the sled in, sliding it easily over the straw. I sit down beside the boy's body and weep.

There is a *wuff,* and I look up to see Woolley's fat golden retriever, Minder, ambling in the end of the shelter. Minder moves slowly and thinks even more slowly.

Wuff, wuff, he says, and sidles over to us. He sniff-sniffs the body on the sled, then snorts in surprise. He extends an enormous tongue and licks a drop of blood off the side of the sled.

The old rage flashes through my mind like lightning.

"Get out of here, Minder", I roar at him.

The dumb, fat dog takes an uncertain step backward and reverses out the other end, toward the house. He emits a sonorous *bow*, then a *wow.*

Woolley calls the dog. He must have come out onto the back porch.

I fling myself up and stomp across the yard. I'll tear Woolley to pieces. He killed Anthony. No, I killed Anthony. No, damn it, the hell-cop killed Anthony!

We stand there and stare at each other. He looks astounded.

"Good God, come in!" he says at last.

I climb the porch steps and shuffle past him into the kitchen. He stares at me and closes the door. My frozen boots crunch on the linoleum.

"Sit down."

I sit.

He places a cup of coffee in front of me. A stereo plays classical guitar music in the background. A John Le Carré spy novel is cracked open, face down on the table. I used to love his books until about five days ago. The house is full of splendid white light. Everything looks horrifyingly normal. Why is it like this when the bottom has fallen out of the universe?

He sits opposite me.

"The elf-prince is dead", I mumble brokenly. "He was only a child."

"Elf prince? What are you talking about?"

"The pawn."

"Pawn?"

"The lamb."

"Where's the lamb?"

"Outside in the shed."

"Oh." Silence.

"He died a few minutes ago."

"Tyler?"

"Thu's oldest boy, Anthony."

"Oh", he says again. I can hear the relief in his voice. It's nobody important to our relationship, he thinks.

"I'm sorry", he adds in a professional tone, sympathetic but detached. It's the worst possible tone he could take. For an instant I almost fire up the engines of hatred, but I don't. I understand now what a broken thing he is. He is no man. At least not a real man. He can't weep. He can't sacrifice. Perhaps a long time ago he was a man, but he lost it somewhere along the way. I refuse to despise him, in the hope that he might find it again. I pity him. I forgive him.

"Woolley, I need you to do one thing for me. Can you take his body to his parents?"

He lights his pipe, and I can tell he's debating with himself.

"It's a risk", he says. "If the police stop me, I'll be in trouble. At the very least my medical license will be suspended."

"It's important. Please do it. I'm begging you."

"I've seen a lot of bodies in my life. Why is this one so important?"

"Because it matters to them. Because the body's not just an old bag we slough off when we've finished with it. It's holy, like a house full of love, or a shrine. It's a home, and there's nothing like it ever existed before or will ever be like it again. It's a word spoken into the void. It pushes back the darkness by just . . . by just *being*. I wish you could have known this kid. He's not just a dead stick you toss on the fire. Please, Woolley."

"I'll try. Where do they live? The family."

"In a shipwreck down on the east shore of Canoe Lake. You can't miss it. It's the last homely house."

"I'll have to make a phone call. I have to let them know at the hospital I'll be late for rounds."

His eyes flicker all over me, the professional diagnostician assessing, weighing, analyzing.

"You're a bloody mess. You'd better go in there and clean yourself up." He nods to the bathroom off the kitchen. "I'll be back in a few minutes."

What a welcome sight a clean, warm bathroom is. I long for a hot shower. I wash my hands in the sink. The blood swirls down the drain. My head is spinning. I look up at the mirror and find a wild-man staring back out of it. A sasquatch. Thinner than I remember ever being. Five days' growth of beard, chapped lips, very red eyes, and scratched cheeks. A torn, stained parka. An intense, perhaps deranged, look in the eyes.

Hot soapy water on the face is indescribably luxurious. I sigh a long, deep sigh. I'm just thinking that this is Saturday, and Woolley never has rounds on Saturday, when I hear the zing go right over the roof and whine into the backyard. Before I can move, the bathroom door bursts open, and three men are hunkered down in the hallway pointing stun guns at me.

Woolley is standing behind them watching me. He puts the pipe stem into his mouth, and a thoughtful look crosses his face.

I walk slowly out of the bathroom. My mouth is open. I stare at him.

"You called them."

He shrugs.

"I trusted you, Doc."

"The mistake you made was in thinking that anything matters", he says.

"No. The mistake you made is thinking that nothing matters. Everything matters. Everything!"

"These fellows here, with the guns, they think it matters too. And there's more of them than there are of you. Billions of them, Eddie. A billion to one. Nice odds, eh? Staggering isn't it?"

"That ratio, Bertram, is the only thing that doesn't matter."

The police have had enough of this. They hustle me out.

* * *

I'm in the R.C.M.P. lockup at Swiftcreek. It's a temporary holding tank, I guess, because they haven't yet strip-searched me—only a customary frisk for concealed weapons. These kinds of guys never suspect that the human mind fits into that category quite nicely. They took everything away except the journal, which is stuffed down the back of my thermal undershirt.

A young corporal brings me soup and coffee in styrofoam containers.

"What's happening, Frank?" I ask him.

"A little argument between government agencies. Three of them want you. S. & I. wants you in Ottawa. Local R.C.M.P. wants you at regional headquarters in Kamloops. And the new boys from O.I.S.—you know, the guys in gray 'n' green—they want you in Vancouver. There's some bigwig flying out to meet you."

"Can you lend me a pen?"

"Promise you won't stab yourself with it?"

"I promise."

"No hanging, either."

"I give you my word."

He pushes a child's soft-plastic pen through the bars. It has ink, and it bends.

"You'd have to saw on a vein all day to draw blood", he says.

Then he spits on the floor. He sees himself as an old-time Mountie, aiming for the spittoon in a two-bit sawdust joint in the Klondike. He's really a Saskatchewan farm boy, a strong, clean sort of fellow with principles. He doesn't like me; he's just interested in what makes psychopaths tick.

"What's the pen for?"

"I want to write a letter."

"Need some paper?"

"Uh, yes, please."

He goes out and returns with two sheets. He hands them through the bars and stands there watching me.

"Why'd you kill Bill?"

"I didn't kill Bill."

He gives me the look I've come to know well. He says nothing.

"How come everybody from here to the east coast is interested in me?" I ask.

"I dunno."

"Got any ideas?"

"Not a one", he says.

"How many suicides in this country every day?"

"Oh, maybe more'n a hundred."

"How many murders are there in this country every day?"

"Maybe eighty, ninety."

"And rising fast."

"Yup."

"So why is my alleged crime so bloody important?"

"I haven't figured that out yet."

"You never will, my friend. They've got it all sealed up tight."

He wrinkles his brow, starts to say something, then closes his mouth.

"Frank, sometime, years from now, you're going to roll over in bed in the middle of the night and ask yourself for the thousandth time if that guy—meaning me—was innocent. On that one night you will know, deep down in your guts, you'll know. I *am* innocent, constable."

"I've heard a lot of guys tell me exactly that story, almost word for word."

"You'll know."

He rattles the cell door. It's locked.

"Look, I gotta go for supper. No hangin', no self-mutilation, no takin' a powder, okay. There's four gray 'n' greens out there in the office congratulatin' themselves on their brilliant manhunt. Take a rest, guy. You look awful."

"Thank you, constable."

"I'll think about what you said. I don't like what's happening to the country."

"Me neither."

"I know you don't. I'm a faithful subscriber. Your paper made me mad lots of times. But you made me think, too. You don't look like the average killer. So maybe I'll think about you some night years from now."

"I'd appreciate it."

"That's all I can do."

"Thanks."

"Yup."

And he's out the door, locking it behind him.

I want to write a letter to Woolley, to tell him that even though the betrayal was more than a final jest between masters of black humor, and even though the hurt is deep, maybe too deep for mending, I can't hate him. The grace of confession is with me; I am strangely free of my habitual rage.

What would I say to him if we could meet and talk?

"Poor, poor Woolley," I would tell him, "you began as an idealist, a lover of life, a bright young adversary of death, proud champion in burnished steel. A scalpel for a sword and a degree for a shield, you charged into the fray with such admirable confidence. But when the medical profession became tainted with death, and you found your hands covered with innocent blood, you ran. You ran from death into the arms of the secret death hiding within yourself.

"You can't defeat it on your own, Woolley. You can't surgically excise it. It's the plague, old boy. You need strong medicine for this one."

I sigh. I take one of the pages McConnell gave me, one infinitely precious and rare sheet. I write on it:

> Dear Woolley,
> I believe in the man you once were, and may be again.
> He's there inside of you.
> I forgive you. Check,
> Mate,
> Nathaniel Delaney

I turn the paper over and write his name on the back. Then I fold the best airplane I've made since boyhood. The cell window is shatterproof glass molded over wire mesh. It's so small not even a child could get through. But someone, perhaps one of the previous tenants, has managed to jimmy the lock and loosen the pins of the hinges. I get the dang thing semi-off, then fire my missile out into the cold night. The wind takes it. It rises and disappears into the dark of the village.

Now to business. I retrieve the plague journal from the inside panel of my undershirt. In such limited time, how can I summarize a life, two lives, three, or the decline and fall of an age? I write with tiny lettering, covering each page both sides, filling every margin. I write for several hours.

But what to do with it? I'll find the right moment. Maybe I'll toss these scraps of text from the Black Maria or send paper airplanes out the window over the backyards of Swiftcreek or drop them from the hatch of a hell-cop. By whatever method that comes to hand, I'll leave these fragments for the remnant.

Or should I hide it under the mattress here? Can that constable be trusted to withhold evidence? Have I inserted sufficient doubt into his mind about the brave new world order? Would he consider giving this to Matthew and Jeanne? I hope so. I want them to know about Anthony. Their surviving children might be able to understand, when they grow up and learn what their brother knew. But they may be swallowed, too. That constable is only a foot soldier in an army of nice young guys who don't really grasp what's happened. He could just chuck the manuscript into the wastebasket. Or even keep it as a souvenir to hand on to his kids, a curio from a vanished era. Some day it might even find a home in a museum of thought-crime.

"I'll think about you", he had said.

Okay, that's good enough, constable. I'll risk it on you—my literary heritage, my last testament. These are the lyrics that Daedalus sings as he plummets, locked in the embrace of love. Falling, falling, fearless in my fear, I have learned that we rise only on the wings of grace. I am a free man. I am awake. I know at last what I am for.

A bell is ringing! Then another! Many bells!

Who set them ringing? And why?

I know that sound. I know it, I know it! I would wager my life that it's Jan Tarnowski's bells.

He's dead, but somehow his word still cries out across a dark landscape—a landscape with dragons.

"Fire, foes, falsehood!" it peals around the valley.

Yes, Natano, Eddie, Poppa, old wrestler, defeater of many private fears—take heart, O discouraged writer. For, in spite of everything there are people out there. Something in them can still hear a word that shatters lies.

Dear family,

So ends the journal of Nathaniel Delaney. If you've read this far, you know that he was accused of killing somebody and spent a few hours in the village lockup before the O.I.S. took him away for further investigation. I never heard another word about him after that.

I was transferred to the coast shortly after the arrest, so I don't know what happened to the author's kids, or to the Thus, or whether Doc Woolley is still around.

The morning they flew him out, I found the manuscript under the mattress of his bunk. Don't ask me why, but I didn't turn it in. I decided to read it first, and then thought maybe I should keep it. Things have a way of just disappearing lately. Things and people.

Cpl. Frank McConnell, R.C.M.P., retired

Fragment

(in a child's handwriting, on a scrap of fluorescent orange paper found in manuscript of plague journal)

Daddy,
Don't be sad. Don't be scared.
Remember Frodo and Sam.
Love,
Zöe

Novels in the *Children of the Last Days* series:

Strangers and Sojourners
Plague Journal
Eclipse of the Sun

Sophia House
Father Elijah
Elijah in Jerusalem

A Cry of Stone

CHILDREN OF THE LAST DAYS is a series of seven novels that examine the major moral and spiritual struggles of our times. Each can be read independently of the others. There are, however, two trilogies within the larger work (*Strangers and Sojourners*, *Plague Journal*, and *Eclipse of the Sun*; and *Sophia House*, *Father Elijah*, and *Elijah in Jerusalem*) that are each best read in chronological order.

Strangers and Sojourners is about the lives of two émigrés in British Columbia, an Englishwoman, Anne, and her Irish husband, Stephen. Beginning on the first day of the 20th century and concluding in the mid-1970s, the Delaneys' story is the foundational novel for the following two titles.

Plague Journal is set in the near future.. The novel is composed of both written and mental notes made by Nathaniel Delaney, Anne and Stephen's grandson, who is the editor of a small-town newspaper. The story takes place over a five-day period as he flees arrest by a federal government agency, during the rise of a totalitarian state in North America.

Eclipse of the Sun describes the plight of Nathaniel's scattered children, who have become fugitives as the government seeks to eradicate all evidence of its ultimate goals. The events of this novel take place during the year following those of *Plague Journal*.

Sophia House is set in Warsaw during the Nazi occupation. Bookseller Pawel Tarnowski hides a Jewish youth, David Schäffer, who has escaped from the Ghetto. Throughout the winter of 1942–43, the two explore the meaning of love, religious identity, and sacrifice.

Father Elijah is the story of a Carmelite priest, Father Elijah (born David Schäffer), and his confrontation with the spirit of Antichrist. The events of this novel take place at approximately the same time as those of *Eclipse of the Sun*.

Elijah in Jerusalem is the continuing story of the Catholic priest called to confront a powerful politician, who could be the Antichrist foretold in the Bible. Now-Bishop Elijah, wanted for a murder he did not commit, perseveres in his mission even when all seems lost. The dramatic and surprising climax underlines that God works all things to the good for those who love him.

A Cry of Stone is the life of a native artist, Rose Wabos. Suffering from deprivation of several kinds, including a physical handicap, Rose is raised in the northern Ontario wilderness by her grandmother. The story covers a period from 1940 to 1973, chronicling Rose's growth to womanhood, her discovery of art, her moving out into the world of cities and culture, her search for beauty and faith.